HOW
FIRE
RUNS

Also by Charles Dodd White

In the House of Wilderness

(Swallow Press)

CHARLES DODD WHITE

HOW FIRE RUNS

A NOVEL

SWALLOW PRESS / OHIO UNIVERSITY PRESS

ATHENS, OHIO

Swallow Press
An imprint of Ohio University Press, Athens, Ohio 45701
ohioswallow.com

Printed in the United States of America
Swallow Press / Ohio University Press books are printed on acid-free paper ∞ ™

30 29 28 27 26 25 24 23 22 21 20   5 4 3 2 1

Library of Congress Cataloging-in-Publication Data

Names: White, Charles Dodd, 1976- author.
Title: How fire runs : a novel / Charles Dodd White.
Description: Athens, Ohio : Swallow Press, Ohio University Press, [2020] | Summary: "A chilling, timely reminder of the moral and human costs of racial hatred. What happens when a delusional white supremacist and his army of followers decide to create a racially pure "Little Europe" within a rural Tennessee community? As the town's residents grapple with their new reality, minor skirmishes escalate and dirty politics, scandals, and a cataclysmic chain of violence follows. In this uncanny reflection of our time, award-winning novelist Charles Dodd White asks whether Americans can save themselves from their worst impulses and considers the consequences when this salvation comes too late"-- Provided by publisher.
Identifiers: LCCN 2020020326 | ISBN 9780804012287 (trade paperback) | ISBN 9780804041157 (pdf)
Classification: LCC PS3623.H57258 H69 2020 | DDC 813/.6--dc23
LC record available at https://lccn.loc.gov/2020020326

For the Boundary Waters Fellers

The mentality that destroys a watershed and then panics at the threat of flood is the same mentality that gives institutionalized insult to black people and then panics at the prospect of race riots.

—Wendell Berry, "Think Little"

I will read ashes for you, if you ask me.
I will look in the fire and tell you from the gray lashes
And out of the red and black tongues and stripes,
I will tell how fire comes
And how fire runs far as the sea.

—Carl Sandburg, "Fire Pages"

SIX MEN arrive at the abandoned asylum on a late March evening. They pull the pair of moving vans into the deep bend of the horseshoe drive beyond the hemlocks, bail out of their cabs, and release the rear trailer doors. The metal shivers, rattles, and slams. Ramps drop from above both bumpers, slap the ground like heavy tongues. If the men communicate at all, it is in some crude agreement of murmur and gesture. Nothing precisely said. Just brusque sound drawn from the throat's center.

Darkness falls, but the men do not pause in their work. They strap headlamps around their skulls and carry box after box into the halls of the building. Beams of light dance and scrawl over the brick walls, the Doric columns, the pediment. At the men's bright glances, broken windows glimmer. Yet the dimensions within remained unexplored because even these men fear the stories of those mad who had been quartered there and they will not cross certain lines. The boxes and larger furnishings mount in the front hall until there is nothing more to unload.

When the trucks are emptied, they stand and smoke cigarettes, loiter with their personal kits and sleeping bags. They consider the advantage of indoors, but settle on a fire and the softest ground they can find. Even so, they keep an unofficial watch, sense the dark pull of something they will not admit. The fire never dies. It shapes itself against the living faces. They find their voices, use them as they would something they do not fully trust.

They used to drown them, one says.

Bullshit.

No, I heard the same. They took the wild ones down to the Watauga. Had a bunch of blacks down from Knoxville do their dirty work. Held them under. Was supposed to separate the ones that were truly crazy from the ones that only pretended.

Why the hell would you pretend something like that?

Because they was crazy, I guess.

You understand how little sense you make?

That's what I've heard said, is all.

None sleep, though they do zip themselves into the mummy bags and shut their eyes for a time, let the gray dawn find them. After a breakfast of bacon and toast cooked over a Coleman camp stove, they divide their labor. Half move the boxes and furniture into the separate rooms. The others spell one another with a pair of posthole diggers, root out a place at the end of the drive fronting the gravel road. By midmorning they accomplish their depth and assemble a metal piece twenty feet long and big around as a girl's wrist. Amid a flutter of curses, they settle the pole into the ground, pour in the sludge of hand-mixed concrete and brace it to settle. They take turns holding the staff and staring up the clean stroke of metal pointing toward the sky.

Once the pole can stand on its own they bring lumber down from the trucks, begin to nail pre-cut boards together and then paint them. After everything dries they carry the assemblage with great care and nail it to the trunk of a poplar tree. They do not hurry. They desire symmetry, precision. They desire impact.

When's he supposed to get here?

Soon, I think.

Should we put it up then?

Yeah, go ahead and run that sucker to the top.

One takes the flag and snaps it to the halyards. It balls and bunches and cracks free in the crosswind. They all look up and salute, sing their patriotic song. Above them a red-tailed hawk wars with an echelon of crows. A good omen, they decide.

Not long after, the man they wait for arrives. He is middle-aged and handsome with thin golden hair and abstracted eyes. He has not driven. He has a man for that. He has men for everything he has dreamed and conjured here in the Tennessee woods.

He beholds it all now and smiles. He smiles at the lacquered sign with its simple and pure statement. He smiles up at the red flag and its brave insignia. He has brought this here. It cannot be undone. Their words match his heart, and he smiles again as they shout with a hoarse fury that sounds like joy.

Sieg Heil.

PART I

1

KYLE PETTUS WATCHED THE SLANT OF LIGHT FOR A SENSE OF CHANGED time. Winter had been a trial for much of what he grew, but he had made adjustments in accordance with the sun and now the season was coming back around. He shifted the cabbages to the rear of the greenhouse, pushed the amaryllis and larkspur to the edge of the wooden crib, pinched the petals of his primroses as he would tender fingertips. They were doing well. They were healthy. He turned on the garden hose and filled the big watering can. The stream played in the metal bottom until the waterline came up a few inches. The rest of the way it filled with a sound like a kind voice.

He heard Orlynne's Jeep grind up from the base of the cove long before she swung around the curve at the bottom of the mountain and chugged up the rest of the way. She drove on around to the side next to the toolshed and killed the engine. He saw that she wore her heavy coat though it was only a cool forty degrees that morning. Permanently cold-blooded, she'd once told him. As a timber rattler, he'd said once, and she'd laughed and it had been their unspoken joke since then.

"Hey, kid," she called, held up a paper bag with damp swatches of grease. "I took care of biscuits for us. I'll only charge you a ten percent delivery fee."

"Take it on up to the house. I'll water this row and see you up there in a minute."

Though Kyle gave her a good five minutes to make it up from the greenhouses, he overtook her short of the front porch. She'd had to rest at the top of the wooden steps embedded in the hillside. Hip going bad. Eighty-five at the end of the month, and still she insisted on coming out to work with him, just as she had his mother and father since they'd bought the property fifty-two years before. All his life Orlynne had been out here, nursing the greenery that would supply other people's gardens. He had thought of telling her to sell the camper she kept on the Doe River, to come up and stay in the spare bedroom of the main house, but he knew she would have refused. She wanted no charity, only the promise of work and to help things grow.

"You go on up. I'll be there in a minute," she told him. "I'm just testing gravity. Making sure the earth is still willing to grab hold of me."

"All right. You want a coffee, don't you?"

"Does the Pope crap in the woods?"

"I don't know. If I see a Catholic grizzly bear I'll ask."

He went up and ground some fresh beans, poured some well water into the back of the Mr. Coffee, and watched it wheeze and spit into the carafe. By the time it had filled Orlynne had made it to the front door, put her rear in the big Queen Anne chair in the front room next to the wood-burning stove. She didn't bother unbuttoning her parka, though her forehead was already slick with sweat. He handed over her coffee.

It wasn't difficult to see that some mornings were harder on her than others. Clear to him that the only thing worse than dragging herself out of bed to a full day working amid the rows was the prospect of doing nothing at all. She was about as tough as anyone he'd ever known. So he wouldn't ever tell her what she couldn't do, that she needed to stay back. He couldn't ever imagine himself being that cruel.

After they'd kicked around the house eating breakfast and letting it settle, they went back down to the greenhouse and began loading the truck with what they would take to the midweek farmers market. The sun was well up from behind the top ridge, so the mild day would grow warmer, likely draw a decent crowd. They needed it. The winter had always been leaner than he would have liked, but for the last couple of years he had noticed several brown patches where people had kept winter gardens in the past. Many of the older people in the Warlick community were aging into assisted-living facilities and their inherited land was going untenanted or else being taken over by younger kin with more of a mind for selling than making their own lives here. He guessed that his forty years made him one of the youngest still holding on, though that didn't bother him particularly. He had enough to keep him busy.

He cranked the Tacoma and fed the gas until the engine skipped past its cold chatter and achieved full throat.

"Let's get while the getting's good," Orlynne said, slapped the dash like a hind end.

The parking brake popped and they rolled downhill.

Once they were off the mountain, the road followed the Doe River for close to a mile, the steep bank pitched like the edge of the world. Kyle always took the bends slow, knowing many Carter County drunks had met an abrupt end in those narrow turns. But once he made the asphalt he opened things up, pushed down through the quick switchbacks that carried them over the southern shoulders of Towheaded Mountain until they could turn for the highway headed toward Elizabethton.

They stopped at a Valero gas station before they got out of Warlick to buy some bottled water and to break a large bill for the sake of change to keep in the cash box. The clerk tried to sell them some lottery tickets but Kyle said he'd had enough experience throwing money away and he saw no reason to make the government rich in the process. The clerk, a man no younger than Cain, said that was a hell of a way for a county commissioner to talk, and Kyle said, "Ain't it though," and smiled as he let the front door swat shut behind him.

It was only another five minutes up the road before they reached the dusty side lot where the other members of the market had arrived and thrown up their tents. He and Orlynne waved and said hello to the few others sticking it out through the winter months, mostly retirees and their underemployed relations, though there were a couple of hippie girls down from a Watauga County co-op with their organic wares. Honey and jams mostly. Kyle liked to watch them work, especially when it was warm enough for shorts and tank tops. Orlynne had noticed his particular attention to these girls who were indecently young and had done her best to ruin it for him when she'd decided they were lesbians, called them "the Sapphic sweethearts" in a whisper so loud that they could hear her from across the parking lot, which caused them to giggle.

Orlynne braced up the tent poles while Kyle ran the guylines and hammered the stakes into the ground with a rubber mallet. Once it was set and held well in the crosswind, he brought out a pair of long tables with folding legs and leveled them with wood chips he kept in the truck bed for that purpose. Ten minutes later they had all the potted plants down on the ground and the lettuce and flowers spread out on the tables. What little remained they placed on the dropped tailgate of the Tacoma, then sat in their camp chairs and drank their waters and waited.

A good flurry of tourists began to stop by after the first hour. They wanted the flowers mostly, talked about how they desired something natural to carry home as a genuine part of their Appalachian driving tour. He smiled and listened to them, gave directions, advised the best spots for snapping scenic overlook pictures, took their money. Orylnne stepped in and told stories to those who looked like they were after a little bit of local color. It was a good and established rhythm and by midday a substantial portion of what they'd hauled off the side of the mountain was gone. Kyle told Orlynne to watch things while he walked across the road to buy them a barbeque lunch.

When he came back holding a handful of hot paper sacks, he saw a county sheriff's deputy standing there talking with Orylnne. The big SUV's engine was still running. What had been hunger in his stomach turned to something else.

"Hey, deputy. What can we do for you all?"

"You ever heard of a cell phone? We've been trying to get ahold of you half the morning," the deputy said. His broad face was mottled pink and he had a look in his eyes like he'd suffered an unfair accusation. Given what Kyle knew about the man the deputy worked for, there was a good chance of that having been the case.

"I must have come off and forgot it. You've turned over the right rock and found me."

"Come on, dang it. I've got orders to pick you up. Sheriff said."

"I hope I don't need a lawyer."

"No, you don't need a dang lawyer. It's Old Man Pickens. Sheriff needs you to talk the old son of a gun down. And I mean quick, too."

Kyle told Orlynne to pack up what was left, to get the girls to help her take the tent down and drive everything back home, that he'd have the deputy bring him back when he was done.

"You sure about that, kid? I'm not too trusting of the po-lease," she asked, grinned wide when she saw that the deputy heard her and didn't appear pleased.

"Yeah, you go on. This one's a good old boy. Ain't you?"

"Can we get on, please?"

"Yeah, we can get on."

Kyle went around the SUV and got into the passenger's seat. He didn't have time to buckle his seat belt before the deputy spun them around and bounced onto the highway, accelerating as fast as he could.

"You care to explain any of this?"

"I don't imagine I'll need to. Anyhow, Sheriff told me not to spoil the surprise."

"The surprise?"

"His word, not mine."

Kyle let his curiosity ride. At the speed they were going it wouldn't take long to get out to the Pickens place and see what breed of trouble the old man had crossed. He and Gerald Pickens were the only two Democrats who sat on the county commission, and the general consensus among the other serving government officials was that only Kyle had an insight into the old man's ravings. Whenever some touch of the inscrutable lit in Gerald's brain, Kyle was consulted in order to determine the cause.

A couple of minutes past the turnoff for Hampton they took the only road leading into the hollow. Not far up the way they could see deputy cruisers pulled off to the side of the road. A bit farther on and they saw a potbellied man wearing aviator sunglasses and a Kevlar vest with Velcro straps dangling loose. When he saw the approaching vehicle he clapped a Stetson on his bald head and waved them forward.

"Well, if it isn't Christ Almighty himself," Sheriff Holston crowed. "Glad to see you could make it up, Commissioner Pettus. I truly am."

"You going to tell me what the damn fool has gotten to or do you plan on window-dressing in front of your deputy a few more minutes?"

"Yeah, I'll let you know all right. Get out and follow me up here a little bit. Tyler, reach out your second-chance vest from the back. As much as I'd like to see a straight Republican commission, I'd prefer it not to come at the wrong end of a Remington."

Kyle and the deputy stepped out and went around to the rear of the SUV. The vest was as floppy and oversized as the one the sheriff wore, though it seemed distinctly more ineffective around Kyle's slender frame. He tugged the straps as far as they would go, then went on with the sheriff until they made the bend of the road where they could see a beige Lincoln town car settled on a pair of flat back tires. Its back windshield was shattered, though he could see a trio of men remained seated inside. They were talking and smoking cigarettes.

The sheriff pointed, said, "Now those boys were backing out of that driveway there when your libtard buddy across the way sniped out one of their tires from his front porch. Bam. Didn't say a goddamn thing, just opened fire like he was back in the Mekong rice paddies. When the driver got out to see what the hell was going on, bam, a second shot half a foot in front of him. He dove right back inside and shut the door. Then a third shot, took out the other tire and one more in the glass. That one must have been for shits and giggles because they didn't even try anything after the third shot. That was about two hours ago. Here's the best part, though. It wasn't any of them boys being shot at that called the law. It was that tar sunk sonofabitch setting up there on his porch! Called dispatch, said he had a bunch of damn wild dogs that needed us to pick up and take in or he'd start wasting 'em. Wasting 'em, he said, like he'd been watching Dirty Harry movies since daybreak. Now dispatch didn't know how to make heads nor tails of what he was saying, but they figured they didn't want to have sanitation come out and scrape somebody's house pets that had gotten out of their fences off the side of the road. So they sent Shirley from animal control out and this is what she seen, a damn bloodbath waiting to happen. She talked to them boys to find out what was going on and when they told her she tried to go and talk to Pickens, but he told her the only man he would talk to was you. Said you were the only one who would understand what was on his mind. Since then we've been in what the news media likes to call containment. Until we could get your happy ass up here, that is."

Kyle went up a few more paces until he could see Gerald sitting behind his porch rail with a scoped 7 mm Magnum. At his right hand a cup of coffee and between his teeth a brier pipe. Kyle couldn't be sure, but it looked like he was wearing a bathrobe over his clothes and his PROUD VIETNAM VETERAN ball cap.

"What if I decline?" he asked the sheriff, though by then Holston had turned back the way he had come and was headed out of the direct line of sight. Kyle recited a few epithets to his back before he went on up the hill.

"Who goes there?" Gerald hollered down.

"I imagine you can see me just fine through that scope you've got trained on me, Gerald. I'd be obliged if you took those crosshairs off my chest."

"Crosshairs ain't on your chest, anyhow. They on your head."

Kyle could tell the old man was enjoying himself. Still, he went on.

Two of Gerald's goats met him on the way up. Molly and Malone, he believed their names were. Each cocked a yellow alien eye at him, stamped a hoof. Malone then bounded into the higher brush like the banished wood spirit he was. Molly, the one with white socks, bleated as she dropped a quick chain of turds before clattering up the steps and peering out from beneath the porch railing. Her nose twitched at him like she smelled something bad in the wind.

Gerald was known to leave the front and back doors of his cabin open all through the course of a day so that his pet goats could come and go as they pleased. He had told Kyle once that he preferred their company to most others who would have had business darkening his door. When Kyle had asked what he did if one of them took a shit indoors the old man told him that he only had to worry about it once. That a butcher knife and a crock pot made short work of any recidivists.

"Hey, Gerald."

"Howdy."

"You care to explain the events of the morning?"

"I'd say you probably have a good idea of it already."

"It's not looking too good for you from what I've heard so far."

"You been listening to the wrong end of a gassy hog then."

Kyle sighed, eased his weight onto the porch rail, tried to get within reach of the deer rifle as casually as he could.

"You can't shoot at people, Gerald."

"People he calls them. This is what he comes up here to tell me."

"It's not civil."

"Wolf is at the very door and he tells me to kowtow."

"The wolf, huh?"

"You step in there to the front door and get that pair of birdwatchers on top of the mantel. You look over yonder and tell me what you'd call it then."

"If I do will you put that damn gun up?"

He mulled this over.

"I'm open to the possibility," he said.

Kyle went in and got the Otasco binoculars from above the fireplace, came back and glassed the neighboring front.

"All I see is three boys who are likely wearing loaded britches."

"Look on further back. Up there in front of the old asylum."

Kyle searched through the shaded distance and was about to set the field glasses aside when a slim languid movement of red slipped across a bright hole of sunlight. The breeze played at the edges of the flag before it fluttered and flung out to its complete length. He saw the swastika.

"Do you see it?"

"Yeah, I see it."

He placed the binoculars on the porch rail.

"Will you hand me that rifle now, Gerald?"

"That's all you've got to say?"

"What the hell else do you want me to say? You've got some rednecks taking up residence across the road from you? That's hardly breaking news. You know how many Confederate battle flags I passed coming out to market this morning?"

"But these are Nazis! This isn't some broke-down sonofabitch who likes to play dress up and yell 'Shiloh, bloody Shiloh.' Can't you see the difference?"

"Only thing I see right now is an old man about to spend the rest of his commissioner term in the county courthouse jail unless he hands over his hardware. Now unload that goddamn thing and give it to me so I can do my best to keep you out of more trouble than you're already in."

Gerald sat there glaring for the better part of a minute, plumes of pipe smoke floating up around his head like vapor cusses. Reluctantly he worked the bolt, kicked out three fully jacketed brass rounds that thunked and rolled across the porch floorboards. Molly came over, sniffed at each one before she popped her heels in the air and danced briskly away, disappeared somewhere inside the cabin.

"Go get whatever you need to get done before we leave. I don't think you'll be back here today."

The old man stood, removed his pipe, spat.

"Let's get on. These animals can see to themselves."

Kyle folded the rifle under his arm with the muzzle pointed at the ground and walked down with Gerald at his right shoulder. When they got to the edge of the road he called out that he had the gun and the old man was coming of his own volition. The deputies appeared from behind their positions of cover and concealment behind oak trees and cruiser doors. Sheriff Holston came forward and idly unholstered his service revolver. Finding it an odd and awkward piece in his hand, he just as idly returned it and waved them on with his empty hand, told them to hurry up and get the old sonofabitch into the back of his patrol car before somebody ended up properly shot and killed.

2

FROM HIS BEDROOM WINDOW GAVIN NOON HAD SEEN THE MAN when he had come off the mountain carrying the rifle, had watched when the three men he'd sent out had come to shake his hand and how he had spoken a few words to them but had not taken their offered hands. This would be something to deal with then. He turned at the sound of footsteps at his door. It was Harrison's woman, Delilah.

"What the fuck we going to do about this, Gavin?"

He smiled, went to his dresser to look in the mirror and comb his hair. He watched her in the slight distortion of the glass. Despite the tattoos, the dark cropped hair and the stray leavings of brightwork pieced into her face, she remained attractive, if primitively so. She reminded him of a mean animal or a sharp knife. He knew that she enjoyed this fact about herself. Mistook it for an advantage.

"There will be ample time to make things right, Delilah. No one can say how time finds its channel. No one can steer it on their own."

"Your men out there getting shot and you stand here at the bedroom window and talk high. That's about what I'd expect out of you, you blind bastard. I think it's time you got those glasses of yours checked. My man nearly died and all you have to say is something that sounds like it comes out of one of these goddamn books," she said, waved her hand at the shelves jammed with volumes of Spinoza, Rockwell, Rosenberg, Dostoevsky, Nietzsche, Moore, Hitler. "You need to realize there's more to this than a bunch of vocabulary. There's people out here ready to die for something that matters. There's people out here that . . ."

"Delilah, enough!"

She stilled as Harrison came in behind her and placed his hands on her shoulders. Gavin could see where Harrison's bandaged forearm seeped with the darkening of blood. He went to his desk and poured out a tumbler of Jack Daniels, handed it to him.

"Does it sting?" he asked.

Harrison shrugged, said, "Only glass."

Gavin nodded, poured himself a tumbler for no other reason than to buy himself a moment to think.

"Delilah, I need to speak with Mr. Harrison alone for a few minutes if you think you might spare us the privacy."

Harrison squeezed her shoulders and she left without a word.

"Is everyone alright?"

"Nothing they won't get over. Nothing but a crazy old man anyway."

Harrison strolled past Gavin, canted his shaven head to study the close rows of book titles pressed together. He was an impressively built man with developed muscles that belied a graceful carriage. The six years spent in the penitentiary had been time put to good use if it resulted in a body assembled into this kind of weaponry. He was exactly the kind of man Gavin needed. Exactly the kind this new nation deserved.

"Do you see anything that interests you?"

"I read this one when I was inside," he said, pointed out the Nietzsche. "I liked it. I liked how it sounded like he wasn't going to take shit from anybody for believing what he did."

"You're welcome to borrow any you like. I would enjoy hearing what you think of them."

Harrison stood, took nothing, his colorless eyes staring into distance. A soldier awaiting instruction. Little more than what circumstances had made of him then. A pity.

"Could you do me a favor, Harrison? Once the tires have been replaced could you have Jonathan bring the car around. I believe I'll need to go into town."

His lieutenant nodded briskly, left the room, granted Gavin the silence that was his most welcome companion.

HE WORE a suit and tie and a brushed peacoat over that. A gray fedora with a black band. He liked the completion the hat lent. He would not have these people make a cartoon of him. There was too much of that already in the libelous media. The jackboots and fanatics let loose on the world to froth barbarously at the mouth. He meant to demonstrate the principles of his community and its democratic right to exist. It was time.

"Here, you can park on the street, Jonathan. I don't believe it should be terribly long."

"Yes, sir. I'll keep the motor running."

He stepped onto the neat sidewalk and gazed up at the quaint brick building with its pediment and tall columns. As apt a picture of the small-town courthouse as could be desired. It touched his own sentimental recollections of his boyhood Kentucky home. He remembered the small-town life that had been the only retreat from the slums of Vietnam-era America. The things that he'd watched in the living room with his mother. The televised horrors of war in the jungle with helicopters and machine guns and Agent Orange and of the more immediate war of blacks tearing themselves apart in northern cities like scavengers ripping apart the flanks of some great dying beast. His father had been a truck driver and would come home telling stories of what he had witnessed and how lucky they were to have a home apart from that failed experiment of racial integration. Gavin was afraid, yes, but thrilled too that his father ventured out among that hazard of men with their razors and cheap wine and women, seeing in his mind's eye those black cities rife with crime.

He mounted the front steps and went on into the lobby, checked the directory board for the sheriff's office listing, then went down the hall and entered the front office. A woman with salt-and-pepper hair and cat's-eye glasses looked up from her desk and asked if she could help him with something. He touched his hat, smiled, said he'd like to speak to the sheriff if it were possible.

"I'll be happy to take your name, sir," she said, turned over an appointment book, started to write. "But it's been busy today. Sheriff's tied up at the moment."

"I'm afraid I might be the cause of his busyness. Indirectly, at least. My business concerns the man who shot out the tires of my automobile."

She laid her pen down, said, "Have a seat over there please, sir. I'll step back there and see what I can manage."

He sat against the wall, turned his hat in his hands as he watched her stride back to the sheriff's private office. She leaned in, said something he couldn't hear, then crossed the threshold and shut the door behind her. It was overheated in the waiting area and he loosened his tie. He hated being delayed, knew that the sheriff would have to see him and that making him wait was pointless. To kill time, he studied the pictures decorating the walls. Images of different municipal buildings, the dam out on Watauga Lake, the railroad stop, all the old Kodak colors blanched.

He knew some of the main facts of the town before he'd begun his search for a place to found his own Little Europe. Elizabethton was a hair under fifteen thousand souls, many of whom hailed from families holding in this corner of Northeast Tennessee since the overmountain men of the Revolutionary War. It was the forgotten adjunct of the Tri-City area of the immediate region, surrounded by Bristol, Kingsport, and most immediately, Johnson City. Those towns had their industry, their highway connections to support them while Elizabethton was one step closer to the big mountains, and though these mountains held no coal, they did have water that could be caught and controlled. So, the Tennessee Valley Authority had come in and made Elizabethton what it was. Built its dams and gatehouses. Made the rivers into a commodity. But even with electric power, the people of the place remained largely unchanged. They were proud white men and women. Gavin counted on them to be.

"Sir, the sheriff's got a minute if you can come on back."

He went in and sat in one of a pair of green leather chairs facing Sheriff Holston and his antique walnut desk. Behind him the two flags of state and nation. The secretary stepped out and clicked the door politely shut.

"Mister Noon, I hope you didn't think we needed anything more from you. If you were under that impression I'll have to apologize for my deputies straightaway. They collected all the statements they needed when they were at your property . . ."

His stream of talk ceased at Gavin's raised hand, his smile.

"Sheriff, I've had a chance to talk to everyone involved. Everyone involved on my side of the affair, at least, and I believe there's been a grave misunderstanding."

"A misunderstanding?"

"Yes, I don't think there's any reason to make this any harder than it has to be. I'm not entirely sure any crime, any crime of intent that is, ever took place. It's my understanding that Mister Pickens is incarcerated?"

Holston leaned back in his swivel chair until it creaked and strained like it was about to give way.

"Yes sir. He's locked up until we can get the judge to see him. Probably won't be until tomorrow afternoon."

"Mister Pickens, he's an older gentleman from what I can tell."

"Yes, sir. He's a codgerly seventy-three if I'm not mistaken."

"I really don't think this is all that necessary then, is it? I mean, it seems like the fact that he's already been brought to the jail, that should be lesson enough, don't you think?"

Holston leaned over a ledger, flipped some pages.

"I'll have to say, Mister Noon, I'm not too fond of locking somebody up that's been as much a part of the community as he has. I might not agree with his politics, but he's served the county the better part of thirty years. Lots of little old ladies wouldn't have their Rotary Club garden beds if it wasn't for him. Still, no one would argue him being in the wrong. But if you realized that it was a matter of him target shooting in his front yard and not knowing you and your group had moved into the old asylum, then that might significantly change the complexion of things. The DA might be open to the possibility of revisiting some of the details of the incident. That place where you've moved in has been vacant for twenty years at least, and there ain't nothing further up the holler until you get to state land. Might still stick a misdemeanor on him, but nothing that amounts to anything. If you're of a mind that that's what may have happened, at least."

Gavin nodded, said, "That's very reasonable. As new members of the community, my family and I are interested in neighborly relations. The last thing I'd want to do is cause any unnecessary friction. There's no reason people can't live beside one another despite whatever difference of opinion they might harbor. Don't you think?"

Holston cleared his throat, said something about the wisdom in such a thought, stuck his soft hand across the desk. Gavin took it as he would a rare and complicated gift.

3

KYLE SAT in front of the woodstove with a bowl of canned chili and drank one of those craft beers made down the road in Johnson City. The beer was good and dark and he drank it with deliberate pauses between sips. Otherwise it would have been hard not to get carried away and slip over into a lazy buzz. He'd been close to useless for much of the afternoon once the deputy had driven him back and he'd sent Orylnne home for the day, told her as little about what had happened as he could, though he knew she'd find out the details soon enough. He was worried about Gerald, didn't see any way out of things getting out of hand as soon as the word got out.

He had been on the laptop chatting with a couple of the guys from the veterans group. They were trying to schedule a time when they could all meet for their next reforestation project. Kyle had already set the seedlings aside in the greenhouse, ready to be loaded up and driven to the new site up on Buckhorn Ridge, but they needed to meet once to go over the map and settle all the particulars. They were working out the best time the next morning when he glimpsed something coming through that dark, the shafts of car headlights climbing the drive. He wasn't expecting anybody, so he went back to his bedroom to get the .380 from his bedside table, tucked it into the back of his waistband and stepped out to see who had come up this far into the country unannounced.

He had to put his hand across his face as the vehicle swung its lights around. After the truck parked the lights stayed on for a minute before they cut. The big diesel engine ceased its chatter. As soon as the door cracked open and the driver hove himself out, Kyle knew who it was.

"I think I've had about enough good news from you today," Kyle said.

"Boy, it's only getting started," Holston said as he came up the steps, his breath coming like it cost more than he was willing to invest. "You mind if we go in and sit by the fire? Any kind of cold is tough on these arthritic bones, and it sure can't be doing your bare feet any good."

Kyle looked down, only then realized he'd come out without his shoes.

"Yeah, come on. Just so you know, I'm armed," he said, turned and lifted his shirttail to expose the handgun grip at the small of his back.

Holston grinned, lifted his jacket to reveal his Colt. He said, "Don't worry. I'm comfortable with a man who supports the Second Amendment."

Kyle showed him to the front room and told him to have a seat if he wanted it. The sheriff backed up to the wood stove and spread his hands out behind him like he was trying to catch a gust of wind, said he was all right to stand for a while.

"Want something to drink? I can put on some water for coffee or tea. There's a couple of beers in there too if you're off the clock."

"What kind of beer you got?"

"Yee-haws. Porters."

"That's okay. I'm a Bud man. That hippie shit does something to my stomach."

Kyle let the fridge door shut.

"Well, now that we've pretended we can get along for half a minute, you want to tell me what's got you up here? I would have figured you've had enough to gloat about for one day without driving to the back of beyond for just a little more."

Holston shook his head like he was trying to get something inside his brain to come loose.

"Charming. A real country gentleman, my mama would have called you, Pettus. A real country gentleman. But I've come out here on what I'd like to call a mission of mutual advantage. How surprised would you be if I told you that Gerald Pickens isn't sitting in county detention? How surprised would you be to hear that he's sitting out there in my pickup as we live and breathe?"

"I'd say you'd developed a heart or a brain tumor, one."

"Maybe. But it's the truth regardless. I was closing up the last of the paperwork when Gavin Noon, the man who owns the property across the road from Pickens, came down and said he thought there was no good reason to throw an old fool in the jail for just being an old fool. Said he didn't want the community to have an idea of him and his people as adversarial to the better desires of the county. I told him I thought that was a mighty philosophical way of looking at things, taken all in all. A little sweet talk with a DA who's already covered up prosecuting pillheads all over Kingdom Come, and you'd be surprised what you can get to happen."

"So you struck a deal with a Nazi? That's pretty Christian of you."

"Yeah, well. Sometimes the law ain't pretty in all of its fine print."

"That still doesn't explain why you've brought him up here. I only sit down next to the man every month at the courthouse. I've got about as much use for him as you do."

Holston passed a hand over his skull, stood there trying to collect himself. A man come to the end of all best intentions.

"I'm going to tell you right now, Pettus," Holston said. "Don't you look this kindness in the face and call it anything else. I'm trying to help you and him both, you stubborn ass. That man could very well end up the majority of his days left on this earth in a damn cage if you don't help him. Now I need you to take him in for a little bit. Not too long. Maybe a week or two. Time enough to give things a chance to cool off. It's a goddamn good thing he's as good a shot as he is. If he'd slipped up and killed one of those boys this would be done before it even got started. You play your cards right, you might even be able to keep him on the commission."

"Babysit him, huh? What's he say to that idea?"

"He's not too fond of it, if you want to know the truth. He said he couldn't much stand the sight of you and that the only thing that redeemed you as far as he could tell was your politics. Then I told him that a man often hated most what he most resembled. He pretty much shut up after that."

Kyle shook his head, went over to the coatrack, pulled on his boots and his hunting jacket.

"Come on, dammit," he said. "Help me convince the old bastard to see to his own best interest."

Holston smiled, said. "See, there's that country gentlemen I was talking about. I think the school teachers call it noblesse oblige."

"Fuck you."

"Well, no thank you, but I appreciate the offer. I surely do."

HE PUT Gerald in the front bedroom just down the hall from where he slept. The old man still wore his clothes from that morning and had nothing else to change into.

"Hell, it's fine," he said. "Wouldn't be the first time I've slept in my clothes. If it gets bad I can always strip down to my skivvies."

Kyle was about to show him the closet where he had some old sweatpants that might have fit, but Gerald waved him away, told him to get on and let him have a bit of earned peace. Just as Kyle stepped out the door slammed shut. A second later the bolt shot home.

Kyle went back to his bedroom and went through some pictures of Laura and him he kept in a password-protected folder on his phone. They were all self-shot, high angled and tight, context excluded from the frame. He wanted to call her, but he knew to text first. That was one of the foundations of their agreement. To never put her in a compromised position. He sent a brief message and waited for an answer in the otherwise dark room.

In a few minues: SORRY CANT TONIGHT. WILL SEE YOU TOMORROW THOUGH. ;)

He placed the phone on its charger face down on the nightstand, tried to put it out of his head. After a few minutes he knew he wouldn't be able to sleep anytime soon, so he put on his slippers and went quietly to the kitchen to warm a small pan of milk. It was one of his mama's rituals for helping his father to bed when he'd been sick with cancer and he couldn't ever rest once the sun was down. Milk with a whole tablespoon of orange blossom honey. Sometimes Kyle could go an entire day without thinking of either one of them, gone now for so many years. Him eight and her six. But then there would be weeks at a stretch that he couldn't get them off his mind. When he'd come back from Iraq they'd been there for him when everything else in his life had come unsprung. The drugs, the barfights, the ugly divorce from a woman he'd met at an off-base bar in Jacksonville, North Carolina. They'd seen him through all that, brought him home where he could remember who he was before he'd given mind, body, and soul to the Marine Corps. Maybe that's what the Corps demanded, but when he earned his discharge, surely he was entitled to take back his mind even if the rest was supposed to remain.

Kyle took the milk off the stove and drank it in a steel camping cup, listened for a long time to a barred owl that often liked to take up around the back shed when he came to visit. Heard him keep shouting, "Who cooks for you, who cooks for you all?" until he flew off. By then, it was well past time to put head to pillow.

The next morning he was up early and made a big breakfast of biscuit and eggs and JFG coffee. He ate his own plate of food and sat there drinking two cups of the coffee until the sun was up. He had resolved overnight to make the old man feel as welcomed as he could, thought the breakfast could be a running start. Despite their differences, he knew it couldn't have been easy to be put in the old man's position. He thought too about what Holston had said about his similarity to Gerald. In many ways it wasn't that hard to see. Each of them had his own way of coming to the truth of things and sticking by what they believed. It was what kept both of them on the commission. People trusted them to see to the best interests of those they represented. But they also set their teeth deep into their ideas and sometimes when others disagreed it was a hell of a lot easier to bite down harder rather than let go. People had a way of remembering things like that too.

When it had gotten to be time to go to work Gerald still wasn't up. A hell of a thing. Kyle had long thought the old kept the same hours as roosters. His luck to have to take care of one that slept like a teenager. He scraped the eggs, wrapped the biscuits in foil, and carried out the last of his coffee in the Stanley thermos.

He had worked his way through the upper greenhouse and was cataloguing some things in the lower one when Gerald poked his head in the door.

"You got any weed growing around here?" the old man asked, scratched at his chin whiskers.

"No, Gerald. I don't grow weed."

"That's a shame. I figured it might be the time to pick up a new habit."

"There's better habits to pick up, I imagine."

"Yeah? Maybe so. I hear that meth is all the rage these days. They like to put it in books and movies. Preachers and teachers catching on fire when their drug labs explode. That seems like something I could get into. Seems like something that might be enough to distract a man from his immediate concerns."

"Think so, huh?"

He showed his hands, shrugged. After a minute of staring around at the plants he stepped down and walked the neighboring aisle, peered down at the specimen tabs.

"You take a sudden interest in a botany lesson or are you out here to help?"

"Hell, I'm not above putting in a hand if you think it could be useful. Reach me that clipboard."

They worked shoulder to shoulder for the better part of the hour, ran the inventory. Pickens took down the species and numbers they needed in terms of transfer and seed. Kyle had known him to have a strong eye for detail, had seen for years how he measured the worth of some proposal or regulation with a bottomless patience for even the most tedious points. His mind remained anchored to whatever held its attention. He never wavered or became distracted. He was serious about things because he understood that a moment's inattention was all it took to rob you of the essence of something, to miss the subtlety that distinguished this from that.

Too much noise, too many competing motives floated a political life, and a man without the ability to cut through it was no more than the people's fool.

"What is it you think that man Noon is up to?" Kyle asked once they had run the numbers and stood there looking over the rows of plants.

"What he's up to?"

"Why he didn't have the DA press charges. Why he's letting this settle as easy as he is."

"Hell, he's not letting a goddamn thing settle. He needs things to be quiet. Why else would you turn somebody loose you had by the short hairs? He wants to make sure nobody is paying attention. That's what every fascist that ever came down the pike needed. Invisibility. For a little while, at least."

"I wouldn't call putting up a Nazi flag invisibility."

"That's nothing. That's lawn decor. He figured there wouldn't be any problems about that because of how far back he decided to settle in. Hell, what are the chances he'd run into an enlightened soul like myself way back there in the way back. Bad luck for him is all. Now he's got to find a way to play the peacenik. He's meaning to install himself somehow. Him forgiving me. Shit. Only forgiveness I need is from Almighty Cthulhu."

Kyle had heard him go on these atheistic tears before. Shouting about Baptists being the modern-day equivalent of superstitious Neanderthal clans howling and beating their breasts at the sky wizard whenever their crops failed. Gerald had preferred to locate his faith in H.P. Lovecraft's horrific mythology of the ancients, he said, because at least those stories were interesting, not mere object lessons in dullness.

Kyle told him he was headed up to wash before he ran down to the vets meeting and asked if he needed him to pick anything up while he was out. He said that he was fine, that he could do well enough with nothing here just as well as he could at his own place, then went just outside the greenhouse to take a leak. Kyle shook his head and went on.

In town Kyle stopped off at a couple of places that kept an order of his plants in their garden shops, took notes for restocking, and chatted with the proprietors. He grocery-shopped at the Food City, picked up a bottle of wine because he knew Gerald fashioned himself as a kind of misunderstood backwoods connoisseur and would appreciate the chance to indulge. Perhaps it would be enough to soften his crankiness, though he doubted it.

When he got to the library he recognized several of the vehicles that were already in the parking lot. Trey Buckner was smoking a cigarette with his car door open talking on the phone with someone. He glanced up and cast a brief wave, mouthed "In five," while he nodded to whatever was being said into his ear. Trey was one of the earliest members of the veterans group and had been to nearly every meeting for the past six years. He ran a car repair place down around Jonesborough and had a couple of foster kids with his wife. He had been an artilleryman in the Army, which explained why he was always leaning in tight with his head dropped during a conversation, his small hearing aid pointed as close as he could get it to the speaker's mouth.

Once inside, he saw a couple of the other guys getting coffee from the alcove and taking it back to the community room. He went on to the back office where Laura was.

"Right on time," she said and smiled. After a quick peek to see that no one could see them, she kissed his cheek and held onto his shoulders for a few beats. Once she let him go, they went back to her desk where they could sit and talk without it seeming out of place to anyone. They'd been seeing each other like this for the past six months, and as far as they could tell they had held up innocent appearances. Still, the sneaking around had started to wear on Kyle. It had never been just a matter of fun for either one of them, but he also understood splitting up a marriage wasn't as simple as a piece of paperwork.

"You need to make some time for me," he told her.

She balanced her chin on her small fist, studied him through those blue Tennessee eyes. Every bit of her was something he would have loved to eat whole. When she was alone with him like this, he couldn't help but imagine her as a fairytale damsel and him the wolf.

"You have a way of talking to me that makes me think it's half love and half hate," she said.

"I suspect that's sort of how you like it."

By her smile, he felt confident he was right.

"You go on in there and talk to the boys. Once you're done you come back here and we'll see what there is to see."

By the time he got his coffee and went back to where the others had already circled up their chairs, he was just about the last one to get in. Only guy he saw missing was Turner Whist.

"Where's Turner?"

The other men shrugged, said he'd been out of touch for the last couple of weeks as far as they knew. Turner was one of the newest members of the group. An Army Spec who had been riding in the loader's position of an M1A2 while they were patrolling some outer suburbs of Baghdad less than a week after it had been taken in the first blitz. They'd cleared block after block and were about to head in to the assembly area when they spotted combatants on the rooftops. What appeared to be an RPG team moving in to take a shot from the corner of a near building. His tank commander had pointed the turret hard left and was about to engage with the target, but he had missed the second team getting a fix on the bottlenecked tank from the opposite building. There was the hiss and slight pop as the RPG struck the top of the turret, a munition that failed to detonate. But when Turner had turned to see if his tank commander was all right he saw that the grenade head had bounced and docked the man's head clean from his shoulders. He did all he knew to do, slammed his hatch shut and pulled the headless body inside while screaming at the driver to reverse.

"Hell, I guess somebody better check on him," Buckner said. "It's not too far out of the way for me."

"No," Kyle said. "He's a grown man. If we don't hear anything between now and the planting day, I'll go bug him just a little. Now, let's all figure out a time when we can get these trees put in the ground."

SHE WAS was helping a patron check out a stack of books on the Civil War when they got done with the meeting. He lingered for a while with some books under his arm, poked through the magazines until she was done and the other woman had come on for the rest of the afternoon. He didn't need to be told to hang around outside after that.

He cranked the engine when she came out and got in her Nissan, followed her the few miles out to their regular meeting place along the road back to Dennis Cove and pulled up beside her under the shadow of the big oak at the edge of a turnaround. He wished he'd thought to bring a bottle opener so he could have opened the wine, but all he had that could be gotten into was a lukewarm six-pack of beer. He tugged out a couple of bottles from the paper sack and cracked them each open with the hard edge of his house keys by the time she had come around and slid into the passenger's seat.

"Well," she said, took one of the beers. "Is this as romantic as you'd hoped?"

He kissed her, arm hooked around her strong shoulders and back. "Look at you, getting mean with me."

"Is that what this is? Funny way of acting mean, you ask me."

They didn't talk for a while after that. Just tried to swim down into each other. Afterward, they sat looking at the woods, drawing breath until it seemed like it belonged in their throats. They talked of things which held little consequence for a while, worked their way by degrees toward what was always the matter between them.

"I'm guessing you still haven't said anything to him," Kyle said.

"No, not yet I haven't."

"You wouldn't be privy to a time line on that subject, by chance?"

Kyle knew the situation well enough to explain all the minute concerns and causes, but that didn't keep him from wanting to hear it said that she was serious, that she would leave her husband and make an effort toward something permanent with him. He knew too that it was all a case of rehearsal and idle desire on his part. She would have to do certain things on her own, and though he was dissatisfied with standing on the boundaries of her life, there was nothing else he could imagine her allowing.

"I can just go home now if that's what you'd rather me do," she told him.

He took a sip of his beer and told her that was the last thing in the world he wanted.

"Okay then. Quit your ugliness."

He caught himself before an edge worked its way into his words.

"You feel like stretching your legs?" he asked. "There's a pretty little creek up this way."

They got out and locked the doors, went up past a lodge and hostel that serviced hikers on the Appalachian Trail and crossed over through a small campsite with a dirt path that hugged the high bank of the creek. A mockingbird flushed and screamed at them. Kyle flapped his arm and told him to go to hell. About a quarter of a mile on they found a big boulder that projected out over a calm clear pool where they could sit and see if anything stirred beneath them. Laura removed her shoes and dangled bare feet that reflected back up at them from the bottom.

"Look, I get it, okay?" she said. "Nobody said breaking up a marriage was meant for the faint of heart."

"I don't want you to do something you don't want to."

"Is that what you think I'm saying?"

"I don't know. No. I guess not."

She took his face in her hands, made him look at her.

"You've got to trust me, you know? I haven't come this far with you for nothing. I love you, Kyle. I'm getting there as fast as I can."

He told her that he understood, took her close to him, and pressed her against his side as though fitting a broken piece back to its whole. He glanced down. The water beneath them was cradled in ancient stone.

4

HARRISON FOUND Gavin's driver Jonathan out around back running a damp rag over the windshield of the white van. Every inch of the vehicle gleamed from its evenly laid coat of detailer's wax, even the stark black German cross emblazoned on the rear quarter panel.

"You wouldn't mind running me on an errand, would you?"

Jonathan's face wrinkled.

"What kind of errand?"

"Gavin wants me to pick up another vehicle so I can start some revenue generation."

"That his word or yours?"

"It's mine, I guess. But the request comes from the man himself."

Jonathan wrung out the rag, wiped his hands.

"I'm a touch thirsty. Any way you might be able to help me out with that?"

Harrison nodded.

"Yeah, I might be able to connect you to a six-pack between here and where you need to take me."

"Alright, gimme a minute to get my cigarettes."

There were times in life when you took such an immediate dislike to another human that you would swear it was as clear as a smell. By the time Jonathan got back and started the van, the impression hadn't shifted.

After they stopped off at the convenience store for a pack of Bud, Harrison talked him through the directions he'd written on a scrap of paper. In ten minutes they pulled up to a trailer park overgrown with milkweed and whorls of encroaching kudzu. He got out and told Jonathan to wait while he made sure they had the right place. Before he'd crossed the yard, a shirtless man no bigger around than a light pole came out holding a can of Steel Reserve in one hand while the other clutched at the droopy waist of a pair of cutoff camouflage fatigues.

"You the one I talked to about the Taurus?" he asked.

"Yeah, that's me."

"Alright then. Step around back here then, why don't you?"

He went and looked at the car. Radio didn't work. One electric window wouldn't go down, but hell, it seemed to run well enough. And the man was willing to part with it without any paperwork. He went back to Jonathan's van, picked up the envelope of cash and told him to head on back, that he was good to go on his own.

"That it, huh? All slick on the side, right?"

"Yeah, I guess so. Tell Gavin I'll be back in a while."

"I'm not your errand boy."

Jonathan backed out, cut across a corner of the lot jumbled with a few road-cast empties that had lain uncollected and bleached by the sun. One can popped and flattened as he drove over it.

Harrison went up to the trailer, gave the seller the envelope of money and declined when he offered him a beer.

"Just the keys. I've got some places to be."

HARRISON HAD been wanting to see Emmanuel since he'd gotten out of prison, but one thing or another had conspired to get in the way. Emmanuel had written for the entirety of the time Harrison had been locked up, done his best to keep him in the world. Harrison did not always write back because sometimes he did not hold onto enough of himself to feel he was able to write down words that matched his mind. Still, the steady diet of letters sustained him there, gave him something that pushed through the steady wash of time, provided something distinct, something with contour.

He drove down 81 and then headed west on I-40 on the way to Knoxville, got off at the Asheville Highway exit and drove past the middle-class stone and brick homes that transitioned to Magnolia Avenue and the depressed commercial zone with its weeded lots, drive through liquor store, Little Caesars, title loan lenders, and AME Zion Tabernacle. There was a motel and some public housing perched along the strip where men draped from porches and stoops and leaned against electric poles while their women pushed thrift-store strollers up and down the sidewalks. Many were African immigrants with their dark skin and bright headdresses. But there were native blacks and poor whites too. Many simply sat there in the afternoon sun and stared at the passing traffic as if it were some repetitive television drama. They smoked cigarettes and toed the edge of the curb, waited for something that never seemed to arrive.

He turned at the corner Chinese restaurant and went back a couple of blocks. The houses were small and shabby, though some were meticulously kept. It had been nearly seven years since he'd been back here, but so little had changed. How many times had he sat out here on Emmanuel's porch and eaten Kung Pao and egg rolls, counting the sparrows and chickadees that had come in the evenings to the bird feeder while they talked and smoked weed? He saw the bungalow now, there at the end of the row, a joyous purple that he would always associate with Emmanuel, like some hue mixed and bettered from anything you might see in a flower bed. Instead, it was its own kind of achievement, something discovered through the electric possibility of art.

He parked behind Emmanuel's old Cutlass, got out and went up the steps to the front door. He knocked and looked in but could see no signs of anyone inside. He knew he should have called to make sure he was in, that he hadn't been out with some of his queer friends, but there hadn't been time, and a part of him didn't want to face the possibility that Emmanuel would take their company over his. Not after all that had happened.

It occurred to him then to check around back. He went to the gate and pushed around where it dragged from its bad angle to the ground and saw him there among the rows of tomato plants and whatever else he was trying to grow. He wore a green kimono and slippers. He hummed something that sounded like a lullaby.

"Well this is a hell of a welcome home," Harrison called.

Emmanuel turned, brightened.

"Oh my God, honey. Why didn't you tell me you were coming?"

That smile of his that was such a freely given gift. He left his things where they were, embraced Harrison and held to his shoulders.

"Are you still alive in there?" he asked.

"Parts of me," Harrison said.

"Well, we can work with that. I'll make us up a special cocktail, love. Just you wait. Come on into the house."

He fell in step at Emmanuel's side and they went in the back and through the kitchen, out to the living room with its Buddha head and the sting of incense. In the corner the easel stood with a paint-speckled sheet thrown over some work in progress. Many of Emmanuel's finished pieces crowded the walls. Some abstract and some of figures but all distinguished by their shocks of unreal color. Harrison had felt better whenever he was around any of his friend's paintings.

Emmanuel came in from the kitchen island with a pair of plated joints and matches. He set the plate on the coffee table and dropped into a recliner directly across from the couch where Harrison sat, kicked one leg over the other and posed himself there like a woman in a tight cocktail dress, the kimono drawn open well up his thigh.

"I see you've added a few pictures since the last time I saw you," Harrison said to him. "You haven't lost the touch."

Emmanuel grinned, said, "That would be about as hard as forgetting how to draw a breath, I'm afraid. Either way, not breathing or not painting, it would end up with the same result for dear little Emmanuel. But that's not what we're going to sit here and do, talk about how your poor nigger love is pining his time away. We're going to talk about big ole Jay Harrison and how his body and soul is mending. But first, first, we have to get all of our equipment in working order."

He leaned forward, took one of the joints and struck a match. Once the weed was going, he took a big hit and motioned for

Harrison to do the same. Harrison picked up the joint and did what made him feel right. That was what he was after anyhow. That was why he'd come.

"This is some of my finer accomplishments, if you can forgive my bragging. I call it Black Lace. That's a pretty good sense of it, don't you think?"

"It is. I'll have to say that it is."

So much of the weight he carried in his body began to slide free. He could feel it coming off him like pieces of something that didn't belong. He had been under this weight for so long. It had been why he'd begun to develop and build his body in the gym as a teenager. He thought it might make the pressure become more bearable. But through the years, though the body shaped itself as he pressed bars over his head and chest, the body could not rid him of this strange and vague and impossible weight. But that first touch of weed convinced him that somewhere he might find just the slightest ease.

It allowed him distance too. The distance to consider what had brought him back here. There was always something that seemed original and safe when it concerned Emmanuel. So different from the life he had led when he'd been released from prison and slid into the easy arms of someone like Delilah and the kind of solace she had to offer. What had been the necessity of survival with the other whites on the inside had ceded to some kind of odd and confusing comfort once he was back in the world. Strange to think of the violence she carried inside her as a kind of comfort, but Harrison knew no other word for it. The habit of conflict, of being pushed up hard against something that threatened you, made a difference in someone over a period of time. It built a room inside you that held a version of what seemed important, even if that importance was impossible to articulate. The question was how could you ever find a way to escape that room. How could you ever manage a way back to who you were?

WHEN HE woke the sun had gone down and Emmanuel's head was on his shoulder, one limp arm stretched across his chest. He saw the discoloration there on the inside of his right forearm, the raised bumps from where the scars had risen over the old wound from when Emmanuel had put his fist through a window as a teenager. Not for any reason other than he was young and gay and wanted to shore himself up with an intense moment of pain.

He gazed up at the ceiling for a long time, tried to force the edges of reality through his eyes despite the soft light of the hour. The bitter but necessary process that would take him back to where he belonged rather than this dream of what he desired. Emmanuel gently breathed in a deep sleep that promised to remain steady. Carefully, Harrison extracted himself, laid Emmanuel's head back in the deep cushions of the couch where he covered him with a light wool throw. He wrote a short note and left with as little noise as he could.

It was late by the time he made it back to Elizabethton and then out past to the hollow that hid the asylum grounds. He parked beside a stand of quince, sat and smoked another small joint while listening to the night. He bundled the drugs he'd bought off Emanuel in a couple of plastic grocery sacks and locked them inside a hard-cased Samsonite. He hefted the suitcase and walked through the front and directly up the stairs to Gavin's room. A pale quiver of lamp light played at the door sill and when he glanced in he could see Gavin at his desk, his ghostly face illumined by the blue cast of his laptop. Harrison tapped at the door before putting his head in.

"Ah, glad to see you're back," Gavin said, glanced up as he closed the computer. "I knew it would take some time, but I was beginning to become concerned. Is that the product you have with you there?"

"It is. Do you want me to have you check it?"

"No, no, that won't be necessary. I'm confident in your professionalism. How long before you think you can begin your operation?"

"Shouldn't be long. I know how the business works. We'll start bringing in a regular income. What's in the case here should pay for the outlay by the end of the week. We'll be making money from there on out. Plenty to keep things going. Plenty to have the cash to get the renovations done."

"Excellent. I knew I was bringing on the right man for the job. Is there anything else then?"

Harrison paused.

"You mind if I clean up in your shower? The one down where Delilah and me are is busted."

"Of course. Help yourself. There are some towels in there too."

He set the case in the corner of the room and went back to the bathroom, shut and locked the door before he turned the taps wide open. Only a weak arc of rusted water that did not strengthen nor warm as a minute passed. He undressed and stepped under the gelid splash. He washed between his legs, rid himself of the smell Delilah might detect, then stood there for a long time until he was numb and able to go on where he knew he must.

He walked down the back stairs wearing the towel around his waist. In one hand he held his clothes and in the other the suitcase. He eased his bedroom door open and quietly put his things away in one empty corner. Though there was little light in the room he could see that Delilah was awake and sitting up in bed watching him.

"I heard you when you drove in," she told him. "That was half a hour ago."

"Yeah, I had to talk to Gavin."

"You and him must have been talking in the shower then."

"He let me use his bathroom."

"That's mighty fucking white of him."

He crossed the space of the room and settled onto the edge of the squeaking bed, put his hand over her thigh. He could tell that beneath the sheet she wore nothing.

"You need to ease off him. He might not be what you want him to be, but he's given us a place to stay. A place to get a start. We need that."

"We don't need him. We need a place with people who care about something bigger than their own comforts. Gavin's a pussy. He plays at being something he's not fit for. He's weak. This is supposed to be about the strong. That's what I want to be a part of. Something strong, something independent. Let the rest of the world burn and I'll take care of mine."

He let her speak, didn't try to counter any of it. He knew she meant these things, meant them with a conviction that would never exhaust itself, but he knew too that such belief had a way of settling down for a time after it had been spoken. He wanted to think that he could make her come back around to the easy habit of themselves outside of being among Gavin and his men. But he knew how hard that would be now that she had a taste for this world and what it promised.

Harrison had met Delilah through letters. His cellmate, a skinny boy named Cole, had shown him her picture while they'd sat together in those long formless hours together and they'd exchanged pieces of their life as a kind of defense against becoming the less than human things that walked the prison halls. He wasn't sure why he asked him if it was okay if he wrote his sister. Maybe it was a desperate cast into a life that was still worth living, something that could be photographed and valued. The surprise had been when she wrote him back, when she told him that the outside had its own kind of confinement too, as real and terrifying as any prison cell.

He felt one of her hands brush at his waist where the towel was knotted and soon it was free of him and he was between her legs, fighting against a desire to leave where he was, become someone else, but then he was inside her and she moaned and clasped his body until he was caught.

5

GAVIN CONTINUED TO SCAN THE DISCUSSION BOARDS LONG AFTER Harrison had gone on to bed. *Storm Front* remained as active as ever, but it was all rhetoric. All mud people and Jewish capital and White Lives Matters and little in the way of practical matters. There were some interesting rumblings about getting a cadre together to oppose the leftist Antifa protestors on several of the California campuses when the student groups brought in climate skeptics, but there seemed to be little money behind it. More promising and closer to home was the beginning of a group devoted to traveling with Richard Spencer through colleges in the Southeast and working to agitate the protesters who would turn up. But even there, confusion rather than cohesion seemed to prevail. Everyone wanting to take credit with no one willing to take charge of the details that would ensure the thing was properly done. Then there was the case of a group running a disinformation campaign against a professor at a small university in North Georgia. He'd posted on some thread and been fool enough to use his real name. A minute on Google and the man's whole life had tumbled open as easily as if it had a combination. Several people had already run some bots with fake Ratemyprofessor reviews that accused him of anti-Semitic assignments, the occasional race slur. Anything that would have got the university honchos all riled up. It tickled Gavin to think that the Left could be so easy to lead by its own nose, so anxious to tear itself to pieces.

He shut down the computer and pushed away from the desk, sat in the darkness of the room until his eyes could adjust. He stepped into a pair of slippers he kept at the door and walked silently down the hall and stairs. He paused at several doors to see if he could hear the others sleeping before he moved on. It was a strange habit, this walking the floors while everyone else was asleep, but he'd been subject to it since he was a child. He would stand for many hours of the night and be aware of the enclosing emptiness of his surroundings and absorb the fact that he was solely aware of it, the others all trapped behind the high walls of their own dreams.

Sometimes it crushed him to realize how alone he was at this point in his life. It happened to everyone eventually, being slowly stripped of the people who made you who you were. But he could never escape the sense that his bereavement was premature, unfair. Both his parents gone by the time he was thirty. Close to two decades now that he'd been without blood ties. Perhaps that's what drove him toward building Little Europe. There had been other factors at play, of course, but maybe it was this keen awareness of being utterly alone that allowed him to recognize the power such a vision could mold. Great deeds could be subverted by a fear of hurting those you loved. But greatness was surely a worthy answer to grief.

He went outside and sat on the front steps, the huge front door left open at his back like a mouth. That's what it was, too, what it was meant to be. A mouth to speak of a truth that couldn't be acknowledged or understood by the rest of America. This place in the woods to bring the possibility of a new country together. A small country within the country. When he had first heard the idea of Little Europe he knew he was the man to make it happen. Not simply the idea of a pure and isolated community as had been tried elsewhere, a commune that would be subject to its own vulnerable politics and struggles for power. No, the necessary difference would come when it was made part of an established government. They would have to entrench politically in a place that would be receptive to the idea of white nationhood. That was true revolution, when the revolution became invisible, when it became part of the routine. That was what would make the ultimate difference.

He had heard of efforts made out in Montana and Wyoming, places where the communities had taken root in the midst of great isolation. Preserves or reservations of people who stockpiled arms and foolishly became noticed by the FBI. But these broke down fairly quickly. They dissolved because of a lack of cogency. It was unclear who they were fighting in the middle of all that wind and tall grass. Their seclusion was easy to ignore or oppress. It failed to become a message. It failed to understand the idiom it needed to speak.

Then he had realized the mistake had been that Little Europe was a place that had to be created rather than one that simply needed to be wakened. Why settle empty territory? Why not simply enter the minds of the sleepers and reveal to them their own self-interest? Wake them and show them the world could be shaped by the imagination of those with the strength and fortitude to do so.

He stood and moved out past the yard and crossed into the tree line until he felt himself muted by the entanglement of trees, the undergrowth. There was a comfort in this invisibility. How to explain that? And yet it took a kind of heroism to accept the role one was destined for, didn't it? To be the mind controlling the hand, the abstract behind the accomplishment. There was nothing wrong in agreeing with the nighttime in his soul. It was where action mounted. It was where the loss of sleep surrendered something more.

6

KYLE CHECKED IN ON GERALD EVERY COUPLE OF DAYS ONCE HE'D LET him cool off for a week and then taken him back to his place across from Gavin Noon and his followers. He took no particular pleasure in the roles of spy and nursemaid, but didn't care to entertain the possibility of another of the old man's ideas about ammunition and its application to ideological difference. Kyle had made him promise to get him on the phone if he felt any risky impulses coming on. He had him hand over all of his rifles for the next couple of months too, though there was no depriving him of his pistols. That would have been like pulling a man's healthy teeth, Gerald had said, and Kyle knew he was lucky to have gotten the concession he had.

After he was satisfied the old man was well disposed, he drove the truckload of seedlings to Buckhorn Ridge where the rest of the veterans group was meeting him. Trey Buckner helped him unload while a few of the others started digging where they were told. This was the tail end of the project on the ridge, and Kyle was proud to see it working as well as it did, as much for the men as the countryside. Orlynne had been the one to come up with the plan—having the veterans work through their trauma by putting their hands in the ground.

"One thing I've learned about menfolk," she had said, "is that the only way they ever give a damn for another's hurting is if they work together a little while. Realize they have that little bit of suffering in common before they get into anything more. Stubborn sonsabitches to a one."

It hadn't taken much convincing the next time the group met. The bad counterfeit of an Alcoholics Anonymous meeting had begun to wear on nearly every one of them. So Kyle had advanced the project to the county commissioner board in order to get access to the reforestation initiative that was coordinated with the state. Surveying the marked rows of small trees going all the way back to the newest seedlings that were being planted, he could see the time up here had been put to good use. The other men agreed.

A little before noon they put the last of the seedlings in and dug into Kyle's Yeti cooler for a cold can of either beer or Coke.

"Looking pretty damn snazzy, you ask me," Trey said, surveying the bristling ranks.

"It'll be an awful nice place to picnic up here in a few years," Kyle agreed. "Deer are going to love it too. Good way to run down to the valley and still keep cover."

Trey bottomed his can of soda, crushed it under his foot and tossed the disc in the truck bed.

"You noticed who was missing out here today, didn't you?"

"Yeah," Kyle said. "I did. I'll run out that way to check on him. Due diligence and all."

"I don't mind going out there with you. Turner can be a special kind of pain in the ass at times."

"No, that's fine," Kyle said. "Special kinds of pain in the ass seem to have become my specialty lately."

TURNER WHIST lived at the back end of a family hollow that could have been split up and sold to a real estate developer for a couple of million dollars, but unlike so many the Whists had kept the property together even if family relations had run as thin as the drought-starved creek you had to cross when you went over the bridge.

Kyle drove up past Turner's oldest brother's place and then past some of the cabins tenanted by his cousins and other distantly connected kin. At each bend, the walls of the mountains nudged in a bit closer, closed much of what was left of the sun, so that by the time he could see Turner's doublewide set back in the deepest pocket, everything in sight lay in a muted blue shadow.

He got out and talked to the geriatric Plott hound that came and licked his hand before it settled back under the house that lacked an underpinning. The dog's ribs were as plain as an anatomical diagram. No one came to the porch to see who had come even though he waited a good couple of minutes before he knocked hard enough to rattle the door in its frame.

Turner's wife Melanie finally answered. She had her boy on her hip. Too big to be carried around like that, Kyle knew.

"Hey, Kyle."

"Hey yourself."

She was a good decade younger than Turner, which meant she couldn't have been much past legal drinking age. Short yellow hair and skin that looked like it had been pulled too tight for too long. The kind of face that might have been called handsome a generation ago but now would most likely be considered hard. A face that held no happy future.

"I think you've got something I've been missing," he said.

"Missing, huh?"

"Yeah, that husband of yours. Is he around?"

"Guess that depends on what you mean by around. He's here, though."

"You mind if I step inside and talk to him a minute?"

She watched him for a while, said nothing. Her boy stared on with empty eyes.

"Shit," she said. "What could it hurt?"

She went back to the couch with the boy and let Kyle close the door himself. When his eyes adjusted to the dim light he could see the domestic congestion—the dirty laundry, the chldren's toys, the erratic scrum of everything else.

"He's back in the bedroom if you're sure you want to talk to him."

Kyle said that he did and went back, stood at the end of the hall listening for anything on the other side of the thin door. He tapped lightly, spoke Turner's name. When he heard an answer he stepped in.

The room, like the rest of the house, had no electric light. Turner was a vague shape sitting atop the unmade bed, limned by the soft strokes of lingering daylight through the blinds. Kyle's hand instinctively went to the light switch but the bulb didn't burn though he flipped it up and down a couple of times.

"Shut off a couple of weeks ago," Turner told him.

Kyle found a place on a recliner that faced him, wedged in between low piles of sour-smelling clothes.

"She tell you about the job?"

"No," Kyle said. "She hadn't told me anything. I just came up here to check on you. The rest of the group, they've been missing you."

"Missing me? I kind of find that hard to believe. Most of them can't stand the sight of me."

"That's not true. You don't know what other people think of you. No one ever really does."

If he accepted that point of wisdom, he did so without comment.

"How long you been closed up in here in the dark like this, Turner?"

"Been a while."

"Couple of days?"

"More than that."

"A week?"

Turner's shoulders made some kind of movement that Kyle took to be a shrug.

"You got a weapon in the house?"

"Yeah. I got a couple of deer rifles in the closet."

"That all?"

He hesitated before he reached a handgun out from beneath the pillow he was sitting against, placed it on a wadded sheet.

"I'm going to come take that from you now, okay?"

"Yeah."

Kyle took the handgun and slipped it into his waistband at the small of his back, then knocked around in the closet until he'd collected both of the rifles.

"Be careful," Turner said. "They're loaded."

"Nothing else in here I need to be concerned about, is there?"

"No, not now."

"I'll be back here in a minute, okay?"

"Yeah."

Kyle left the bedroom door ajar before he went back to the front of the house. His voice was shaking despite his trying to keep it quiet when he talked to Melanie.

"Don't you think you could have called somebody?" he said hoarsely.

"With what?" she spat back. "Telephone bills don't pay themselves. Nothing around here does. There's not enough gas in the tank to get as far as the highway."

"You all live right out here with another half a dozen families in walking distance."

"Yeah, well, it'll be a cold day in hell before I go to any of them uppity motherfuckers playing white trash."

"They're his family, for Christ's sake."

Her laugh was even and mean.

"You don't understand shit, do you?"

"No," he said, "I guess maybe I don't."

HE CALLED and got the deputies out to execute the welfare check and have Turner transported to the hospital psychiatric unit for twenty-four hours observation. After that, they'd just have to play it by ear, but maybe changing up his meds would help. He hoped to God so. He asked Turner if he could come by and check in with him once he got settled. Turner said that that would be fine before the deputies took him out of the hollow in the back of their car.

Melanie cussed at him for a while after her husband had been taken, but when Kyle told her he would give her a ride to somewhere she might be able to stay until things were all right she told him to wait while she packed a few things. She had a sister over in Kingsport she wouldn't mind seeing.

It was dark by the time he got home. Dark but the house was not empty. As he topped the final rise of the drive he saw Laura's car parked down by the greenhouse. When he pulled in beside he saw her walk down from the front porch.

"I'd about given up on you," she told him, encircled his neck with her arms.

"What are you doing here?"

"You want me to leave?"

"I didn't say that."

They kissed. The night paused.

"I can't stay, you know. He expects me back."

"You got time for a drink?"

"A glass of wine if you've got any."

He told her she was in luck and led her to the house. She sat in the living room thumbing through a couple of *Oxford American* magazines while he uncorked a Côte du Rhône and poured it out in a pair of water tumblers. As they drank they sat there listening to the ticking of the old tall clock. She got up to study it.

"Did you grow up with this?" she asked.

"I did. It was a wedding gift to my parents. My father's mother gave it to them. Hell of a gift to give somebody considering they didn't have a house to put it in at the time. But there it was. Had to haul it around from three different places that weren't much more than shacks before he finally got the money to build this place."

"I like the sound it lends to a house," she said. "Makes things seem more permanent. When I was growing up everything was just drywall and shag carpet. Seemed like we were being moved around like luggage through our own lives. I could see how it wore my mama down. I did. My dad didn't, but I did. He never cared about a house. To him it was just a place you went when you were done working selling tires. I think that's why I was in such a hurry to get out on my own. I love my parents, but by god I think I'd lose my mind if I ever became them."

He came up behind her and held her shoulders. She eased beneath the weight of his hands. Together they listened to the steadfast sound of what had once been unwanted.

7

ORLYNNE WAS UNEASY ON THE MOONLIT PATH. TWICE SHE'D LOST the trail and had to guide herself back by the awkward angle of the cabin's lights on the side of the mountain. It reared like a vessel on a black ocean and she aligned herself to it, made her path depend on direct opposition. By the time she reached the front steps her breath whistled high in her throat and her body felt like a heavy suit that did not properly fit. She waited until she had collected herself and tapped at the front door.

He fumbled from the back of the cabin, knocked over an object that thudded and clattered and he then came on and unbolted the door.

"Oh, Orlynne. I'd thought it was too late for you to come. Please," Gerald said, stepping aside to usher her in.

She went back to the den where he had a television on. It made a sound like a stream of water in the room. He asked her if she would like something to drink.

"Tea if you have it," she said.

"I do. Sit down."

This was the first time out here among his things. A strange solace. How long had she known the old eccentric, even if by reputation alone? But she had never imagined what his home would be like, how he would arrange the finer details of his daily life. It was only when he had come to stay with Kyle that she'd seen him as a man, a lonely old man, who was no longer anything but another human within reach. How that made a difference in their talks. And quietly something had begun, something she felt giving way in the frozen passages of her own body. Still, this was theirs alone. This didn't belong in the mouths of others. She knew how the talk would get around, how it would be reduced to an idle bit of humor, even among those she cared for and who cared for her in turn. There was an unintentional cruelty people committed against the old, laughing at what was a silent torment of the heart. So she had kept it from Kyle. Would keep this contentment to herself as long as she could. That was what you did with something you stole. And she knew that anything you had this late in life was a kind of theft.

He came back in and silenced the television, placed a cup and saucer with a Twinings tab hung over the rim. She lifted it and sipped.

"It's very good," she said.

"Good. I usually drink coffee. Are you hungry? I could find a snack."

"No, I'm fine. I just came to see you. Like I said I would."

He smiled, sat there with his hands heavily in his lap, without an idea of what else to say. It amused her to see him at such an awkward end with himself.

"I'll have to admit, this is all pretty exciting," she said.

"Exciting? How?"

"Coming out here in secret. Kyle doesn't have any idea, I'm pretty sure."

He laughed, the lines in his face beginning to relax.

"I'm sure Kyle would be scandalized. Some kind of rift in the Democratic Party would ensue, no doubt."

She weighed this a moment before speaking.

"He cares about me. Wants me to be safe, but sometimes being safe can just be so goddamn boring, don't you think?"

He said that he did and asked if she'd mind listening to some music. When she said that she'd love it he dropped the needle on a Leonard Cohen record and the mellow tones of "Suzanne" leaked from the speakers stuck at each end of the bookcase. She leaned her head against the back of the chair and shut her eyes. Cohen's young voice was tranquilizing and she knew if she allowed it she could let it do something to memory, but she didn't want that. She wanted to remember exactly when and where she was.

"Why don't you come over here and hold my hand a little while," she told him.

SHE WOKE in the middle of the night and immediately sensed his absence next to her in the bed. She sat up and saw him silhouetted against the bedroom window, a pistol clutched in his right hand. When she first tried to speak, her voice seized but she was able to make enough noise to turn his head.

"It's okay. I'm just listening," he told her.

"Listening?"

"I heard them out there for a while. They've been coming up to the back of the house the last few nights. Trying to either scare me or make me think I'm crazy, I guess."

She swung her legs over the side of the bed and pulled her tennis shoes on. She had gone to bed with him fully dressed and they had lain there close together, made a signature of their companionship against their sleeping bodies, but with the feel of the floor beneath her feet, the good memory of that abruptly fled. It was all ache and strung nerve now. A sudden return to how the real world had the capacity to hurt.

"Have you seen anything?" she whispered.

He shook his head.

"They don't want to be seen. Not yet, anyhow. They figure this is more effective. Trying to get inside my head."

She strained to listen, tried to hear what he had, though the silence she gathered threw back dissolving echoes of itself. An ever-descending bottom that created greater depths the further she delved. She touched his arm.

"Come back to bed."

He placed the pistol on the nightstand and pulled the covers up to his chest. She lay beside him, watched his eyes glisten in the dark.

"You think I'm crazy, don't you?"

"No. I don't think it, Gerald. I've never had a doubt."

He tried to laugh but it didn't quite come out that way.

"What the hell is happening to us, Orlynne? How did it get this bad?"

"Are you asking in the general or the particular?"

"Either one. I'm not sure there's a hell of a lot of difference, though. I don't feel like I know this place anymore. I don't feel like I belong."

She tried for a long time to say something to quiet him, but instead they remained like that until his eyes closed with undesired sleep.

GERALD WAS stove up the next morning and had to take three ibuprofens before he could put himself in motion. She asked where everything was to make coffee, though all he had in the pantry was some Folger's instant, so she needed only a pan of water and a mixing spoon. Still, after she'd poured it out in a pair of mugs, he told her it was the best coffee he'd had.

She sampled her own and winced.

"Lord, honey. That's something a Confederate cavalryman would have drunk in the winter of '64."

"Well, I guess I need to be a little bit more particular in my shopping in the near future."

"You sure do if you plan on keeping me around."

Despite what had woken her in the night, the morning seemed expansive with promise. While Gerald piddled with his record collection Orlynne said she was going to do some yard work, something to tidy up the immediate environment of the house. He told her not to bother but she wouldn't listen, claimed it gave her pleasure to work the ground while she could.

"Time to get the rules straight. Don't try to tell me not to do what I mean to do. I could use some music, though. Why don't you occupy yourself as deejay?"

He smiled, went back inside and began playing some Pete Seeger, and later, one of her favorites, Bob Dylan.

After she had hunted through the work shed and found an old pair of canvas gloves she started tearing out the long runners of

English ivy that had grown down the back slope of the property. She worked with method, winding the vine around the crook of her arm and using the entire leverage of her upper body to rip the rooted systems from the dusty ground. The growth gave way in small cloudy bursts and soon she was covered in a fine powder of earth. She couldn't remember a spring like this. Days that grew hot but failed to yield afternoon thunderstorms. It was as though the country had forgotten its own established cycles, refuted all laws that ensured balance. She had spent her life close to the natural world, learned to decode its messages, but this was a new confusion. Everything gone dangerously dry, as if prepared for some necessary eradication.

When she was finished she went around the side to wash herself at the spigot. She saw it then in the soft and sandy soil and her heart dropped in her chest. Just within the wedge of corner shade pressed into the otherwise undisturbed and talc-like ground. A pair of boot tracks that led to the bedroom window before straying away into the surrounding brush.

8

HARRISON PAID THE MAN AT THE MARINA FORTY DOLLARS TO RENT the jon boat for the day. Said he didn't need rods or reels because he'd brought his own, though he loaded up only two small coolers and a backpack before he and Delilah climbed aboard and cast off from the dock.

He piloted slowly around a few pontoon boats and a small sailboat riding at anchor before he opened up the throttle and bounced over Watauga Lake, headed away from the swimming area and toward the distant shore with its pines, deadfall, and steep banks. The wind was strong on his face and it dried the sweat as soon as it rose to his skin. He turned his head to see Delilah leaned back in her chair, elbows struck out wide so that her chest rolled forward under the thin wedge of her black bikini top. She saw him looking and smiled.

The first time they'd met in person she smiled like that. Like she withheld something of value beyond estimation. It had worried him then as much as now. Six weeks before they met her brother had been killed after he'd gotten Jesus and decided he didn't need the other whites inside prison. And then she had turned up to see him, to meet the man who had been nothing more than a signature on a piece of paper. It scared Harrison to think what kind of woman did that. But he realized even then that the things that scared him were exactly what he would need once he was free.

They swung around the back of a scorched-looking island with a line of footprints and a burnt campfire circle and slowed as the lake narrowed into little more than a dark stream, coins of light slotting through the breaks of overarching evergreens. The wind was blocked by the land and now there was a new and immediate world surrounding them. Something spooked from the near bank and Harrison turned to see a beaver slipping from its perch, the water closing over its totemic head. He slowed the engine further so that they made as little noise as possible. He wanted the music of what belonged here, wanted to study it as you would a foreign language.

"You sure you remember how to get where we're going, baby?" Delilah asked. She trailed one languid hand in the water, carved a slender second wake.

"Yeah, just on a bit further."

They passed out of the narrow cut and the sun caught them as if they'd been struck. He throttled up and they cleared the next broad opening, passed only a rowboat with a pair of old men fishing and a young woman sitting on a paddleboard watching them. They then entered a second narrowing where the water began to shoal and clouds of minnows attacked their passage. Once he had to push off a bar with the end of a paddle before the water deepened into a clear pool that continued to the backside of the island with its small but empty beach.

Delilah splashed over the side as soon as he cut the engine and ran the bow up on the shore. When she stood near him he could feel the metallic coolness of the lake.

"Hungry?" he asked.

"No. Pretty thirsty though."

He slid one of the coolers open and handed her a can of Coors Light. He got a bottle of water for himself and laid out two beach towels a few feet up from where the waterline lapped. They stretched out alongside one another on their stomachs, their ears pressed to the warm ground.

"Why's it taken you this long to bring me out here? You know how much I like sitting in the sun," she said.

"It hasn't been long."

"Seems like it to me. Just sitting around that creepy place all the time."

"There's no reason you can't get out if you want to."

"There's plenty of reasons. A couple of them even got names."

He didn't like the way she was tending, knew it shaped toward no good end.

"Hey, you're getting pink around the shoulders," he told her. "I'm going to put some sunscreen on you."

He got the tube from the cooler and warmed the cream in his hands before straddling her. She relaxed somewhat under his hands. Behaved in that animal way he knew she thought was attractive. And even now as she gently flexed her tan legs beneath him he could feel the muscles of her ass ride into his pelvis and he began to harden. He rolled off and washed his hands in the chill lake.

"Why you stopping? It was just starting to get interesting."

"We haven't got time for that. This is a business trip, remember?"

"Hell, we got half an hour, don't we? That's plenty of time for what I've got in mind."

He didn't let her catch his eye. Instead, he pulled a pack of cigarettes from the backpack and lit one. He didn't like to smoke anything aside from weed, but he had learned the convenience of tobacco in prison, knew it had a way of carving a segment of space, gave you a place to occupy. He just needed a little time to think, to sift things out.

Too much had happened too quickly. Only eight months earlier he'd been sitting in the correctional facility computer lab, checking job postings open to ex-cons through the state-sponsored release program. And then one of the Aryan brothers, he'd shown him how to bypass the browser's security settings, directed him to the *Storm Front* discussion threads. A new world opened with a single mouse click. There were men on the outside who needed help establishing new communities, who were willing and able to set people like him up on the outside, who saw their convict status not as a stain but as an asset. Inside, he had no choice but to belong among the whites, with their swastikas, sieg heils, and Ghost Face Gangsters. It was simply membership and a matter of protection within those walls. He hadn't felt himself change when he joined, not his truest self. How would it be any different on the outside?

It was different, of course. He soon realized that. Gavin Noon had not been what he expected. At first, he had been unable to determine what bothered him about this man who was offering him a chance at a new life. But then it became clear. He was not a man of violence, not in the way the others were. Gavin was a coordinator, a theorist. His interests were conceptual and measured, attached to ideas rather than memories, and Harrison could think of nothing more dangerous than that.

Delilah sunk her empty beer can in the water and went to the cooler to get another.

"You want one?"

"Yeah, reach me a can out."

She placed it in the sand beside him, let her hand stray to the back of his neck. Her palm remained there like it was something she meant to grow in place. He wanted to say something to her, something that she could carry away and understand, but he knew that was impossible. Unlike Gavin, Delilah was full of the hurt that had brought her here. Hurt from when her brother had been killed in prison and hurt again when she'd found what was supposed to be a sanctuary in this fantasy of Little Europe. She had been drawn to him because she'd thought him strong. He had needed her to think that, so he'd done his best to make it true, though he had learned that what was true yielded so quickly to what was not.

He heard the approach of jet skis and walked out to the wooded point of the island to see them coming on, a pair of men with women tightly hugging their backs as they raced across the placid green water. They swung around and entered the channel, their engines going silent as they neared the beach. The man in the lead, short but muscled in bright orange board shorts and Oakley sunglasses, swung a leg over the side and came within a few feet of Delilah, stood over her, dripping.

"Howdy, darling. You wouldn't know a man by the name of Harrison now, would you?"

"I might."

He laughed, wiped his forearm across his jaw.

"He must favor a smartass then, if you're any indication. He here or not?"

Harrison came forward from the tree line.

"He is. He may even have a set of ears on him."

"Glad to hear it. I was worried you'd gotten shy on me."

"Nope. Looks like you're missing something in your hand though."

The man laughed again, went back out to the jet ski where his blonde girlfriend handed him a bulky envelope sealed in a Ziploc bag. He opened the seal and counted out five hundred-dollar bills, laid them there on the beach towel next to Delilah's feet.

"A gift for your little redneck mermaid then."

Delilah picked up the cash and folded it into the cleavage of her top. Harrison fished the weed out of the backpack and set it on the beach.

"That's a pile of fun right there," the man said as he sat down in the sand and slit a Case knife blade up the plastic seam. "Come on, everbody. A party of one ain't no party at all."

The other three came out of the water and joined him. The other man from the jet ski had a small glass pipe. He was fat and had a permanent scowl. His woman giggled when she plopped down so hard it looked like it hurt. She grabbed the pipe, packed it and they each took a hit.

"Pretty fucking solid, brother. I'll have to say I didn't really know what to expect. You mind sharing some of those beers? We're fresh out."

"Sure. We're about to leave anyhow."

"Come on now," the man said. "Why is it I get the feeling you two think we smell bad? We just come up here and dropped half a grand and you don't even want to spend a little fellowship. That seems decidedly uncharitable."

Harrison had already seen the shape of a revolver tucked in between the man's shorts and life vest. He gathered the beers and handed them over.

"Get yourself a couple," the man told him. "You and the mermaid both. Maybe she'll loosen up a little bit with a touch of lubricant in her."

The girls tittered.

"She's fine. I told you that we're both fine."

"Boy, the way you say it seems more like you're telling me to go fuck myself. What do you think, Taylor? Am I imagining it or does it sound like this wayfaring stranger is telling me to fuck myself?"

The one called Taylor grunted, pawed at the sand. Harrison picked a beer for himself and squatted a few feet away from the others, sipped and waited.

"That's better. I feel relaxed now. I don't feel like I'm being rushed. A terrible thing for a man to feel his leisure is rushed."

The man took a deep toke from the pipe before passing it along. Harrison wondered how long the man had stood in front of a mirror working on his hardboiled personality. Every gesture and word like something he'd gathered from a pulp paperback. He'd seen what happened to men like that, men who acted as though the force of their bluster would make up for their lack of attention, their failure of intelligence.

"I've noticed something about you," the man said.

"You have?"

"Yessir. I've noticed your eyes. They don't look like the eyes of someone who lets much get by him." He reached down and patted the grip of the pistol. "I saw that you noticed the old hog leg here just as soon as I stepped up on the beach. But you acted like you didn't notice it. Didn't want me to know that you knew. I find that pretty interesting. I find it interesting that you'd still stand there and act like you were the one in charge of how things were going to transpire despite the fact that you knew I was holding the cards that mattered. That tells me you're pretty confident. Tells me you think you don't have too much in this world that gives you any concerns. And I'll tell you, that makes me think you're a dangerous man. The kind of man that makes me think it was a prudent idea to come out here toting a piece in the first place."

"You've got it all figured out, sounds like."

The man smiled, shifted so that he could draw the handgun from his waist and set it in the sand beside him.

"I don't mean nothing by that," the man said. "I just want to sit here and be comfortable. I hope you don't mind?"

"I'm just sitting here."

"That's true. You are just sitting here. Not a troubled thought in the world, I'll bet. You look like somebody who may have spent plenty of time sitting and waiting. Probably know the inside of a small room pretty well, huh?"

"You got a point you want to make?"

"I'm just getting to know my friendly drug dealer. There's nothing wrong with that, is there? I'm a friend to the working man. There's no reason why people can't discover common ground across class lines."

The man showed a small file of hygienic teeth.

Harrison cut his eyes to Delilah, told her to get their stuff in the boat. She bunched the towels and began to load the remaining cooler. Harrison slipped the backpack over his shoulder and turned to go. He was already walking when he heard the footsteps of the man behind him, heard him exclaim, "Now hold on, you goddamn dumb redneck . . ."

Harrison pivoted and grabbed the man's wrist above the pistol, twisted down sharply so that the gunman lurched over Harrison's planted foot. They went to the ground hard with Harrison on top, the pistol kicked loose. Delilah was there within a moment, holding the gun on the others who were mute with shock. Harrison pinned the man between his legs and rained down half a dozen quick punches on the man's unguarded face. The man's eyes went distant and sleepy with concussion. Harrison stopped when his hands began to register hurt, sat there over the unmoving lump while he leveled his breath.

"Was this worth it? Was this fun for you all?" Harrison shouted to the others. Though they did not answer, he took their silence to mean they thought it was not. He grabbed the pistol from Delilah and tossed the remaining cooler into the boat, started the engine and wheeled out of the channel and around to the island's point. As they passed he could see that Taylor and the two women remained sitting where they were, looking at the fallen man but afraid to approach him, as if his condition was somehow communicable. Harrison tossed the handgun in the water and throttled up. The bow rose.

"You could have killed him," Delilah said into his ear so she could be heard above the noise of the engine.

He nodded.

She kissed him at the back of his neck, put her hand over his sun-cooked thigh.

"I wish you would have."

WHEN THEY returned to the compound some of the men had dragged a big Weber grill around to the side and were grilling ribeyes and tight cylinders of corn in aluminum foil. The smoke moved over the big back lot. Jonathan stood sweating over the flames with a long fork, stabbing the cuts and flipping them over every few seconds.

"That smells good," Delilah said.

"You go ahead and get you some," Harrison told her.

"You don't want to eat?"

"I'm going to go lay down for a while. You're hungry, though. I'll be down there in a little bit, don't worry."

Harrison kissed her briefly and went up to their room. He could feel her watching his back as he left.

He stripped out of his clothes and washed himself with a cloth and a bowl of water that had been left out on the pine dresser. Pulled on a clean T-shirt and a pair of torn but laundered jeans. He took out the two hundred he needed, folded it into his hip pocket and returned the rest to the envelope he would take to Gavin. Somebody had turned a radio on outside and he heard Johnny Cash and Willie Nelson singing about their many reincarnations and lawless deeds. He went to the window and looked down. Delilah had moved in among the circle of others, one hand on her hip, the other holding a can of Bud. She seemed to fit there as exactly as though she had been cut to form.

He lay down and closed his eyes, let his mind reel free. Before he realized it he was asleep and dreaming of a kinder life.

9

THOUGH THE SUN WOULD NOT RELENT, THE MEN CONTINUED marching along the broad shoulders of the highway. They dragged large plastic sacks behind them and gathered whatever did not belong. Aluminum cans and assorted wadded rubbish fattened the bags until they were misshapen burdens that needed to be tied off. The old moving van came rolling behind then and Jonathan grabbed what remained and loaded it into the back. Gavin walked along behind that, ensured that no single piece was overlooked.

At the top of the hour he waved his hand to gain their attention, shouted for the van to be shut down, to have everyone come on and get water from the cooler.

"We won't get the job done if we're heatstruck, gentleman," he cautioned. "Make sure to get some ice as well."

The men stood in a conversational circle, drank deeply from red Solo cups. Some smoked cigarettes. Gavin drew fresh water whenever someone needed a refill. It moved him to see that they worked without complaint. These were good men. How could anyone see them as anything else? Good men who cared for the betterment of their small corner of the world. All they required was the hand to tend and correct them.

He recalled how often across the years he had stood aside when among other men. An aid far more than a participant. As a boy he was obsessed by his own physical weakness. The asthma attacks taught him to be afraid of what his body couldn't handle. His father was a bluff, hearty man, and though it was never directly addressed, Gavin could see how it pained the old man to recognize the insufficient creature he had fathered. That was what had driven him to know things, to observe and learn how people behaved. If the strength wasn't in the body, he could discover it in the mind. And the best way of doing that was to make himself indispensable in some way. Give them something to believe in—that was the only way to make sure you could be dependably admired and loved.

After the sun had slid past its hottest zone they resumed the policing and cleanup. Heat came off the asphalt in distorting waves. Cicadas whirred.

Gavin turned at the sound of gravel crunching behind him. A marked SUV with its blue lights stirring and folding in the humid air. The door swung open and Sheriff Holston dragged himself out, fanning his Stetson a few inches from his ruddy face.

"Mister Noon."

"Hello, Sheriff."

"Looks like you boys are out here busting your ass."

"They've put in a good day already."

"Looks like it. I hate to come out here when it's plain to me that you mean good by what you're doing, but there's been complaints."

"Complaints?"

"Well, a complaint. But it was to the effect that you had come out here as a party without requesting proper paperwork. This area, it's part of the Adopt-a-Highway program, and there's a method for applying for permissions. I know you didn't mean nothing by it, of course . . ."

"And how do I go about by applying for permission?"

Holston clapped his hat back on his head, winced up at the sun.

"It really is powerful hot out here anyhow. It's just best to call it a day and make sure your folks are back home sitting in the shade, you ask me."

"We'll be happy to do that, Sheriff. As long as you tell me who I need to talk to."

THE FOLLOWING week Gavin had Jonathan drive him down to the county courthouse and accompany him into the boardroom where the county commissioners' meeting was being held. It was a plain little room at the back end of the facility that had a single window looking out over a courtyard with a pair of locust trees. The ceilings were high and plaster, cracked down the middle from the stress of age and thin budgets. At the front a long table where the seven members of the commission were seated behind name placards and microphones attached to flexible metal necks. The gallery seating was arranged in aligned rows of folding chairs, and as the audience began to file in people were having to get up and shuffle around so as to allow adequate room. That, together with the poor ventilation, quickly turned the air hot and hard to bear. Gavin felt the sweat along his ribs and spine, felt his skin becoming as slick as if it were freshly painted.

The chairman of the board rapped his gavel on the sound block until the few listless comments of the audience trailed off. He opened the meeting with a few procedural remarks and a review of the evening's agenda. From the corner of his eye, Gavin could see a young man in a blue cotton blazer feverishly recording these particulars in a small moleskin book. A reporter from the local paper, he surmised.

The chairman opened a thin file of papers and began, "Now, I would like to get to a few pieces of board business that are fairly run-of-the-mill in the name of expediency. Once we get through that we can move on to more Byzantine matters. Are there any objections to that?"

The board raised no complaint.

"Very well. Let's attend to all new business as it concerns the sanction of the county. I believe there's a bill here regarding participation in the highway cleanup program. It appears that an organization under the name of Little Europe of Carter County has posited an application to take care of a three-mile stretch of road that runs from lower Elizabethton down to the Warlick unincorporated township. Do we have anyone in the gallery who intends to say anything in support of the application?"

Gavin raised his hand.

"Yessir? Are you Mister Noon?"

"I am."

"Very good, Mister Noon. Could you please approach the podium? I believe the microphone is already switched on."

Gavin pardoned himself as he moved past the young newspaper reporter and assumed his place at the lectern, tilted the microphone toward his mouth.

"Good evening. I'm Gavin Noon, the individual who has submitted the request. I'm sorry that we didn't understand the need to put this paperwork forward when we began collecting the trash. We were simply trying to practice good stewardship as part of being new members of the community. We'd certainly not intended to violate any codes. I explained this to Sheriff Holston, who has been very gracious and understanding in the matter."

"That's fine, Mister Noon. Could you speak to us briefly about your organization?"

"Yes, I'd be glad to. We are an intentional community that believes in reclaiming ethnic distinctiveness as part of our cultural identity. As part of that goal, we firmly support the laws and principles of the American ideal of individual expression and the right to self-protection. To that end, citizenship is at the forefront of our collective interests. We see the health of the local government as complementary and essential to our own. To that end, we desire to be part of giving back to the area and to establish our investment in its continued betterment through volunteer efforts and other charitable activities."

"Thank you, Mister Noon. Does anyone have any questions or comments for the gentleman?"

The old man Pickens covered his microphone and said something unintelligible, though Gavin could see that it drew glares from several of the other commissioners. After a brief exchange of whispered conversation, the younger commissioner, Kyle Pettus, edged his microphone closer and spoke into it in a mild, controlled voice.

"Mister Noon, could you please elaborate on the name of your organization? I believe you said it was called Little Europe? Can you tell us a little about that?"

Gavin cleared his throat, tightly wrung the edges of the podium.

"Yes, Commissioner. Little Europe is an acknowledgment of historical precedence. It informs our sense of cultural and philosophical distinctiveness. It is merely a unifying term for a larger ideology."

"Yes, I understand that. I was wondering, though, if you might clarify that ideology somewhat for members of the commission."

Gavin paused, pressed ahead.

"It is a community founded in pride not apology. It declares itself along lines of genetic identity without reservation."

Several members of the board traded looks.

"Mister Noon, does your Little Europe community have any ties to neo-Nazi parties?"

"Absolutely not. That is a categorical falsehood. There are many entities in this country that do not associate themselves with any violent or discriminatory sects that seek to break the law. Our community is self-sustaining and contributes to the ongoing prosperity . . ."

"Yes," Pettus broke in. "I've heard you say so. However, is it true that a Nazi flag, that is a red flag with a swastika symbol, was flown from the flagstaff at your current residence?"

"There was a mistake when we first arrived. Some of the community members were overzealous and did not act wisely."

"I see. I've heard that flag is no longer flying. Do you confirm that?"

"Yes, I've made sure it was removed."

He could feel dark moons of sweat soaking through his shirt under his arms.

"But since then there have been reports of a new flag. Is that true?"

"Reports?"

"Yes, other county members in the area have made note of it."

"Yes, I made the change myself."

"Could you describe the appearance of the current flag?"

"Yes, it's a cross. A black German cross, what's commonly called an iron cross, on a simple field of white."

"And what's the significance of this flag?"

"I'm unaware of any significance other than it demonstrates a sense of pride in white identity. There is nothing malevolent intended by it, if that's what you're implying. Every other ethnic group in this country is encouraged to exhibit pride in their heritage. We are simply part of that collective movement in order to preserve what we hold dear. I have no guilt for being a white man, no shame. That doesn't make me a threat. It merely makes me honest. Let me remind the commission that neither I nor any direct members of the Little Europe community have participated in any violence. In fact, we have been quite consistent in our opposition to violence, even when it may have been directed toward us . . ."

"Thank you, Mister Noon. I'd like to ask the board that we table this issue for further discussion in closed session. Would that be all right, Mister Chairman?"

"Yes, yes, I believe that would be the best course of action for the moment. Thank you for your comments, Mister Noon. We will pick up this issue again as soon as it is feasible. If you would please take your seat."

HE STRODE into the hall with Jonathan unable to keep an easy pace beside him, banged through the outer door. Stood there holding his arms like he was pinned by something he couldn't name. His anger a tumor in the hollow of his throat. It was all that prevented a hoarse scream.

"Mister Noon, sir. If I could talk to you a moment?"

A voice from inside the courthouse, as the door was quickly closing. The door was flung open and he saw then the damp face of the young reporter appear, his hands still busy writing in his notebook. Gavin composed himself, assumed a beleaguered smile.

"Yes, can I be of some help?"

"Yessir. I'm Karl Sealy. Municipal and crime reporter for the *Carter Citizen*."

Gavin extended his hand and they shook.

"Delighted to know you, Mister Sealy. I subscribe to your publication. I'm sure I've enjoyed several of your contributions."

The young man actually blushed and stammered before continuing.

"I was hoping we could talk about something you said. Something about acts of violence that have been directed at the members of the Little Europe compound."

"Not a compound. A community. There is a significant difference. A compound suggests militancy, which is not at all the case. Words like that matter, Mister Sealy. That's the sort of thing I need people to understand so that fear and assumption don't color people's opinions before they have a true sense of what Little Europe is about."

"Yessir, I understand. Is there something you might want to tell me?" he asked, folded the notebook shut and tucked it in the inner breast pocket of his sports jacket. "Something that doesn't necessarily have to go on record?"

Gavin touched his fingers to the shallow cleft of his chin as he considered.

"You said that you were also tasked with crime reporting?"

"Yes."

"Well, what might interest you is something that may not have received any official paperwork. An incident at Little Europe involving members of the very same governmental entity as the one deciding the fate of our application this evening. And even though this incident might lack formal documentation, I'm certain that the several members of the sheriff's office who were summoned will not have lost all memory of what they witnessed. Does that sound like something that might prove worth your attention?"

"Yessir, it absolutely does. Is there a number I can reach you at, Mister Noon? In case we ever need to sit down and talk a bit?"

"Absolutely. Jonathan, please hand Mister Sealy one of our cards."

THAT NIGHT after the house had succumbed to the quiet of the late hours, Gavin sat up at his desk with a cup of herbal tea, scrolling through the familiar *Storm Front* threads. He clicked through and read some of the creative writing that had been posted since he last checked. His favorite was a series of Batman fan fiction that portrayed the Gothic vigilante in a steampunk world of the Reconstruction South where Bruce Wayne was a dispossessed Virginia planter. The author's name was WhiteGallah00d, and his stories had sharp dialogue and charismatic villains, including the grandson of Nat Turner, a grandstanding fiend called The Emasculator, who practiced a strange mix of voodoo and Zoroastrian ritual after he murdered sleeping tenant farmers and raped their wives and sometimes their children, regardless of sex or age. It thrilled Gavin to read these kinds of stories. They seemed truer than the source material somehow. More than simple comic books in that they had generated these distinct and different lives from their mainstream origin. These stories were owned by the people, had become part of something entirely new.

He had begun to try writing something of his own. Nothing he had taken too seriously, but still he recognized a certain therapy in the recording of these ideas, worked out as they were in the frame of a dramatic story. He wrote about Captain America, what he would have been had he known the truth of the holocaust lies.

He opened the file of the first story, one he'd called "The Dresden Massacre," and uploaded it to the fan fiction thread. He would be curious to hear what the other members of the community might make of it. He refreshed the screen three or four times before he grew bored and shut the computer down, listened to its motor cease and cool.

He checked his phone several times as he sat there and thought. He had sent Jonathan back to the commissioners' meeting. He needed to understand more about that man Kyle Pettus. Told Jonathan to follow him and make a record of the man's actions. A simple enough task, he hoped, but still he had received no word despite several texts.

Men could be so disappointing. The idea of what he wanted to accomplish was pure and full of such promise. But there was always this intervening thing that seemed to wreck it all. A lack of common purpose, a desire for empty appetites. He wanted these people to recognize that what they were trying to do was as important as when those first European explorers staked their claim in the American wilderness. It took such extraordinary faith to create a country that could endure. That was where abiding strength could be found—in a community that looked beyond the glib advertisements for beauty and sensuality and superficial gain and saw the inner content in being among others who shared the common roots of race. No fear or misunderstanding of what some other tribe might hold as dear. Only the deep satisfaction of being finally at home in the world.

Sleep was beyond him now. He realized there was no need to attempt it, so he went silently down the stairs carrying his shoes and put them on only after he had crossed the dusty front yard. He turned and looked back at the old asylum. A ghostly and imperial edifice there in the overall mountain dark. It was an extraordinary thing to have made this happen, to make others see its viability. A restoration to something they had believed irretrievably lost. He needed to remain patient, that was all. The one thing that could undermine his efforts was haste. Instead, he must remain deliberate, measured. He must not allow others to make him the caricature they would have preferred him to be.

At the road he paused as he waited for the quarter moon to enmesh itself in the tree branches. Once it did he slipped through the mottled light, a creature of mere shape and motion, who left just the slight signature of sounds as he went across and climbed the trail that led to Gerald Picken's cabin. He circled around to where he could see into the bedroom window and stood there for a long time to let the wilderness settle around him. Inside no lights burned. Still, he gained suggestions of outlines and angles. The old woman wasn't there this evening. This could be it then, if he chose. He touched the barrel of the pistol riding in his front pocket. This could be a quick decision. Kill the old man while he slept and make him a victim of his own self-righteousness. There was a certain justice in that. But he did not draw the pistol. He only watched Pickens sleep. The old man oblivious to the charity he was being granted. There was a power and dignity in that too.

10

KYLE HAD A FULL DAY IN TOWN. HE HAD DRIVEN OUT TO THE HOSPITAL to sit with Turner Whist for a while, played gin with him in the visitors' room for the hour they would allow, then came back to meet a man from the seed supplier to figure out how best to plan his summer orders. It was all a scratch of numbers on yellowed tabs of paper and that kind of patient give and take between men who, though each had a thousand items of account in their heads, nevertheless persisted in the illusion that they had all the time in the world, and they would be content to walk away if the deal fell through, though neither man wanted or could afford that. Eventually, they put the business to rest, pleased that neither seemed too proud or abused and that they parted on good terms, the future orders settled.

He drove around town aimlessly for a while, considered drinking a couple of beers to linger in the warm feeling of accomplishment before going back to the empty house. He got as close as sitting in the parking lot of a little out-of-the-way place off the highway where he could see a couple of guys shooting pool under the honky-tonk lights when he decided it would be better to look in on Gerald once more, make sure everything out there was as quiet as he wanted it to be.

All the house lights were blazing. Even so, he made plenty of noise coming up the side of the hill. Wanted to be sure the old man knew that whoever was coming had no surreptitious designs. Once he made the final crest, he could see Gerald had come out to the front steps, was scratching one of the goats behind the ears while he pondered the evening.

"Hard to recall a season this dry, ain't it?"

Kyle took a moment on the bottom step to catch his breath before answering.

"I thought it was the green thumb's business to worry about turns of the weather. You aim to run me out of business? I don't think I could stand the competition."

Gerald joggled his head, laughed.

"You want a pinch of snuff?"

"Yeah, why not?"

Gerald's vague hand moved in the dark to his shirt pocket, pinched a small take for himself before flipping the tin of Skoal to Kyle.

"First time I ever took this stuff I felt like I was going to puke my guts up."

"Why hell, son. So does everybody. That's why we keep at it."

"And why's that?"

"To prove we can take it," Gerald said, spat.

They sat there listening to the night for a while; the flying bugs thumped themselves against the naked porch bulbs.

"You know, when somebody brings up the weather, it's usually as a way of getting toward something else," Kyle said.

"Hell, weather is all we have to talk about. Seems plenty enough to me. Land out here scorching under our feet. Damn hurricanes every other week down in Florida. We've made this hell we're living in. This, this is just the epilogue. Makes unnatural things natural. Makes people like these across the road, makes these cockroaches know it's time to come out and feed."

Kyle was wary of the way Gerald's mind had turned.

"I don't need to be worried about you out here by yourself, do I, Gerald?"

The old man's eyes crawled the dark.

"They been sneaking out here, spying on me."

"Spying on you?"

"Hell, I know you think I'm crazy, but I know what I know. Don't worry, I'm not going to shoot them. Not dumb enough to play into their hands. Dumb enough for plenty of things, but not that."

Kyle stood and stepped to the edge of the porch, listened for something out there that might lend credence to what the old man believed.

"You feel unsafe out here, Gerald?"

"Hard for a man my age to care too much about that, idn't it? Every morning I wake up I imagine I've found a way to beat the odds. No, I don't worry too much about what might happen to me. I think they just want to let me know that they could do something if they wanted to. Want to show that they're young men and I'm not. Nothing too unusual in that, is there?"

Kyle ignored the question and the accusation it implied.

"You got my number in your phone, you know that?"

"Yeah, I know it. I might even bother to dial it once I need to."

Kyle nodded, stepped down. "That's good," he said. "You want me to step out here in the yard and look things over?"

"Naw. You get on home. I imagine if anybody can, it's me that can find some peace in the evening dark."

KYLE DROVE back through Elizabethton slowly. It had gotten late and much of the town had succumbed to one of its habitual early nights. There was no surprise in that. So much of what happened here was as dependable as a timetable. Some despised life in small towns because of this predictability, but it offered its own pleasures, its own particular support. Perhaps that was at the heart of why he worried about what this involvement with the people from Little Europe could mean.

His conversation with Gerald had worked something slow and nagging inside him. Gavin Noon didn't belong, and by trying to wedge himself into their community he had started something. Gerald had been right. There was a difference in how this outsider meant to steer the future. You could see it on him as clearly as if it had been stamped. And once it would be allowed to start there would be something dangerous born in people's minds. The world would begin to seem like something that could split and reveal inner poison. Hatred could take hold of a place like a virus, and once the mutations began to multiply and infect, it would turn everything inside out. Noon represented what people buried in their shame. Kyle wouldn't let people forget their conscience just because someone played a clever sleight of hand.

He cleared town and took the country highway. The looming dark of the mountain blocked out the town lights and he switched on his high beams. As he did so he caught sight of a vehicle trailing him. Not too close, but enough to note as he turned onto the riverside gravel road. There were only three other houses this far out in the hollow and they belonged to families who would have been abed at a far more decent hour. He crept through the deep curve above the falls and pulled the .380 from the glove box. He rested it on his right thigh while he wheeled down the straightaway with his free hand.

The headlights pressed in nearer until he could feel himself silhouetted in the truck cab. The entry to his drive was only a few yards more. Before he came to it he whipped abruptly in to a patch of hard ground, cut his lights and slid across to the passenger's side. He dropped out just as the following vehicle slid past, so that he had the cover of his truck between him and them. His nerves went tight when the car swung up into his driveway and stayed there, raced the engine. It was too dark to see how many might be inside the car. Could only tell that it was a sedan of some kind. He slithered down a few steps and chanced a quick glimpse across the truck bed. If they came at him now he had time for three maybe four quick shots from the semiautomatic. But in the dark, accuracy couldn't be counted on. The car remained where it was, made its high racing threat. He aimed at the passenger window, snapped the safety free.

The car swung back wildly in reverse, struck the truck's rear quarter panel and bounced with a tremendous shower of gravel. Kyle touched his finger to the trigger and two quick reports went somewhere into the night before the car was away back the way it had come, brake lights flashing. He stood there for a long time, until he vomited into the ditch, steadied himself so that he could climb back into his truck.

The moon was up but it was like something he'd never seen before. It lay tracks through his eyes. He felt it had the power to split him.

PART II

11

JONATHAN HAD WATCHED HER FROM HIS HIGH WINDOW IN THE evenings when she went by herself to the edge of the property to walk beside the softly breaking tree line. At first, he had tried to stay to the interior shadows, but with each repeated appearance he began to believe she wanted him to see her, so he stood at the sill and gave her what she wanted.

He'd been with women like her before. With a man for convenience, protection, or perhaps simple habit. But always looking for a chance to slip the leash. Still, Harrison wasn't someone to be casually overlooked. Even if he didn't want anything to do with Delilah, the shaven-headed muscle freak wouldn't abide the humiliation of open betrayal. It would take strategy then, finesse.

"Hey, you gonna share one of them cigarettes?" she called up.

He leaned forward from the open window.

"You want me to throw it to you?"

He was smiling, having fun with her. He saw the smile returned.

"Hold on a minute. Let me get my boots on."

He sat on the edge of his military-made cot and snugged the black leather boots on. Popped, wrapped, and tied the laces and was down the stairs inside of a minute. The crisp drills of basic training still held their mold somewhere inside his head. All that hurry up and wait had evidently written itself into him in such a way that he was always ready, always responsive. Army was good for that, at least. Harrison might have the hard schooling of being locked up, but Jonathan had this ability to duck and move, react to other shifting pieces on a board game table. Find out where he needed to position himself in relationship to everyone else in order to gain maximum advantage.

She had drawn up against a pine tree, one leg cocked back while she waited.

"You're johnny on the spot, aren't you?"

"I know better than to keep a serious woman waiting."

He held out one of his cigarettes, lit it for her.

From the house they could hear Gavin and a couple of others talking on the front porch. Mostly just Gavin, which was the way he preferred it.

"How'd you ever run across him?" she asked.

"People with a purpose have a way of finding each other, don't they? I could ask the same about Harrison, couldn't I?"

Her smile thinned, though she still held his eye.

"I don't want to talk about him right now."

He couldn't tell if she was wounded or merely pretending to be.

"You haven't had much chance to get out into town, have you? Why don't you take a ride with me for a little bit. Run the roads."

"Don't you need to ask somebody for permission before you go running off?" she teased.

He knew he had her then.

"No," he said. "Do you?"

THEY STOPPED for a sixer of Natty Light and drove out past Hampton and the lake, just to put miles behind them. It was soon dark, and Jonathan parked down an old logging road. It was warm out despite the hour and sitting inside the van without air-conditioning wasn't comfortable, so they tore off a couple of beers to take along on a walk to get fresh air.

"You like walking out in the woods with attached women?"

"Is that what you are?"

She made a movement with her shoulders.

"Seems like a reasonable question. Just so we can understand how things lie."

"I feel like we're both beginning to get a pretty good idea of that."

Her silence didn't contradict him.

The ground steepened and the loose soil underfoot began to roll and squirm as they trudged toward the switchback. Jonathan steadied her by the bicep as they climbed. He could feel the live strength of her jerk beneath his touch like closed circuit. Even so, she didn't discourage his guiding hand.

"Look at that there," he said, pointed above the ridge at the scimitar moon.

She went on ahead to get a better view. She pushed through the low branches until they came to the ridge crest and all the mountains were patchworks of shade and cool moonlight. He settled his hands around her hips. She turned to face him, did not pull away. She had a smell that made him want to hold her hard enough that she couldn't breathe.

"That's nice," she said.

"What is?"

"The way you touch me. Like you mean it."

After a while she worked free and went out to a higher rock to get as close to the sky as she could. She sat down, drew her legs to her chest, and began to talk.

"One of my mama's boyfriends, he used to take us both out into the woods at night and teach the constellations. He had a telescope he'd take with us and we'd run through everything. Even now I can tell direction on a clear night."

He came up and stood next to her, his hand placed on the stone, just beyond the warmth of her thigh.

"I've heard a compass is pretty good for that too," he said.

"I didn't come out here for you to make fun of me."

"I didn't mean to."

"Yeah, you did. You think that makes you better than me, talking like that. That's what men do."

He saw no profit in contradicting her. In a minute, she slid off the rock and started back toward the van.

She turned her head over her shoulder.

"You coming or you want me to leave you out here for the bears and coyotes?"

He had been ready to laugh when he heard the step of something heavy in the brush. Without a word, he hurried back.

12

HARRISON WHEELED DOWN 75 WHILE EMMANUEL DOZED IN THE SUN. The day was hot but he ran with the windows down while the wind played at his chest and face. They were down to the Georgia line by noon and into the commuter sprawl of Atlanta by the end of the lunch hour. Harrison prodded Emmanuel awake. He sat there under the heavy influence of sleep for a few minutes before he was able to give directions.

"It won't take long. I remember the place pretty well."

They got off the interstate and cruised into midtown, where they parked in a stucco deck. Harrison picked up his gym bag from the trunk and left the car itself unlocked. It was empty and besides, the only vehicle in the parking area worth less than fifty thousand dollars. They walked down the smooth dark concrete of the ramp into the tremendous city light and heat and it was if they were cast onto the blister of a completely new world, but they moved through that too, past all the glass and Gucci until they found the sidewalk and began to make their way through the midday crowds.

Ten minutes later found them in the climate-controlled lobby of the hotel where they stood waiting for one of the glass elevators. When it arrived it made a sounds like expelled breath. No one else was inside, and when Emmanuel pushed the button for the top and it began to lift them they could see the lengthening dimensions of the inner building rush away.

The doors opened into a dark corridor that held a single door framed by a rectangle of sunlight. They walked toward it as they heard the sound of lapping water and people talking. The door opened and a naked bodybuilder stood blocking the way.

"Are you here to see Mister Sterne?" the bodybuilder asked. As they got closer they could see that he had touched up his cheeks with the suggestion of rouge. Also, he smelled good, some expensive perfume dabbed along his neck or chest.

"We are," Emmanuel said. "He's expecting to see us."

The bodybuilder stood aside and waved them through.

As they crossed the threshold they came into a large area contained with a high glass ceiling open at the peak. Several nude men wearing sunglasses sat sunbathing around a turquoise swimming pool sipping cocktails from zinc mugs and long-stemmed glasses. At a recess a black man wearing a woman's single-piece swimsuit served drinks across a lacquered bar.

"Emmanuel, my savior, there you are!" an old man wearing a terry cloth robe crowed. He wore a hemp beach hat pulled down on what must have been an enormous skull. He reminded Harrison of Marlon Brando in *The Island of Doctor Moreau*.

He stood and took Emmanuel in a full embrace and did the same to Harrison as soon as they were introduced.

"Excellent to finally meet you, my boy. Your reputation does you many favors. Would you care for refreshment of some stripe? A Mai Tai or something more butch perhaps? We do have an entire cooler stocked with Samuel Adams."

"I'm fine, thank you."

"Of course you are, my lad. But please, before we get to any significant discussion, I'm absolutely overheated. Let's all retire to the pool for a few minutes."

Without waiting to see if his visitors were in agreement, Sterne loosened his belt and let his robe pool at his feet, releasing pale bulk unguarded by the mercy of clothing. He strolled past and cannonballed into the pool with a tremendous splash. Emmanuel and Harrison disrobed and lowered themselves into the water via the ladder. They tread water as they watched Sterne make two laborious laps before waving them over. The beach hat, though streaming, remained clapped securely to his head.

"Much better. Thank you for your indulgence, gentlemen. Now, with all propriety served, I suppose it would be efficient to go ahead and discuss the vicissitudes of our business arrangement. I understand, through Emmanuel here, whom I implicitly trust, that you may have means of distributing product into a region that remains relatively undeveloped, is that correct?"

Harrison nodded.

"Well, I am certainly open to the idea of diversifying all my assets, though I am a little hesitant, if you don't mind me saying so. It was my understanding that the lovely hills of Southern Appalachia were rather saturated with distraction of the prescription variety or otherwise that scourge known as methamphetamine. Both nasty strains of human suffering, from what I've seen. Something I'm not at all interested in becoming entangled with. The powder that we move is at a price point somewhat beyond the grasp of the working classes as well. I'm uncertain, in short, that there's a sufficient market to support its distribution."

Harrison watched the fat man's limbs flapping in the water. It was as though the air of his words alone were what buoyed him up.

"There's plenty of tourists. Plenty of college kids," Harrison told him. "I know how to unload what you give to me in good time. You won't lose a dollar."

Sterne pinched his nose and slipped his head beneath the waterline. He reemerged with tears in his eyes.

"Your confidence is inspiring, Mister Harrison. I must say it does make all the difference in the world to discuss these details in person, it really does. I wouldn't dare contradict a man of your . . . conviction. Nevertheless, I must remain prudent. Why don't we start with a reduced amount? Conduct something of an environmental scan before going the whole proverbial hog. I think that would put my mind at rest while allowing you time to secure a smooth infrastructure on your end. Is that something you might find agreeable?"

Harrison, knowing that he had no choice, said that it was.

"Excellent. I trust the gym bag you've left over by the beach chair is your end of the bargain, so I'll have my people exchange what is a fair market value while we enjoy a little more time in the water."

Sterne raised his hand to call the attention of the bodybuilder. The man briskly approached, and seeing the bag of money, took it with him out a glass door at the far end of the swimming pool. Harrison followed the man with his eyes and was caught unawares when Sterne splashed him across the face and giggled.

"So intense! I can see why you've collected him, Emmanuel. He really is something else."

Emmanuel said nothing.

The bodybuilder returned in a few minutes and settled the bag where Harrison had left it before. He and Emmanuel swam to the pool's edge and heaved themselves out. They stood dripping while they waited on an attendant to bring them towels. They had dried off and dressed by the time Sterne ascended the shallow stone steps and stood basking in the refracted pool light with hands on his flaccid hips. Harrison collected the cocaine and nodded his farewell as they left by the door through which they had entered.

They walked around the corner to an expensive steak house and sat in a deep booth next to a view of Peachtree Street. Commerce and transit in its full urban flower. They ordered martinis and ribeyes and ate hunks of hot buttered bread while they looked through the window at men in suits and tight shoes flustering past.

"This is the kind of people we have to work with?"

"It's the price of efficiency, honey. I wouldn't lead you astray. I hope you remember that. It's been enough to keep me out of the big house working with people like that."

"Hey, now. No need to get rough about it."

"Sorry, I wasn't thinking. Anyhow, the last thing I want to do is sharpen up my pen pal skills all over again. I've done enough of that already, don't you agree?"

"I do."

The martinis arrived. Harrison popped one of the olives in his mouth as he drank.

"It's fine. As long as he doesn't run scared we should be able to do respectable business. Nothing like what you do in Knoxville, but still something halfway justifiable. Then we'll see from there."

"You're using the royal we, I take it?"

"I don't know, Emmanuel. I told you things are complicated with Delilah."

"Sounds to me as if you like them being complicated."

"Is this the part where you play the pissy queen?"

"I only do that when you decide to play the part of the closet faggot."

Their steaks came and they ate without speaking. Their utensils hard against the metal plates.

"I have obligations. I thought you understood that."

"Yeah, obligations. You and your cracker whore. Don't you ever get worn out by all that shit? Doesn't it get confusing?"

"Look, this is the way my life is right now. You've known that. I never pretended any different."

Emmanuel watched the smooth blur of outside life, slowly chewed.

"Order me another fucking drink, please," he said. "I absolutely cannot tolerate being blind sober just this very minute."

AFTER DROPPING Emmanuel off in Knoxville, Harrison drove on toward Little Europe and made it back in the hour of the last good light. Civil twilight was the term. Emmanuel had named one of his paintings after it. That time when the sun was gone but light enough remained to live under its natural blush. A kindness in what remained of a lapsed day. The painting was a landscape, a picture of a river slicing through the base of a mountain, the sun gone over the ridge but still present. Harrison had thought of that, thought of what Emmanuel must be expecting from him and how the colors of the world were at work on what it would make of them. How ridiculous it must have seemed, how trite. A black man in love with a white supremacist. Could have been a joke if he ever managed to figure out the punchline.

There was still the question of what to make of himself with Delilah. Time spent with someone had an effect on who you were and what you could become, as surely as a tool held long enough would wear a callus. Harrison knew Emmanuel sensed the kind of people he'd been forced together with in prison. Too much of the then and now working inside Harrison's head to sort it out in a way that made sense. Delilah offered an extreme. A desire for belonging, but belonging that demanded you reject the rest of the world. Hate was love. Hard to see it any other way once you were inside and breathing the different kind of air that everybody else did. Hard to imagine surviving any other way.

He parked around the side of the building and tucked the gym bag under his arm, walked up to the room and stowed the drugs behind the removable panel at the back of the closet. He pressed the wood back in snugly and piled some of Delilah's shoes in front. It was far from perfect, but he had no better options. He had just shut the door when he heard Delilah coming from the end of the hall.

"Hey."

"Hey yourself. I was wondering if you were going to get back tonight."

"I told you I was."

"Yeah, you told me."

She stepped past him and flung herself across the bed. The box springs creaked. He eased down beside her, put his hand on the pillow next to her head. It seemed like a foreign member there, dark and encumbered.

"Look, I'm tired of this being mad at each other."

She turned her face toward him, said nothing for a long time. He took that as some measure of agreement.

"Can you just please leave me alone for a while? Please?"

He thought of asking her where she would want him to go, but instead he simply rose and left the room.

13

KYLE WAS WORKING THE GREENHOUSES ALONE, WAITING FOR Orlynne to turn up, though it was already late in the morning and he was beginning to worry. He went in to call her from the land-line, but there was no answer. He was getting ready to get washed up and head off the mountain when he heard her Jeep climbing the drive. When she pulled into sight, he saw that she had Gerald riding along in the passenger seat with her. As peculiar a sight as he could have imagined. Kyle went up to the porch and sat there waiting for her while she parked. When she came on it was alone, a newspaper folded under her arm. The old man remained slumped in his seat like he'd taken root there.

"I was about to send the sheriff after you."

"I'm sorry. I didn't think it would take as long as it did or I'd of called."

"Well, I guess there's a story behind it."

"I'm afraid there is, though it's not a good one. I'd meant to tell you about me and Gerald before now, but it just never seemed to come out right. I want you to know that. I wasn't trying to hide nothing from you."

"It's your business, Orlynne. You know that."

"Well, I'm afraid you're more a part of this business than you might think you are. You haven't heard what the paper published?"

"I'm afraid to ask."

She reached the newspaper across, her thumb highlighting the front page headline and the file photograph of Gerald. COUNTY COMMISSIONER FIRES ON CITIZENS. He skimmed the details. They were, in the main, accurate.

"Goddammit."

He wrung the paper between his hands a minute while he tried to think.

"You get him out of your Jeep and inside. I've got to run into town about this. Don't let him off the mountain, you understand?"

"Of course I do. Why do you think I went out to his place and got to him as quick as I could? You want me to call anybody?"

"No. Just set here a while. Boil up some coffee and wait to hear what I can find out."

He pulled on a clean T-shirt and a pair of tennis shoes and drove down to the county courthouse. He went straight into Holston's office without a knock or announcement.

"You want to tell me how you can't keep your deputies from running their mouths?"

Holston glanced up from a small tower of stacked incident reports, leaned back in his chair with his coffee cup held aloft in the exaggerated gesture of a gentleman at leisure taking his ease.

"Look here. It's my favorite Dopeocrat. Why don't you cop yourself a squat? I imagine I have a pretty good idea about your concern already, but why don't you enlighten me?"

"Running your goddamn mouth to the press? Are you serious?"

"Now, let's not make assumptions. And please do refrain from taking the Lord's name in vain. We are still a few of us Christian men and women in this godless modern age. If you'll care to remember it was me who came with every intention of keeping the old man clear of public scrutiny. And the fact that it has remained so is no small achievement in and of itself. People have eyes and they have mouths. It is awfully difficult to keep them from using them, especially with the passage of time."

"This will ruin him. You understand that, don't you?"

"Would you please sit down? You're making yourself hysterical."

Kyle sat and watched Holston turn the coffee cup in his hands.

"Now, I realize why you're upset, alright? I commiserate. And no, I didn't tell my deputies to run out and tell tales out of school, but this little pissant at the paper decided he wanted to have something to print, something that might get a little attention over in Knoxville or Chattanooga. Maybe he's looking for a pay raise or a gig in something bigger than a backwater. Be that as it may, this is something that's going to have to be dealt with, both on the personal and the political level. But it can be done. If I know one thing it's that Gerald is a tough old bird. He's not above being able to shoulder a little bit of disgrace. What's that anyway but a little bit of trampled pride? You do realize this is going to force him to resign from the commission, don't you? Enough digging and there's no way in hell we can keep this a secret. You need to start thinking about what your next move on the commission is going to be, what kind of concessions might be reached in order to soften the blow."

"Concessions? You mean letting Noon and his racists have their way?"

Holston shook his head, set his cup down so that it thumped the desk with a dull ringing.

"Why is everything such a hard line with you, Pettus? How can you sit there and tell me this is a case with definite edges? Do I want these sumbitches out there praising Himmler and Goering and every other jackbooted killer that ever came down the pike? And yet, what have they done? What have they really done to infract the law? They're protected citizens, Kyle. As much as you and I are. They have every right to participate in the community. You can't run them out of town just because you don't like what they believe. You've got to remember where you live. You know as well as I do that there are plenty of folks out in the county that don't really disagree with the fundamentals of what they're saying. Just a little difference in word choice here and there, but it's no accident that people like this picked Carter County."

"You're telling me they're harmless? Is that why one of them followed me back to my house?"

Holston leaned forward.

"What are you saying?"

"The other night. After the commissioner meeting. I was followed right up to the base of the driveway. I pulled over and then he slammed into me hard. Put a hell of a dent in the back end of the truck."

"You get a license plate?"

"In the pitch black, blinded by headlights? What do you think?"

"And no positive ID either, I'm going to hazard? Look, all I've got is an unverified report of a hit and run with no outside witnesses. You expect me to run somebody in for that? You're smarter than that, surely. You come back with something I can work with, then that's different, but until then all you have is an accusation that makes it look an awful lot like somebody trying to cover his associate's tail end. That won't turn out well, I can promise you that. You need to cool down and figure out your next move. I can send a deputy out past your place ever so often to keep an eye on things but it's a big county and we've got a lot bigger concerns at the moment than Gavin Noon and his group of white boys. There is this little thing commonly referred to as the opioid epidemic that has my present attention. Now, I think we've both got enough to keep us busy. Why don't you see to your business and let me attend to mine?"

Kyle left and spent the next half hour placing calls to the other sitting members of the commission. They agreed that they'd have to arrange a special informal meeting as soon as they could. They agreed to get together that afternoon at Shepard Dixon's law office and use one of his conference rooms. Shepard was the longest-serving member of the commission, and though he held no political allegiance to either Gerald or Kyle, he said that he despised the idea of making things into something obscene. Above anything, Dixon despised needless gossip.

By the time he got back home, Orlynne had Gerald out helping her water some small pear trees that they'd just transferred into larger crates. Standing there working at her side without the slightest sense of worry or concern. It made Kyle want to knock him flat on his ass.

"Gerald, I need to talk to you a minute."

"I'll be there in a while. Orlynne needs my help at the moment."

"Now, goddamnit!"

His face turned like it had been struck.

"Go on, Gerald. It must be important," Orlynne said. "I can handle this just fine."

They went up together to the house and found themselves across from one another in the living room. Gerald refused to sit.

"Go on and say what you mean to. I'm not accustomed to being talked to that way. Damn sure not from some buck half my age."

"I'm sorry, Gerald. Please, just sit down. I was wrong to use that tone," Kyle said, showed him a pair of empty hands in contrition. "Please, we need to talk."

The old man relented, though once seated he maintained as soldierly a posture as he could.

"All right, I'm listening."

Kyle told him of what had happened, how the other commissioners had agreed to meet in order to discuss the inevitable fallout. As the words hit him, a certain change in his demeanor and even in his complexion began to take place. The facts almost appeared to have a certain mass to them, as if they were capable exerting physical pressure against his personal resolve.

Gerald shook his head, leaned his elbows fully to his knees so that he looked like a man on the verge of collapse or penitence or some disagreeable hybrid of the two.

"Those sonsofbitches. I played right into their damn hands, didn't I? I went and did the one thing they wanted—to be persecuted."

"Let's just wait and see what everybody at the board meeting has to say. This is by no means something that's set in stone."

Gerald laughed a tired old man's laugh.

"Of course it is, Kyle. I'm stubborn but I'm not a fool. Not a complete one at any rate. They've got me nailed to the tanning board as clear as if I was a damn jackrabbit. Them letting it go, I should never have bought that for a second. I'd thought them snooping about my place was going to be the end of it, but clearly that was just their way of having some fun."

"What are you talking about?"

Gerald's eyes lifted briefly before turning back to the floorboards.

"They come up at night, set out there in the yard just beyond the tree line. You can hear them calling to one another in what is supposed to be sounds like owls or whippoorwills, but nothing makes sounds like that but men. They wait until we're asleep before they come all the way up to the house. You don't ever see them, just their boot tracks the next morning. There's no note telling you what that means, but it doesn't take much of an imagination to figure it out, does it?"

A column of connected events assembled themselves in Kyle's mind. He could see the architecture of things as clearly as if it were sketched out and arranged at a drafting desk. The silent pressure of Noon's people. Working in the shadows while the world of daylight tried to go on as though it were untouched by suspicion. This was how someone who wanted a deviant reality had to operate, he supposed. Be something harmless and familiar until you weren't. Perhaps that's all this really was—a failure of imagination. A failure to see how quickly things could go wrong.

They drove over to Shepard Dixon's law offices and entered around back. They were the last two members of the commission to show up. Everybody else was sitting around a long mahogany table drinking glasses of water or cups of coffee. Dixon stood up and greeted them, shook their hands.

"I am relieved to see you both. This has weighed on me all day," Dixon told them in that odd syntactical refinement that seemed at direct odds with his otherwise hard-nosed demeanor. Kyle wondered if this mix of appearance and behavior was a self-conscious style developed to keep his legal opponents off balance. It had certainly served the man well in his political battles.

They all took their places at the table and Dixon asked the rest of the commissioners to please remember that all comments at this unofficial meeting were not being recorded nor would any formal minutes be kept. Once they had assented, he turned the floor over to Jack Hogan, the recently appointed chairman of the county commission.

"First, I want to thank everyone for making time on such short notice. I know we all have plenty of things going on in our own personal work days that makes that more than a simple matter of routine. Additionally, I'd like to thank Commissioner Dixon for the gracious use of his space here . . ."

Gerald popped up from his chair.

"Jesus, Jack! The man just told you there wasn't a recording. Let's be honest for once, step clear over all these platitudes, okay? I screwed up. I get it. I screwed up royally and I need to pay the price. I recognize that. I'll tender my resignation at the next meeting. There'll be a special election. You all need to figure who it is you want to run. There's always old Bud Cannon over next to Hampton. He might be up to it."

"Bud Cannon talks like he's got marbles in his mouth," Seth Buchanan, who owned the highway movie drive-on interjected. "His chances of being elected if opposed are about as good as my wife's house cat. Hell, maybe Pickle would fare better."

A few men laughed.

"I'm afraid if Gerald quits, the election won't be unopposed," Kyle quietly said. "I'm afraid we'd be looking at this problem head on."

"You mean Gavin Noon?" Dixon asked.

"I do. I can't believe I'm saying it, but that's exactly what I think. And I'm afraid of what that means, about how that changes the complexion of things. How does that affect the place we live when we allow a man like him to make a claim on the public office? How do we reconcile that to the country we've all grown up in? I talked to the sheriff about this. He told me something that maybe shouldn't have surprised me, but it did. He told me that there's not a hell of a lot of difference between the kind of community Noon wants and what a lot of people out here in Carter County would agree with. That's not the way I like to think about my home, but maybe it's not entirely untrue either. You don't see a lot of black families itching to move out here, do you? A scattering but that's all. Rebel flags no further than a quarter of a mile apart even though just about every family up here was pro-Union during the Civil War. But history doesn't have a damn thing to do with it anymore. Doesn't matter if your great-great-grandpa ambushed any butternut home guard he could, what matters is that even if your life has run down the backside of a toilet, at least you're a white man by God, and you're going to let the world know it.

"What happens then when a man like Noon can run for a position of government? It makes all of those racist jokes and hatred legitimate. It makes the whole ugly violent mess of who we are something to ignore and it makes it acceptable to do anything we please because we are just protecting what makes up our genetic code.

"And that's why you can't resign, Gerald. That's why we can't afford to let you."

They sat for some time before Jack Hogan tapped his knuckles on the table in lieu of his gavel.

"We need to decide something," Hogan said. "And I believe it would be best if we proceeded in agreement. Does anyone have anything else to contribute?"

"I do, Mister Chairman," Dixon spoke in his mellifluous voice. "I believe Commissioner Pettus has arrived at the most important juncture of this concern. This is not so much a matter of the law or politics as it is a sense of moral obligation. Gerald, I've known you a very long time and I disagree with just about every position you've ever taken, but I recognize your commitment to the people of the county, your desire to serve them to the best of your ability. I, for one, will not see that undone by a cadre of Nazi revisionists, because make no mistake, that's exactly what they are, regardless of what nomenclature they might adopt. I think every man in this room would agree to the same."

A subdued nodding of heads circled the table.

Jack Hogan then cleared his throat.

"Well, Commissioner Pickens, you've heard the opinion of the board. Will you reconsider your decision to resign?"

Gerald, who had remained standing throughout the duration of the discussion, slowly lowered himself into his chair, sat there with his hands folded like a man ready to be sentenced.

"I will do my best in continuing to serve at the pleasure of my peers," he said. "If they judge that to be the best course of action."

"We do."

"Mister Chairman, I would like to add one thing," Dixon interposed. "This is something best dealt with in the open. I believe we need to hold a special public session in order to state our position regarding this issue. Put the fire out before it gets going, so to speak."

"What do you think, Gerald? You ready to claim a bit of the spotlight?"

"Hell, I ain't afraid of a bit of spirited debate. Makes democracy strong, don't it?"

"All right. Let's work out the details over email in the next couple of days. I think it's about time I shuffled on to the home front. Let's consider this meeting adjourned."

GERALD WAS silent for much of the ride back to Kyle's place. Just the jostle of the truck chassis and the long green slideshow of passing scenery. Kyle had offered to stop off and grab something quick to eat but Gerald had said that he wasn't hungry.

Kyle was beginning to see something in Gerald he had not expected—weariness. In the time they had served on the board together, he had been irritated by but admiring of the old man's zeal, his ability to follow an argument of procedure or regulation. Though many of the other commissioners considered Gerald a professional contrarian, Kyle had recognized his eye for detail wasn't a simple matter of fastidiousness but an ethical concern. Not to stick to precision and nuance was to fail as a gatekeeper of the law and what it sought to protect. But something in him had begun to change, something that seemed to have shaken him at a basic level. Perhaps it was age, though he suspected it was more than that. Perhaps he was just ready to remove himself from the obligation of a public life and enjoy the time he had left, to have some quiet moments in the sun.

Orlynne met them out front as they drove up, said she'd finished the work that needed to be done for the day. It was clear that she wanted to be alone with Gerald. Once the old man had gone out and gotten in her Jeep, Kyle pulled her aside, asked her to make sure he didn't go back to his cabin for a while, not until things were better sorted out. He told her that he could drive out and check on his animals in the meantime to make it easier on everybody.

"We've already took care of it, honey. We've got Molly and Malone tied up by my camper. I've always wanted a couple of breathing lawnmowers down there anyhow. I'm about tired of pulling weeds all day as it is. You'll know where to find both of us if you need us."

He said that he did and stood there on the porch, watching them go off the mountain.

14

DELILAH KNEW THAT SHE WAS BEING FOLLOWED. SHE'D KNOWN IT since she'd first begun slipping down past the tree line in the heat of the day and following the long piney shadows as far as the banks of the Doe River. At first she'd been unsure who it might have been, and at any rate, it was hardly the first time she'd had a man want to see her without her clothes on. But it didn't take long to figure out.

She took a different path down to the water each time she went. It was the secrecy she wanted as much as the shade. And there was that added risk of becoming lost, the chance of becoming swallowed by the wilderness that attracted her. Maybe it wouldn't be so bad if she never found her way back to that old place anyhow. She never had a shortage of men who would take care of her, and all most of them ever really expected was little more than a few minutes of sweat and a couch of flesh to throw themselves on like a whale stranding on a shore. Just another transaction. One that didn't need to be fair because why should she ever find herself at a deficit? But she knew Jonathan was still following her. Since the night of the moon up on the ridge she knew he wouldn't be able to turn her loose. She had seen to it.

Harrison was a different breed of man though. She sensed it the first time he'd sent one of his letters. There was something skewed in him, something that was able to knock her off balance. Maybe it was just the mystery of a grown man who knew what he thought of things, who knew how to go after them. There were few men where she grew up who seemed to have any ambition other than the next government paycheck or prescription bottle. But Harrison wanted more for himself and the idea of attaching to that conviction thrilled her, made her feel capable beyond measure. Harrison was strong in ways she'd only begun to understand.

That was what caused the trouble with Cole, of course, him being as runty as he was and trying to pretend to something he couldn't keep. Always under the shadow of their daddy who had died too early, his heart just going like something that had been set on a timer. Then Cole had taken it into his head that he was the one who was meant to take care of her and their momma. That long string of men hadn't thought too much of that, nor much of Cole either. Though they did pay plenty of attention to her, the kind that made her momma turn jealous and hateful.

Still, when Cole had turned up dead it touched something off in her. She'd gone up to the penitentiary to visit him and they'd sit and talk. She was his only visitor, he'd told her, and she'd been glad to have that between them, a feeling of two people who had come through something and survived and who were maybe making a future worth looking forward to. Then that had been snapped. A telephone call from her momma blubbering, telling her Cole had been stabbed to death in the prison workshop. Because Momma suddenly cared about what happened to her children now that there was a chance to cry and to get to carry on. Now that is was a good way to have people feel sorry for her. She even went and got saved, started going to church and asking for prayer requests. She'd tried to get Delilah to go along too, but Delilah had told her the only thing she had in common with the Bible was the name she was given and she imagined she was likely headed to the same hell as her namesake.

She took her top off and her bra, a ratty black Kmart thing that looked like it was made from a T-shirt. She didn't need it much anyway. Her body was good. That was the one thing she'd gotten from her mother that was worth a damn. She slipped her shorts down and considered doing the same with her panties, hang it all there on one of the tree branches like a flag, but she decided that would be too much. Make him ask her to, even if the asking was with his eyes more than his mouth.

The water was cold but she could bear it. The current had some life, and that made the chill a complication that invited her in. She'd always liked to swim in the woods. Gave her a chance to forget what she wanted to. She pushed off from a rocky bar until she was in a good deep pool where her toes would barely brush the bottom when she tread water. Around her the slick flashing shadows of startled trout. Above her the scattershot cries of jaybirds.

"I know you're out there," she called up toward the bank. "I've known it for a little while. Why don't you come out so I can see your face and not hide up there like a thirteen-year-old boy."

Jonathan came in little halts, stood there at the river edge holding a small plastic bottle of liquor in one hand. He squatted down and watched the play of the water, wouldn't look her in the eye.

"Why you acting shy?" she asked

"I ain't acting like nothing." he said.

"You afraid of the water?"

"I don't guess I am."

"Why ain't you swimming then?"

"I forgot my bathing suit."

"You don't need a bathing suit in the woods. Come on, I'll even close my eyes."

She screwed up her face, made a big show of scrunching her eyelids. She heard the whisper of jeans being shed from his body and then him coming into the water with a sharp intake of breath as the cold hit him in his middle.

"Is it safe to look?"

"I never said you couldn't look, did I?"

When she opened her eyes she could see that he was up to his chest in a feathering of water, the bottle at his lips.

"You gonna share some of that? I figure you owe me for not going and telling on you."

"Telling on me for what?"

"You know for what."

She swam a few strokes toward him until her feet had purchase on a flat of sand. She stood and reached her hand out, her breasts pinkened by the cold water. She took the bottle and turned it up until the sweetened liquor rolled down her throat and then was gone. She filled the bottle with water and let it sink and settle to the bottom. She saw him take in the fullness of her.

"Why are you acting this way all of the sudden?" he asked.

"What way?"

"Since that time up on the ridge you've acted like I barely was alive."

She tilted her head, like she was appraising something of dubious worth.

"Why are you men always such goddamn fools?"

"I don't know what you're talking about."

"Of course you don't. You and every other dirt-digging sonofabitch in this country doesn't know what a woman wants or thinks. You've got to have everything spelled out for you like it was chalked on the board by a Sunday school teacher. Don't you think women ever get tired of that, of having to wait on you to figure the world out?"

"Seems pretty clear to me that you've decided you belong to somebody."

Real anger flashed in her eyes.

"I don't belong to a goddamn soul," she said, baring her teeth. A moment later, she remembered to ease up, to let him think she'd forgotten his words. "Besides, who said one is ever enough or enough all the time? A woman has her own mind, her own way of sifting out what matters to her. Come here a minute."

He pushed himself through the barrier of water, came to where a placid patch of sun on the quieted current showed the pale flickering shapes of their bodies beneath the surface. She took him by the wrist and placed his hand against the base of her throat, closed her hand over his fingers until his grasp was a tightened crown against her jumping pulse.

"Can you feel that?" she asked.

He nodded and tightened his grip.

"That's what you're doing to me right now. Making me live quicker. Making me want something I don't get as much as I need. Whose business is it but mine and yours?"

"Nobody's," he said.

She kissed him, wrapped the stringy wet tails of his hair in her fingers, tasted the shared liquor and musk of his mouth with the deeper scents of mud and moss and old deadwood in the woods around them. She had him then and she knew she would go on having him as long as she needed.

15

GAVIN HAD BEEN SLEEPING POORLY. HE BLAMED IT ON THE SUMMER heat and the dry air. So many weeks without rain and the country was baked down to its thinnest parts. Some of the men would go up to the lake in the afternoons to cool off on the beaches and banks and drink cans of beer, but that had never held much appeal for him. Though he was glad to have these young men with their energy and belief in what he was doing, he never felt truly joined to them. He preferred the occupation of a hermit, took his contentment from important moments of solitude.

No hour was more meaningful and lonesome than the middle of the night. He knew many engaged their greatest fears and anxieties when waking at some insomniac hour, but it was never that way with him. Time froze when he awoke and could not go back to bed. Everything aligned and took on firmer substance. It wouldn't be really truthful to say that he suffered sleeplessness as much as endured it as one endures a temporary ailment before rising to greater strength.

He realized that he had taken a preoccupation to bed with him earlier in the evening. Though he'd not consciously registered it at the time, he carried it into his dreams and wrestled with it there in dissolving and occluded images. The stories he'd read on the message boards, the soft blue glow of the computer screen like some pale lamp on his mind.

There had been a change in the Batman fan fictions he was reading and he couldn't understand what about that change gripped him so intensely. What was strange about it was how much he disliked the direction the new tales had taken. He had been upset that the vigilante, The Emasculator, had been written off casually, being dispatched with little more than a few indifferent descriptions of a quick and clinical death when Bruce Wayne had trampled him under the hooves of his horse on a deserted road and crushed the former slave's spine. There were no final words between the foes, no satisfying collision that typified their mutual hate. Instead, it was if the writer had simply lost interest in their relationship and couldn't be bothered with the trappings of suspense. It made Gavin angry to have become so invested in the outcome and then to be emotionally cheated.

But that anger then became confounded when the next story featured a different kind of villain for Batman to face. Her name was The Dreamkeeper and her powers were far more insidious that anything The Emasculator had ever been able to wield. She was a former slave who one day appeared at Wayne's war-scarred mansion and offered her services. He had taken her on as a matter of philanthropy without thinking much of it until she had begun appearing to him in a starkly different form during violent nightmares. Though the woman was meager of flesh and bone, in the dream world she was immense and commanding. More animal than woman, and more avenging spirit than either. She towered above Wayne, becoming a titan that struck a primitive and impotent fear in him, so that even when he woke and walked the length of his plantation during the day, he shrunk from the sight of the small shuffling woman. He began to doubt himself and withdrew from his commitment to the Virginians he had sworn to protect, a mere shadow of his former heroism.

It was then that The Dreamkeeper began to speak to him. She no longer loomed in the same sinister way. Now, she reduced herself in his presence, invited him to approach her. He did so, though not through an act of self-directed will so much as if he were drawn to her through some psychological magnetism or spell of witch-craft. Regardless of how the distance was bridged, she and Wayne now entered into a diabolical intimacy wherein she revealed the extent of her weird abilities.

She told him that she could grant any wish he might have, that it would indeed become the literal truth of the waking world, though he would never be able to witness the fulfilment of the desire with his own eyes. Wayne, under the delusions of his fever dream, did not question the consequences, and immediately cried out for his parents to be allowed to live once more. The Dream-keeper smiled broadly and announced that it was done.

As soon as Wayne woke he could hear the sounds of conversation downstairs, and he recognized his father's booming laughter and his mother's measured tones. He did not rush down at once to see them. Instead, he absorbed their presence, these living ghosts that had been brought back into his life. He did not even fear the strange magic that had allowed the past to be rewritten.

He gradually dressed, stood before his long mirror and contemplated his own middle-aged appearance. He wondered what his father would make of him now that he had a son older than he. What his father would think of him when he learned of his dual identity and how the two halves had sought to solve the riddle of darkness, both outer and inner.

He went unhurriedly down the stairs so that his parents could hear him, could prepare themselves for their reunion. But as he rounded the balustrade and entered the hallway that would take him to the dining room, he heard them recede, their footsteps carrying them with great swiftness toward the back of the house. He paused, tried to make sense of their sudden flight, but when he went on to find them deeper in the gloom of the house they once more eluded him, their banter carrying in from the verandah. Wayne then bitterly recognized the meaning of The Dreamkeeper's words and sat down to a solitary breakfast brought to him by the old slave woman, her rheumatic gait belying this new power she held over him.

"You will never see them, Master. Never!"

Gavin closed the laptop, sat there in the room with all of its silent darkness, let time break over his strange and furious helplessness.

THE FOLLOWING week a notice was put in the paper that the county commission would be holding a special meeting behind Rhineman's BBQ, a place just at the edge of Elizabethton that backed up to the Doe River. It was described as a gathering to "hear public concern," which doubtless referred to the story about Gerald Pickens. Gavin had been curious how the board would play its next move and now here they had.

The evening of the meeting he brought two of the men who had been in the car when Pickens had opened fire. Harrison had intended to come as well but had some business out of town that prevented it. These two were both Southern boys who did no favors for breaking stereotypes. Big and dull-featured, with cropped hair and a propensity for elaborately incorrect grammar. Still, they were material witnesses to what had happened and their attendance would be an uncomfortable reminder.

There was a sign out front advertising the event, white Christmas lights strung up in the trees. Reminded him of a Sunday afternoon picnic more than a civic meeting, which was exactly the point, he realized. Show that they had nothing to apologize for. A hard stone of resentment began to form somewhere deep inside Gavin's throat.

Gavin and his men found folding chairs under the limb of a big dogwood tree, sat and watched as the community members began to arrive. Most of them stopped off at the long table where the commissioners stood serving out heaping platefuls of pork barbeque, ears of corn and cornbread baked in cupcake tins. All on the house, they told everybody as they smiled those political smiles of theirs, steam rising from the spoons.

Once the seats had filled and everyone had begun eating, the commissioner chairman went up to a stand where a microphone was lying. He fumbled with it a minute, asked if they all could hear them, which they could.

"It's a mighty pretty night out here tonight, isn't it?"

A few voices agreed that it was.

"I appreciate everybody coming out on an evening like this. First, I'd like to say, as the chairman of the board I'm proud to belong to a place that has folks in it that care about their government, about the details of what goes on with the people they elect. I want to let you all know too that we've got someone out in the audience with a microphone so that if you have questions you want to ask, we all will be able to hear you. This is meant to be a time when all voices are heard."

He kept talking like that for a while, speaking expansively of very little while the crowd chewed and gazed on. After a while though, one older man sitting up near the front waved his hand for the microphone. A girl who worked for the restaurant brought it over.

"Come on, Jack. We're down here to hear the straight damn story about Gerald. You've already been elected. We don't need to hear a stump speech tonight."

Several people laughed.

"Sir," the chairman responded tightly, "would you mind saying your name so everyone has a chance to know who holds the floor."

The old man laboriously came to his feet. He was wearing overalls and a Bank of America ball cap. He briefly turned to the crowd, said, "I'm Jim Turner. Own Turner Feed Store just this side of Warlick." He faced the table where the rest of the commission sat, pointed and said, "Tell us, Gerald. Did you shoot at those boys like it said you did in the paper?"

The old man leaned to one side to listen to something one of the other commissioners spoke into his ear before he said, "I did discharge a firearm on my property."

A ripple of astonishment went through the rows.

"Well, you got anything to add to that?" Turner asked.

"Yes, sir. I did so as an act of conscience."

"Godamighty man. Well, in that case I've got a question for the sheriff. And that's why you weren't locked UNDER the jail?"

The crowd made a restless and confused sound as several independent and contrary comments sounded.

"There weren't any charges filed by the district attorney," Commissioner Dixon broke in. "As a result of that action, the board has come forward to declare its support for Commissioner Pickens. We are proud to take a stand in an issue the board believes deeply matters."

"A stand in support of criminal assault!" a voice shrieked above the general clamor.

Gavin turned at the sudden cry to see the journalist Sealy had come to his feet. The girl with the microphone circled around to the back and handed it to him.

"Karl Sealy, general assignment reporter for *The Carter Citizen*. Can you explain why the board is not demanding the resignation of a member of its committee for blatantly disregarding the law and in effect committing assault with a deadly weapon? Can it explain how this isn't a textbook case of small-town corruption!"

A few people bristled at Sealy's concluding sentence. Dixon took the commissioners' microphone and smiled.

"Mister Sealy, where are you from?"

"What's that got to do with anything?"

"It's just that I'm trying to figure what constitutes a small town to your mind?"

"Not that it matters, but I'm from Atlanta. North Atlanta."

"There's some nice places in North Atlanta. I've heard the Braves just built themselves a billion-dollar stadium down there in Cobb County."

"Can you please answer the question, Commissioner Dixon?" Sealy demanded, his face coloring with heat.

"Well, I'll tell you something I've learned about corruption in my time serving this community, the community where I grew up and came back to after my time away, being educated in the ways and means of a metropolis. Down there in your native land, as a matter of fact, where I studied at Emory. It's far more common to allow corruption take root in a city so large that people don't take the time to greet one another when they pass on the street. More common to let corruption thrive when an ideology is allowed to prevail without understanding its eventual human cost. More common for ambition to override empathy too, even in a field in ostensible support of the principles of democracy. A field such as journalism, for example. Whereas, people that commit to service in small towns do so because they can see the result of their good work. The quality of life is appreciable. So, if you want to challenge our decision as a body as a result of something that issues from corruption, I'm simply going to have to assume you don't truly understand the meaning of the word. Nor, do I think, do you understand the meaning of good civic-mindedness."

A few shouted their approval and clapped. Sealy stammered something about serving the best interests of the public before he slumped back in his seat. Gavin put his hand up in the air and the girl handed him the mic. He stood and introduced himself.

"Mister Chairman, it's a pleasure to have the chance to address the board once again. And I'm glad to hear Commissioner Dixon raise this issue of civic responsibility. The people who live in the Little Europe community wholeheartedly agree and abide by the tenets of said responsibility. If we did not, these circumstances would be quite different, as many of you in this gathering might be able to imagine. It's true that no criminal charges were filed because I was under the impression that there was a misunderstanding on the part of Commissioner Pickens. Perhaps this was due to some age-related cognitive impairment or some other set of circumstances that I simply didn't understand. Regardless, it was my impression that the best thing for the county at large would to allow the board to self-police, to keep things out of the strict eye of the law. I thought this because as newcomers to the area, we want to be a force for good, for stability. We have tried to reinforce this commitment by our participation in the highway cleanup, an initiative that was blocked by this same governing body for undisclosed reasons, though it seems clear now that it is a simple matter of personal grievance. The actions of the board tonight do nothing to dispel that. I must say too in light of tonight's declaration of support for Commissioner Pickens that I feel a very clear threat to the safety of those who live in the Little Europe community has been signaled. And I would like it to be fully understood that such threats, physical or otherwise, will be met in the strongest possible terms."

Half a dozen people came to their feet. One bearded man in a pair of cargo shorts and an unzipped fishing vest said that he was itching to knock a Nazi on his goddamn ass. Chairman Hogan pleaded for a semblance of order so that everyone had a chance to speak their piece, but the meeting was busted wide open by then.

People surged out from the rows, chairs knocked askew and toppled over as they argued and jabbed accusing fingers at one another. Hogan finally gave up and set the microphone down. As he did so it rolled from the table top and the speakers squealed. The girl from the restaurant rushed to switch the amplifier off. Randy Travis then came over the speakers singing about endless amens.

Someone threw their Styrofoam cup at Gavin and then a throng of people stepped in front of him, some shouting threats and others encouragement. He told his men that it was time to go. By the time they had cleared the front parking lot and made it to the car where Jonathan waited, the whole place looked like an overturned colony of ants, constituents breaking in all directions. He told Jonathan to not hurry as he drove away. He wanted to see as much of what he had created as he could. He wanted to see what it looked like when people ate themselves.

16

HARRISON HAD TWO DAYS FOR HIMSELF. HE HAD TOLD GAVIN HE HAD a pickup arranged in Little Rock, though the truth was that he'd needed to go only as far as Nashville. He'd stopped at Knoxville and convinced Emmanuel to come along. It was far enough away that he didn't fear being seen, and he knew it would settle things if he went out with Emmanuel in a public place. It would convey certain commitments and he knew that was what mattered if there was to be any way out of where they were.

They got a room at a Knight's Inn just off the interstate at the edge of the city's limits. It was dark and humid when they checked in and Emmanuel counted half a dozen roaches scuttling in the bathroom when he switched on the overhead light.

"And these ain't the right kind of roaches here," he said holding his nose and slamming the door shut.

Harrison took the hint and started rolling a joint. They smoked it while they sat on the edge of the bed and watched an episode of *Law and Order*.

"I hope you didn't haul me across the state with you just to mash bugs and watch TV."

"Come on," Harrison said. "I told you I have a place in mind."

They drove into town and parked in a deck off Printer's Alley, walked a squalid gauntlet past a strip joint before they turned in at an opening and entered a shallow nook that led to a brick fronted bar with a rainbow flag draped from the window. They went in and showed their IDs to a bouncer wearing a T-shirt of Che Guevara in bright orange lipstick and passed on toward a busy dance floor beneath reddened light. They turned and shifted their way past the dancers until they could wedge into a space at the bar. The music was just turning over into La Roux's "I'm Not Your Toy."

They took their drinks and found a corner where they could hear one another.

"I'm impressed," Emmanuel said. "When you go gay you really fucking go gay."

"You like it?"

Emmanuel laughed.

"I'm not sure like it is the right word, honey. But an A for effort, by all means. How did you find this place?"

"I can use a telephone."

"A telephone? How old are you? Eighty-five?"

"What do you mean?"

"I mean people say phone, not telephone. It's a good thing you're as cute as you are stupid. Come on, you want to go out there and shake your ass a little with me?"

"You go ahead," Harrison said. "I'll hold your drink."

Emmanuel said nothing, betrayed no disappointment, though he knew it remained there just beneath the surface. It had always been hard for Harrison, though he knew he should have gotten over it by this point in his life. He'd known he was different when he was a boy, and it wasn't something he'd tried to deny to himself like so many other boys from his background did. There had been times in the past when he and Emmanuel would slip off to some house party and he was free to behave as though he belonged to the body he did, but that had been rare. So often he was aware of the possibility of being seen and something getting back to his family, something they'd lack the equipment to comprehend.

"You look thirsty," Harrison said once Emmanuel came back.

"I can certainly partake."

He drank the cocktail down.

"Another one?"

"Yeah. Just one more. Let's go walk the city after that."

"Okay."

Once they'd had one more apiece Harrison cleared their tab and they turned out onto the humid streets, surged past the bleary streetlights and beery tourists. Emmanuel laughed at the country music piped in through the occasional public intercom, called Nashville the closest thing he'd ever seen to a cracker Kingdom Come.

They stopped off at a convenience story a few doors down from the public library and bought two tall cans of Steel Reserve. Awful shit really, but their tastebuds were well numbed by now. They found an empty bench in a park next to a church. The sky was busy with the stuttering of bats. Emmanuel's head eased into the pocket of Harrison's shoulder.

"This is crazy, you know?"

"Yeah," Harrison said. "I know."

Harrison kissed him so they wouldn't have to talk anymore like that.

Shortly after midnight they went back to the motel. Emmanuel slept in the car while Harrison drove. They'd both drunk too much but Harrison argued that he was the better drunk driver and Emmanuel had been too tired to put up much of a fight. As he drove, the wheel felt insubstantial in his hands and he briefly considered how easy it would be to let it float free from his grip and let the car coast from the road and deliver the two of them into oblivion. He wondered if that was an evil thought, to take the life of someone who had no way of expressing consent. At least it would be merciful. No pain, just the final easy glide.

He pressed his fingertips along the side of his nose until he could feel sinus pain. It revived him. He reached his arm across the back of the seat. Emmanuel said something that made no sense in his sleep and rolled his head back until he pillowed against Harrison's forearm. The rest of the ride back was long, but Harrison was in no hurry to cover the distance.

WHEN HARRISON was young there had been plenty of reasons to suspect something. A few members of his family had picked up on the subtle signs of who he really was. If it had been a kindly aunt or cousin, things might have turned out so much better than they had. But he'd had no such luck. His uncle Robert and Robert's son Daniel had been the ones who recognized him and they had been ungentle in the recognition.

Robert was his father's older brother, a big and strong man, whereas Harrison's father was always smaller and often suffered from shortness of breath that was precipitated by a chain-smoking habit that verged on suicidal. Robert had stayed in Lafollette his whole life, worked as a mechanic until he'd saved up enough money to open his own garage, where he worked on anything that had wheels turned by a motor. Harrison's father had moved to Knoxville when Harrison was five years old, got a job as a shift manager at Alcoa manufacturing. Robert had always poked fun at his little brother, said it was a hell of a thing to make a living managing men who did actual work while he kicked his heels up in an air-conditioned office. Harrison's father suffered the ribbing well enough, though Harrison could see in his father's eyes that it did real hurt, and when Robert would leave the room a heavy silence fell over him.

When Harrison turned thirteen his father started taking him up to LaFollette on weekend turkey hunts in the spring. The family had a sixty-acre tract of land back in some deep coves where Harrison's grandfather had built a small frame hunting cabin that sat next to a nameless creek. For many years the cabin had been primarily used by the old man for telling lies and drinking in the absence of women, perhaps justified by the infrequent wetting of a fishing line. But that had changed one morning when the elder Harrison stumbled out to relieve himself after a night of head-pounding whiskey drinking. He heard a picking and scratching in the nearby brush. A twenty-five-pound tom turkey with a beard that dragged the ground stood ten feet away. Without a fleeting thought to sportsmanship the old man pulled a .45 Derringer and shot the bird twice through the breast. Though it wounded the turkey mortally, the tom kicked and cried for a minute before the killer stepped over and ground his boot heel into its blood-enflamed head. Despite the gift of mercy, he soon realized that the pistol had done significant damage to the meat. Though by the time his sons had begun hunting the land that detail had been ignored. What mattered was that the woods there were full of turkey and the Harrison men considered it as much a part of their inheritance as the property deed itself.

Harrison's grandfather was dead by the time his father began taking him on the hunts, though a picture of the old man still hung above the cabin's mantelpiece. Next to it was nailed the wispy black beard that had grown from the legendary turkey's breast. When his father and uncle would sit up playing spades with their sons they'd often fall to drinking and comparing that relic to the other turkey beards they'd cut from their own kills. Robert was the better hunter of the brothers because he was committed to rising early every morning regardless of the weather and putting the time in walking the ridges. But Harrison's father was the better caller. He practiced endlessly with the diaphragm mouth caller, yelping with that long seductive hook that lured toms to his hypothetical hen. So each had several trophies to boast, though Robert was loathe to grant any parity. And when he was drunk, the competition got mean, and there were few moments at the hunting camp he wasn't drunk.

One night Robert had gotten particularly bad, insisting that Harrison's father had been cheating at cards.

"I've caught you two passing signals," he said, including Harrison in his accusing gaze. "Bunch of fucking table talk. You all work up some kind of father and son code before you came up here? I imagine I would too if I was getting whipped like a runaway slave ever time I came up to the woods. But shit, man, you ain't supposed to treat family that way."

His father said he was drunk and talking crazy, but Robert became more enraged at the denial. His fist came down so hard on the card table it knocked Harrison's half-full can of Coke to the floor.

"Clean that shit up, boy! I don't want a bunch of fucking ants running around in here because of that sugar. Jesus."

Harrison did as he was told. His father did nothing to stop him.

Robert sat there shuffling the cards. Daniel scratched at a pimple until it started to bleed.

"Now there's only one way to handle this, little brother. And that's for you to catch up with me on the whiskey. I've always found a little brown liquor is about the best guarantee of some truth-telling in this round world. Danny, go pour your uncle a cup of that Jack Daniels and don't go stingy on it."

The teenage boy hitched his overlarge jeans as he strode to the pantry and filled a coffee cup full of the whiskey. He took a quick sip himself before setting it on the card table.

"If I drink this will you stop being such a shit?"

"Drink up, brother."

Harrison's father gulped the liquor until his face reddened.

"All right. Deal those cards."

They played late into the night. Whenever the whiskey cup ran low, Robert nodded gravely at Daniel, who went and topped it off. By the time the game was done Harrison's father could barely speak. Robert and Daniel carried him to his bunk and threw him there like game set aside to butcher, giggling as they went off to their own beds. Harrison went over and spread a wool blanket over his father before he pulled out the sleeping sofa and crawled inside his sleeping bag.

A brusque shake of his shoulder brought him awake in the pre-dawn. Robert stood over him. He was fully dressed and holding a shotgun.

"Jesus, Miss Priss, wake your ass up. You hunting or playing with your clit under the covers?"

He sat up, saw that his father was still passed out.

"He ain't going to be able to hack it, Daddy," Daniel said. "Look at his own daddy over there. Sawing logs."

"Is that right, boy? You ain't able to hack it? I think it's high time somebody sends you to hack it school then."

Harrison quickly pulled on his jeans and a short-sleeved camouflage shirt, grabbed his single-barrel .410 from the gun cabinet and shoved his pockets full of shells on his way out the door. Robert and Daniel said something to one another he couldn't hear and laughed.

They walked up to the old turnaround and stood at the edge of the woods in the dark and listened for a tom to gobble. Robert called on his box and when that elicited nothing he hooted like an owl and that set one off, maybe three-quarters of a mile away. He hooted once more and when the tom responded again he marked its direction and they plunged into the brush after it.

It was hard to keep up. Robert and Daniel moved with easy strides and an uncanny ability to avoid shadow-locked branches and vines, whereas Harrison seemed to find every snare and exposed root along the trail. He scuffed along, stubbed his toe every few steps. Robert whirled around and told him through tight teeth to not make so goddamn much noise. He tried to, aware of his crashing footfalls and his uncle's brimming anger.

At daybreak they stopped and cut small branches and stuck them in the ground to erect a hasty blind. Robert called on the box. The third time the tom answered, some few hundred yards distant, though remaining out of eyesight. Harrison measured his breaths, tried to make himself as small and still as he could. He was close enough to Robert to smell the sour sweat coming from his body, the electric musk from Daniel. They were a small pack of animals there, as much a part of the wilderness of the bird they'd come to kill. This predatory idea sharpened inside Harrison and he felt his senses quicken. And though this made the immediate reek of the man and boy harder to bear, it accessed something within him. He leaned in, felt his surroundings register, became dizzyingly present.

So, he was surprised when the others failed to see it as clearly as he did. The turkey strutted from cover at the far ridge and came straight on toward the creek bed. His mouth dried and he felt shaky. He cut his eyes to Robert, but his uncle was concentrating on a different quarter of the woods. Daniel had taken the turkey caller in his hands and was chalking it for its next use. Harrison was the only one who saw the bird.

"Uncle Robert, do you see it?" he whispered.

"See what?"

"The turkey. He's right over there."

"What the hell are you talking about?"

"Right there," he said reaching his arm out and pointing.

Robert slapped his hand down.

"Don't move, you goddamn moron. Shit."

The tom released a quick series of agitated clucks and trotted back toward the ridgeline. Robert put the butt of his shotgun to his shoulder, but the range was already too great. He lowered it and grabbed the caller from Daniel, tried a series of turkey talk that received no answer. A moment later the tom topped the ridge and disappeared over the other side.

"Come on, dumbass. Now we've got to chase him."

They picked up their gear and started down toward the creek, tramped through the water and up the opposite hill. Harrison's sneakers were soaked and he could feel where his sock rubbed a blister along his heel, but he was able to keep up better now. He watched the backs of Robert and Daniel, saw how they weaved past the lower branches and raised their feet to avoid the stumbling traps of deadwood and crawling undergrowth. At short intervals they paused and Robert would call again to see if he might slow the tom, but the bird remained silent and all they had to guide them was the endless cross work of traveled game trails. In half an hour it seemed like they'd gone nearly two miles. Harrison's legs burned and he began to fall behind once more. He began to wish that he'd stayed behind with his father, but recognized too the need to last on the trail as long as he could.

An hour later they still had not sighted the tom but Robert and Daniel continued hiking the steep hillsides. They did not slow as they grew more distant. Harrison sat and rested against a granite outcropping, knew he was lost, but his legs shook with each step and he felt on the verge of collapse. He leaned his shotgun against the stony flat and pried his sneaker off. The blister at his heel had split and a crusty patch of blood darkened the sock. He pinched the fabric to draw if away from the skin and it made a sound like plastic tearing. With the shoe in one hand he crutched his way with the shotgun after the others.

He walked on for another half hour without any signs of where they might have gone. The day had become hot and the only water he had to drink was from the slow-moving pools of the creek. He had been told not to drink from these, but as his thirst became overpowering he had no choice. Finally, he made it to the highest ground he could see and broke open the action on the .410 and removed the shell. His father had shown him how to blow into the muzzle of the gun so that it made a distinct bugling sound that could carry over a great distance. He put his mouth to the barrel and blew down into it until his face lost its color but the sound never came. He sat and cried.

He stood once more and tried to gather the direction he'd come, but the shifting daylight had merged the woods into an impossible similarity. He raised the shotgun and fired it into the treetops, broke open the action, reloaded, and fired twice more. Then he sat there with an empty gun and waited.

It was midafternoon before Robert and Daniel found him. They came out from the higher country and straight to where he sat as easily as if they'd located him by the point of a compass.

"Miss Priss get lost?"

"Where's my dad?"

"He's back there at the cabin nursing that hangover of his. Man that age and still not able to hold his liquor, I swear."

"Why you got your shoe off?" Daniel sneered.

He turned his foot, showed the bloody heel.

"You need to run to the store and grab a maxi-pad for that?"

Robert laughed at his own joke. Harrison got up and followed them as they headed back the way they came. Soon, however, they had resumed a quick pace that straggled him as soon as they mounted into steeper country. He didn't want to ask them to slow, knew it would do no good if he did.

"Well goddamn," Robert said as he turned and stopped at the base of a granite outcropping. The land rolled away on all sides. "Why don't you drag that sweet ass of yours up here so we don't have to do this all over again? Come on, Miss Priss. We ain't going to maroon you."

As soon as he caught up, Harrison's toe caught on a hidden catch and he went sprawling. Without thinking, he threw his hands out to brace his fall. The shotgun clattered through the brush.

"Get that gun, Danny. Hand it here,"

Robert took the .410, broke open its action to find it empty, snapped the action back closed.

"Get that boy's belt down," he told his son.

Daniel straddled Harrison, pressed his face down into the muddy leaves while his free hand snaked around to the boy's belly. Harrison bucked and tried to push up but the teenager was too strong to move him off. Daniel's fingers slipped under his T-shirt and found the brass clasp. It came loose with a hard, gasping sound. Harrison yelled and kicked but Daniel had him then, yanked the tight denim legs down to the bottom of his thighs so that he lay there hobbled by his own clothes.

"Stop squirming, you little shit!"

Later, he would never understand why he didn't try to get to his feet once more and run, but as Daniel stood and Harrison was exposed there in the clearing, it was as though a greater weight pressed him down, one that was as unopposable as the strange gravity of bad dreams. Some new creature had him in its hold, something interposed between his uncle and cousin and him. He realized then that something as light as air could contain the mass of the world.

The cold nose of the shotgun muzzle jabbed up between his ass cheeks and rammed just above his scrotum. With that jolt of pain he felt like his stomach was going to empty. His fingers arched down into the soft dirt as he tried to pull away. He gained just the slightest distance when Robert pulled the shotgun back and pressed it sharply forward, this time ensuring that it ran up inside him. Harrison screamed and cried.

"Hush. Get up now you punky little bitch. Get up and stay up or I'll keep this big old black dick up inside you all the way back"

He said he'd keep up. He said it as many times as Robert wanted him to.

Daniel looked away when Harrison stood and pulled up his jeans. Robert looked on and shook his head.

"Quit your blubbering, honeysuckle. The goddamn thing wasn't even loaded."

17

KYLE WAS IN TOWN DROPPING OFF SOME PLANTS AT THE INDEPENDENT grocery when he got a call from Orlynne, telling him to get down to the courthouse as quick as he could, that somebody was likely to be killed if he didn't. He dumped the crates in the parking lot and skidded his tires on the way out. The manager yelled at his tailgate, said he wouldn't pay full price for busted product, by damn god.

He saw the police lights before he reached the square, a couple of deputies already suited up in their assault gear and carrying AR-15s at the ready. They were talking into radios clipped to their shoulders. He could hear Sheriff Holston squawking back. There were no empty spots along the main road so he drove up onto the sidewalk and left the truck there next to a memorial bench in the city park. He walked straight on when he saw the deputies were unhurriedly heading up the middle of the street.

He got his phone out, dialed Orlynne.

"Where are you?"

He could hear her talking over her shoulder to someone before she answered.

"We're up here inside the courthouse. We're sitting with the sheriff."

"What the hell's going on, Orlynne?"

"Go on up to the square. You'll see."

He rounded the corner. Four of Gavin's men stood in a small diamond formation with Gavin at their center. They blocked the courthouse's main entrance. Across their bodies hung assault rifles similar to the ones carried by the county deputies. Roadblocks had been put out on either side and several people were standing there looking on. The police light flashed across in long silent swathes.

Kyle raised his phone.

"Orlynne, let me talk to Holston."

She told him to wait a minute. A fumbling across hands.

"Morning, Commissioner Pettus."

"You care to explain what I'm looking at right now?"

"I imagine that would depend on where you're standing. But if you're in the immediate vicinity of the county courthouse then I imagine you're seeing a small group of men gathered in a protest of Commissioner Pickens's recent decision to remain seated on the county commission board."

"This isn't a protest. It's a naked threat."

"Calm down, Pettus. Do you think I'm stupid enough to not see what's going on here? Do me a favor and take a closer look at those rifles. Look at their chambers specifically."

Kyle could see that each of the chambers was locked in the open position and that the magazines had been removed from the receivers. The rifles were empty.

"Do you see?" Holston asked.

"Yeah, I see it. That still doesn't mean it's not a threat."

"Of course it's a threat. It just isn't a technically illegal one. There's nothing in Tennessee law that says you can't be in public with an unloaded long gun. You know, the law is my business after all. While you might have the advantage of following it as a part-time distraction, it is how I earn my grub."

"You're making no effort to get rid of them?"

"I'm exercising what the diplomats call strategic patience. It has the advantage of not getting anyone killed even if a few people get their feelings hurt. I do hope that's alright with you. I worry about the health of our working relationship when we have these little disagreements."

Kyle ended the call, told the dead phone line to damn itself. He approached the street blockage and stood among a few of the on-lookers. One woman had drawn up a sign on a piece of poster board that said NAZIS HATE AMERICA. She had set the message in front of her, resting against her belly. She had her hands free to smoke.

"You mind if I bum one from you?" he asked.

"Sure thing, bud."

She tapped out a long filtered Camel and lit it for him. She was maybe thirty years old with dreaded hair and wore a T-shirt of an Indian head in profile. Above it was an oil pump jack attached to the back of the skull where what appeared to be blood was si-phoned out.

"I like your shirt."

"Thanks, I bought it up at the Dakota pipeline protest last fall. They had a lot of cool shit for sale up there. I wish I'd gotten more."

"You were part of the winter camp?"

She shook her head, jetted smoke from her nostrils with ap-parent ease.

"No, I was just on vacation. Wanted to be part of it though, you know. Some assholes call it protest tourism, but that's bullshit. That money, from this shirt, that went to the cause. I mean it's not much, but it makes me feel like I'm doing something, being part of the resistance. We all do what we can do with the pussy grabber-in-chief holding office, you know?"

He nodded, smoked.

It took a few minutes before Gavin Noon saw him. When he did, he told his small band of men to part so that he could get through to the barricade. As he neared, the crowd momentarily shrunk back, the woman next to Kyle among them.

"Good afternoon, Commissioner Pettus. I'm glad to see that you've taken an interest in the schedule of events. It's important the people have an opportunity to express their opinion. I'm sure you agree."

"Fucking pig!" the protesting woman shouted, now recovered from her initial shock. "Fucking fascist!"

A few others muttered something along similar lines, though nothing caught into a full-throated chorus and the disturbance soon quieted. One of Noon's men began to sing the "Star Spangled Banner." Some booed, but that too quickly diminished.

"You're enjoying this, aren't you?" Kyle asked.

"Enjoying what?"

"This," he said, raised his hand. "The spectacle."

Kyle thought he might have seen the thinnest of smiles, but it was gone before he could be certain.

"Ah look," Noon said, nodding past Kyle's shoulder. "The cavalry has arrived."

Kyle turned to see a marked news van from Knoxville's NBC affiliate swing onto the sidewalk next to where he'd parked his truck. A second later a cameraman sprung from the side door as a man in a suit who touched the wings of his hair followed close behind. The crowd began to stir.

Noon now addressed himself to the protesting woman at Kyle's side.

"What is your name, my dear?"

"I'm not going to tell you my name, asshole. I'm not here to make nice."

"Well, could you tell me why you hate me so much?"

"Are you fucking kidding me?"

"No, I believe in trying to understand one another. Can you tell me what your profession is, at least? What is it that you do on a daily basis?"

The woman paused, unable to determine if answering him betrayed some principle she couldn't immediately pinpoint. The ash on her cigarette had grown precipitously long. Kyle noticed Noon glance toward the news crew.

"I'm a professor. A sociology professor."

"Ah, at East Tennessee State, I assume?"

"Yeah, A-plus and all that happy horseshit. I teach students about social problems in America. Stuff like neo-Confederates, neo-liberalists, et cetera."

"Well, I'm sure you're very passionate."

The video camera was mounted to its tripod. The man with the impeccable hair was facing it and speaking. Kyle laid his hand on the woman's shoulder to try to get her attention, but she shrugged it off, riveted now by her confrontation with Noon.

"You and your Nazis need to go home. Go home!" she shouted.

The crowd reacted to the cry and the chant was picked up, sustained itself. Noon turned to Kyle and briefly winked.

"I'm afraid I'm already home, miss."

And then, what he'd clearly been anticipating happened. The slender ash from the forgotten cigarette clenched between her fingers collapsed and scattered softly on the ground.

"Look at that," Noon said. "You've dropped a Jew."

The woman's fist connected with Noon's jaw and he staggered back. Kyle couldn't tell if the reaction was genuine or more of Noon's theater, but by then it didn't matter. The crowd thrust forward and several hands grabbed for Noon. His men rushed forward to shield him, but as soon as they were there the sheriff's deputies stepped in, pushed back against the crowd, slapped cuffs on anyone who was standing in the immediate area. Kyle got clear and made his way back to the truck. The television reporter called to him, asked if he'd like to say something to the viewers. He got in the cab and drove.

LAURA GOT hold of him just as he was pulling up to the house. He sat there for a minute letting the cell ring before deciding whether to pick up.

"Hey."

"Hey yourself. Tell me I imagined seeing you in the middle of a Nazi protest on channel 10."

"Afraid not."

"Jesus, Kyle. What is happening here?"

He hesitated.

"I miss you," he said. "I was hoping I could see you sometime. You know you can come up whenever you can get away."

The line held its silence for a while. He thought he should hang up.

"It's good to hear you say that," she said. "I can be there in a little while, if you want."

"If you think you can."

"I wouldn't say it if I didn't."

He went up to the house and spent a quarter of an hour straightening up the living room, walked back to the bedroom and tugged the sheets taut. There was a Dixie Chicks CD in the stereo. He skipped it up to their cover of "Landslide" and pulled a Rick Bragg book from the shelf, took it back out to the front porch with a bottle of zinfandel and a glass tumbler pinched between his fingers.

He read for a while with his feet propped up in a chair he'd drawn across from him. The wine disappeared in smooth gulps and by the time the bottle was half drained he began to lose his place in the sentences. He set the book down on the floorboards and watched the slow retreat of the sun across the front of the yard where the ground was baked hard and brown and in the trees around him the cicadas screamed.

He dozed there until sometime later Laura's Subaru chugged up the drive. The sky was bluing toward eventide but the light was still strong and with the sun behind her he could see the long lines of her body. As she got closer it became more than that striking image, turned into the woman he knew, which made her look even better.

"You made it."

"I did. You get an early start on me there?" she said, nodded at the empty wine bottle.

"Maybe just a little."

She pulled up the empty chair, sat across from him.

"You want me to open another bottle?"

"I'm fine. Get yourself some if you want it."

"Well, if you insist," he said and smiled, though he made no effort to rise.

"Are you going to tell me what's wrong?"

"Probably not. I hope that's not a deal breaker."

"God, you should know by now that it isn't."

SHE STAYED over that evening, had even brought a tote bag with a change of clothes and a hairbrush. He didn't ask her what that meant concerning her husband or her job, figuring she was enough of a grown-up to attend to those concerns. Maybe he was being a coward by not pinning her down, getting her to tell him where things could possibly go, but the question didn't bother him enough to say something.

He woke up several times during the night from bad dreams and lay there looking at her, breathing easily in deep sleep. It was a comfort to have her here in the house. Since they'd first started seeing one another it had been hard to get a reasonable idea of how they could make sense of what life would be like together in its quietest moments. They'd never really had the chance to understand what that might mean because of their fear of discovery and the need to evade. That was the appeal of the affair at the outset. It broke through the walls of what was routine, sharpened their desire like blades, but over time that had changed. He had become curious about her, wanted to know more than bare details of her personal history. The simple tally of affection succumbed to something else. He wanted to understand her habits, know the shape of her presence, something that was beyond articulation. To be intuitively content because of the fact of her.

He got up and cooked a breakfast of eggs and buttered toast, cut up a bowl of fruit. By the time she was awake, he'd laid it all out on the kitchen table with coffee and juice. She had showered and wore his plaid robe from the closet. Her wet hair was combed back in neat decisive strokes so that it looked like it had been primitively painted.

"I like the service in this hotel," she said, sat down.

He sat next to her, rested his hand on her thigh as he poured cream in his coffee and stirred it.

"I'd like to show you something today. If you've got the time, that is."

"Yeah? I was kind of hoping you might," she said, leaned forward to be kissed.

"Well, that too. But I want to take you somewhere."

"I'd like that. I hope jeans and a short-sleeve shirt are okay. I didn't pack for the opera, you know."

"That's perfect. Go on and eat now. You'll need your strength."

"That sounds promising."

He went outside to get things ready while she finished up. The weather was warm but crisp. A little bit of wind in the trees that relieved the midsummer listlessness. A good morning to be on the water. He turned the combination lock on the shed and unslotted the clasp. The aluminum door swung open on a sheen of old cobwebs that spun in the early light. He went over to the rack, lifted the canoe and squared the yoke across his shoulders. Once it was balanced, he walked it out to the truck. It wasn't that far to the water, but he decided it would be easier to drive everything down. He picked a pair of paddles out of the pile, placed those in the truck as well.

Laura met him on the porch in a few minutes, her hair tied up under his Braves ball cap.

"Hope you don't mind me stealing a hat. I didn't want to get sunburned."

"No, I like it. Hop in."

They drove down off the mountain and took the first dirt road that split from the hardtop. The truck pitched over the deep ruts and bottomed once in a dried wallow, but it wasn't long before they'd come through the thick boundary of mixed hardwoods and could see the gently rounded banks of the Doe River. He parked up under a big black walnut tree and cracked the windows before he killed the engine and got out.

"It'll be hot before long. It's good to get as much shade as we can."

She helped him unload the canoe, the life vests, and the paddles, walked the boat down to the sandy put-in. The water was low but swift, white creases of current shredding itself in a cream against the humped black stones. She sat at the river's edge and turned up the cuffs of her jeans, waded in calf deep to get a sense of what she had agreed to.

"I'm not much of a swimmer, you know."

"Well, that's alright, I guess. If you're swimming I imagine I'm not doing a very good job of driving this thing. Why don't you get in?"

She carefully stepped over the gunwale and dropped into the front seat. Kyle edged the boat a few feet into a pool until it ground softly past a sandbar and floated free. He came up easily in the stern and then they were moved along by the current. He dipped the paddle in, straightened them as they came into a riffle that thumped and slapped the bow. As they rocked through Laura began to paddle and the water gurgled and swirled where she planted in and pushed as naturally as if she had done it her entire life.

They entered another run close to the bank and angled toward the center of the river. Kyle steered and corrected their movement without thinking. He had traveled this stretch of water so often that he carried the map of it inside his head. No danger of missing a V or forgetting a shoal. His mind could settle somewhere else while the water took them, and now he dwelled on Laura, watched how she met the river. She paddled when they moved through rapids but when the water was calm and slow she watched the banks for plants and birds, called out the names of those she recognized and wondered at those she didn't.

"You make a pretty natural hand at this," Kyle observed.

She smiled over her shoulder.

"My daddy used to take me on his sea kayak down in Tybee Island. We'd paddle out to the sandbar and he'd fish all day. Sometimes he'd send me back into the sound to get a bucket of iced beers from the waterfront seafood place. They weren't supposed to sell them to me but they knew who we were. Used to call me his Budweiser taxi."

"You sound close."

"We were for a long time. He died nearly five years ago, but we didn't really see much of each other once I was out of the house and on my own. He and Peter never did get along, and that made things hard."

Kyle braced, surprised at how the mention of her husband's name bothered him. She must have felt it.

"I'm sorry," she said.

"You shouldn't be. We've got to be honest about things, don't we?"

She said nothing, knew she didn't need to. He pushed down and twisted on the T handle of the paddle, kept them running the deepest water he could find.

"He's not a bad man," she said after a while.

"I never suggested he was."

"I know. I just didn't want you to think that I was going to try to turn him into something else, something that would make this easier on us. I can stop talking if you want."

"We can talk about it. That's what we're doing, isn't it?"

It was midday before they came around the bend and the forested bank thinned, marking the natural takeout. A few tall pines and a flood of golden daylight, the sight of Orlynne's camper and truck. She and Gerald were sitting outside together at her rough-hewn picnic table eating lunch. Kyle took the canoe into the shallow water until they ground against the shoal. He got out and pulled the boat up so that Laura had water no deeper than her calves when she stepped over the side. By the time they'd carried the canoe up to the bank Orlynne had spotted them and come along to offer a hand, though there was no need for it.

"The river bears strange gifts," she said, smiled. "If you would have called ahead I would have saved something to eat for you."

"That's alright. I didn't know exactly when we'd be along," Kyle said, tugging the boat up into a soft bed of pine needles before lowering it.

"I have a hard time believing that, as many times as you've made that run."

"Water's low. Can't remember ever seeing it so bad. I don't even remember what rain feels like anymore."

"Well, at least you can introduce me to your friend."

"Laura Carson," Laura said and stuck her hand out before Kyle had the chance to answer.

"Nice to meet you, Laura Carson. I guess you enjoyed the river even if it has gotten lower than a trickle in a teapot?"

"Yes, ma'am. It's still pretty out there even if it's not what it's supposed to be."

"Well, why don't you have some iced tea up here with Gerald and me? I'm sure you're both plenty thirsty."

They stripped out of their life vests and followed her across the clearing to where Gerald sat sucking on the bony dregs of fried chicken.

"Can't seem to get away from you, Pettus. Even out here in God's country."

"Good to see you too, Gerald. Have you met Laura?"

"I believe I have. The librarian, is that right?"

"Yessir," she said, nodded hello.

They sat across from him and thanked Orlynne when she poured them each a tea from a glass pitcher.

"Have you asked her?" Gerald said to Kyle, motioning toward Laura.

"Asked her what?"

"About that business yesterday." He folded his arms and leaned on the table, addressing her directly. "What do you think, ma'am? How would you say all this Nazi nonsense is playing to the general public?"

She shrugged.

"We haven't really talked about it, but it doesn't look good for anyone, does it?"

"What do you mean?"

"I mean those men look like what they are—racists, hate-filled racists. But look at what it does to the town. It makes us into cartoons. Especially now that it's on television. I'm sure that video's all over the internet by now."

"Indeed," Gerald smiled brightly. "I believe there were 78,000 views on YouTube this morning."

"82,000," Orlynne said, glancing down at the black mirror of her cell. "And climbing."

"It makes me wonder how spontaneous any of it actually was," Gerald continued. "I've already made the mistake once of underestimating this man Noon. It's easy to do because he comes here looking like something we know from the inside out, but we don't. He's part of something new, something one step evolved from its source. Not all evolution is necessarily positive, you know? Humans in general are proof of that if you ask me. But he's shrewd. He understands how important it is to craft appearance, to tell artful lies. That's why he's so dangerous. He has all the traits of a gifted politician."

After that the talk turned in an easier direction. Orlynne took them around back and showed them where they had Gerald's goats staked down until they had time to build an enclosure. Both creatures regarded them with unblinking lunatic eyes. Laura laughed when she tried to pet Malone and Molly cut in between them and baaed like a spurned rival. Gerald told her to hush, which caused the goat to holler even louder.

Once they had visited for a while, Kyle asked Orlynne if she could give them a ride back to the put-in. On the way back Laura rode shotgun talking with Orlynne about some of the gardening books she had at the library that Orlynne might be interested in seeing if she ever had the time to come down and browse. Kyle liked listening to them talk. It made him feel like he was sitting with family. Once they got back to his truck he started to transfer the canoe but Orlynne told him not to bother, that he could drive his vehicle back and she'd haul the canoe the rest of the way. Laura told him she'd just go ahead and ride with Orlynne so they could keep talking.

Once back, Laura told him she had to go, that she had plenty she needed to get straightened out.

"All right," he said, bent forward to kiss her. His hands felt like they belonged there at her waist, and she seemed to agree, not trying to move as he encircled her in his arms. Finally, he let her go.

"Call me," he said. And then added, "If you need me."

"You too," she said and kissed him good-bye.

Orlynne had come around from the side of the house where she unwound one of the long watering hoses. She waved to Laura's car as it swung around in the driveway on its way off the mountain.

"You don't need to fool with that, Orlynne. I can manage today without any help, I think."

"Yeah, it looks like you're managing quite a bit on your own these days."

He didn't like her tone.

"You have something you want to tell me?"

She shrugged her shoulders, kept dragging the hose out like some wayward script drawn across a page.

"I imagine you can gather my feelings."

"You don't like Laura? You all talked like you were getting along."

"I didn't say I didn't like her. You're awful stupid for a man your age, you know that? I'm worried about you, is all. Worried about her too, for that matter. You'd be surprised the nasty things that can turn up when you start sleeping with a woman who wears a ring on her finger, or do I really need to explain that to you?"

Kyle took a minute before he answered.

"No, you don't need to explain that to me."

She started to mess with the hose again.

"I told you I don't need any help today," he told her. "In fact, I'll let you know when I need help again. You don't need to come up here unless I call you."

The look she gave him could have slammed a door. She flung the hose aside.

"Lose my number."

He could tell that she meant it.

18

GAVIN POSTED THE VIDEO OF THE WOMAN ATTACKING HIM ACROSS every active discussion board he could find. The number of hits simply cascaded. He watched it spread across the internet with its own kind of furious intelligence, drawing praise and condemnation. But most importantly, it gathered notice. It was becoming big enough that it couldn't be ignored.

He settled back in his chair and watched the clip crawl across social media. Occasionally, some moderator would delete the content, citing it as inflammatory, but a few minutes later it would appear somewhere else like a regenerated limb. His email began to ping. He moved his hand to the mouse and silenced the speakers.

His phone buzzed. The name he'd been waiting on appeared on the screen.

"Hello, Mr. Sealy. I've been expecting your call."

"Hi, Mr. Noon. I'm writing a follow-up about yesterday. I've already got something about the event, but I wanted to work something in about what's going on online. Especially with what the lieutenant governor had to say . . ."

"I'm afraid I haven't seen what you're referring to."

"Are you near a computer?"

"I am."

"Go to Tom Sheeply's Twitter account."

Gavin opened the browser and clicked over. There, pinned to the top of the page, was a retweet with the video attached. Headlining it were the lieutenant governor's own words: FREEDOM OF SPEECH MEANS FREEDOM FOR ALL SPEECH.

Gavin smiled, said, "Mr. Sealy, you should come over. This really is the sort of thing that demands a face-to-face exchange. I'll even have a cup of freshly brewed coffee waiting for you."

THEY HAD been clearing thorn since daybreak, but now it had grown hot and each swing of the machete felt more useless than the last. A dry rattling as the blade carried through, lopped without any sense of progress. Just sun and the lack of effect. Jonathan straightened, hurled his blade into a patch of earth. Its point stuck in place.

"What, you quitting?" One of Gavin's lesser men, Conner Polk, wanted to know. Like an animal with no greater use, he had been sentenced to the present task. Laboring like something broken.

"I suggest you watch your tone of voice, young man," Jonathan offered.

"You ain't my daddy," Polk spat. "Neither you nor Gavin. At least I can say I'm not afraid of work."

As if to prove this, he turned back toward the thorn and crashed through with wild strokes. The looping brush shuddered but little broke or gave way. Jonathan had ceased clearing now and watched as Polk attacked the thorn as though it was something capable of suffering pain. He shook his head and smiled.

"I believe you're tiring out."

"Shut up, you motherfucker. I know what I'm doing."

Despite this claim, he soon spent himself and slung the blade on the ground. It bounced and flexed in the relentless sun.

"Let me ask you something," Jonathan said. "You ever been told you remind them of the burnt fuse of a dud firecracker?"

Polk told him to shut up, turned back toward the thorn patch and yelled, "Goddammnit! How are we supposed to get this done?"

"Now you're beginning to ask the important questions," Jonathan said, nodded. "Now you're making that important first step."

"The hell you talking about?"

"There's easier ways of doing things. You remember that gas can in the back of the van?"

"Yeah."

"Why don't you go grab that? Why don't you get me one of those rubber bands out of the console too?"

Polk loped up to the side of the asylum and pulled the vehicle's side door open. A minute later he came back with the metal can under his arm.

"You are shitting me."

"I wouldn't shit you. You're my favorite turd."

Jonathan uncapped the can and it made a gentle puff when he upturned it and the gasoline fed the ground with its blue stream. He walked the line of thorn, wet it all until there was nothing left in the can to pour. Once it had all dribbled out he stepped back a few paces and squatted, gave it time to soak in.

"You're crazy, you know that? What makes you think you won't set the whole woods on fire?"

"You see anything between here and the river that ain't something needs chopping down?"

Polk looked, shrugged.

"No, I don't guess so, no."

"Then shut your goddamn mouth and give me your cigarette lighter."

He reached down into his hip pocket and pulled out a particolored Bic. It said WILD LIFE in graffiti style letters.

"Why you need my lighter? You smoke cigarettes too. Why don't you use your own?"

After he had taken the lighter in hand, Jonathan struck it and then double-looped and snugged the band around the lighter so that the flame stayed lit. "Because," he said as he tossed the lighter toward the brush, "I still want to smoke."

The lighter and its small twist of flame arced and dropped amid the thorn. There was a sudden bump of heat and light. Polk felt the warmth push into and then past him. He staggered back and watched the fire enlarge itself on the supply of fuel. It crackled and snapped and sputtered. The air around it bent into waves like pieces of distorted and dripping glass.

PART III

19

KYLE WAS sure there was something wrong. Laura hadn't been herself for much of the afternoon. They'd driven up to Abingdon, Virginia, together, walked the downtown and had a nice steak dinner at the restaurant, but when it was time to go to the Barter Theater she'd said that she wasn't well, that she needed to go back to the hotel. He didn't press her about it, but once they were in the room she turned over in bed to face the wall, and he could feel the gulf between them as clearly as if it were something registered on a map. He placed his hand on her hip and let it stay there over her silk nightgown, but nothing in her nor him moved.

"We going to talk?" he asked.

"You're already doing it, aren't you?"

"It kind of takes a little something on the other end of the line, you know?"

"I'm sorry. I'm just feeling sad."

"I know you are. I just can't figure out why."

"Can't you?"

He knew not to answer too quickly.

"There's nothing that says we can't change things, Laura. Can't make arrangements to have something together that's more than slipping off to a hotel from time to time."

She sat up, looked at him.

"Don't start promising things that you don't mean," she said.

"I wouldn't do that to you. I wouldn't say I wanted things different if I didn't mean it."

She placed her fingers over her closed eyelids, pushed hard there.

"Goddammit, I wish I smoked."

He swung his feet over the edge of the bed and slipped his hiking shoes on.

"Where are you going?" she asked.

"You said you wanted to smoke, didn't you? There's a convenience store next door."

"I said I *wished* I did, not that I wanted to."

She turned her head over her shoulder; an approximation of a smile had worked its way into the corners of her mouth. Good, at least he'd found something to pry out a portion of the gloom.

"You just wait here, girlfriend. I'm a man on a mission."

She sat up, shook her head and said, "Come here, stupid."

He kicked off the shoes and spread out against her. She relaxed into him.

"It's not going to be easy, is it?" he asked.

"No, none of it is going to be easy."

But as she answered, she closed her hand over his and brought it around to her breast, held it there at the clavicle. At that moment, whether it was easy or not seemed utterly beside the point.

THEY LEFT early the next morning and rode back to where they'd left her car in the parking lot of a Kingsport Kroger. They sat there and talked for a while, drank their cups of McDonald's coffee until the sun was well up. Laura said she'd need a little time to figure out how to phrase things; she didn't want to be needlessly cruel to her husband. There was still a lot of history there, after all. Kyle had said that he understood, that he wouldn't want her to do things but how they felt right to her. Then they had kissed and held each other for maybe half an hour without saying another word.

When he drove back home he stopped into his office at the courthouse. Because his position as commissioner was merely part-time,

Kyle was allotted little more than a junked corner of a subdivided section that had once served as a holding area for overnight drunks and other misdemeanor offenders who were deemed harmless enough to avoid detention in the more secure basement level. The bars had been pulled, though the walls still bore the scars of heavy duty bolt holes that spackle had failed to plug.

He went up the hall and filled the coffee carafe from the water fountain, then came back and flipped the coffee maker on, sat and read through a short pile of new business the commissioners' secretary had left for him. By the time the coffee was ready, he was pretty much done with what he had to do, but he sat and drank the coffee, watched through the slim grimy window what passed in the courtyard. He could see the American flag flap, its halyards thunking against the pole. He thought of calling Laura, just to hear her voice really, but he decided to let her have a little time to herself. He didn't want to make things any harder on her than he already had.

Sheriff Holston dropped by after a while, went and poured coffee into his personal cup. In block letters it said BAD COP. NO DONUT.

"Go ahead and help yourself," Kyle told him after Holston had already begun to sip the Folger's and pulled up a chair.

"You decide to do your service for the taxpayers, I see," Holston said, pointed at the skinny leavings of paperwork. "Glad to see it's not above your attention."

"Is there a reason you're sucking up all the air in here?"

"Nothing in particular. Simply keeping the lines of communication open with my legislative colleague. Working for the commonweal, you know. How about you?"

"How about me what?"

"How are you managing your late problems with Mister Noon?"

"My problems? Funny you put it that way. Seems like he'd be your problem as much as anyone's."

Holston tipped his head back, studied a long damp crack in the plaster ceiling. When he next spoke, it was as though he were addressing the building's rift itself.

"I deny we have a problem, Commissioner. We had a disturbance, yes. But when you allow things to expend themselves, to run the course they're destined to run, then you are practicing a kind of husbandry. You are protecting the people from shortsightedness and immediate gratification. That's our charge as public servants. If, however, we overreact or countermand, then we give those who would oppose good order the means to subvert the rule of law. They need inconsistency because inconsistency of government gives these men the means to resist. Consistency then. Consistency and understanding is what keeps communities like ours safe and true."

"You really believe that?"

Holston faintly smiled, polished off his coffee.

"Don't get weighed down in the particulars, Pettus. It's enough to drive you to the loony bin."

KYLE STOPPED off at a few places in town to tally stock and keep up to date on refilling standing orders before he drove back home. He passed Orlynne's trailer on the way, tried his best not to dwell on her and what had passed between them, though the spot of woods there was like something pressing up hard against the wall of his brain. He pulled off the road just above the river, sat there and watched it long enough to finish the Diet Coke he was drinking. He put the truck back in gear and turned around in the road and drove down the driveway where the goats were pegged on either side of the porch steps. When he stepped out from the Tacoma they yelled.

"Hush your cussing," Gerald called down to them. They cocked their heads in a contemplative moment before they turned and unleashed their screams on him. The old man brayed in turn, his lungs as full of satyric rage as perhaps uttered by any man. Completely baffled, the pair fell silent.

"Glad I had you here to translate," Kyle said as he stepped up on the porch.

"A man picks up many pieces of small wisdom across the years. Are you looking for Orlynne?"

"I am."

"What the hell got said between the two of you? She come back over here the other day mad enough to chew a drill bit."

"Yeah, it was a bit of a two-way street. I was hoping I might come over here and say a few words that might be taken for a truce."

"Well, good luck. Woman is a mystery with depths no man is meant to fully discern."

"That more of your small wisdom?"

"Naw. I think I read that on the internet somewhere. Anyhow, she's not going to be back until later this evening. She got her some part-time work at the Walmart. Working over there in the garden center."

Kyle would have laughed if it didn't hurt him as much as it did. He said he'd need to go on then.

"You not going to set here with me for a while? Figure out the inner riddles of existence?"

"Not right now, I'm afraid. I've got some work to do up in the greenhouses."

"I'll tell her you came by. I'll be up to see you at the meeting next week."

"All right."

ONCE HE got back to the house he worked through the afternoon, took his supper of a tuna fish sandwich onto the porch steps while he watched the sun bury itself behind the ridgeline. Afterward, he cleaned up in the outside shower so he wouldn't track everything onto the floors. He made a note to look up a cleaning lady somewhere in town. Things weren't disreputable yet, but they were headed that way in a hurry. To his own embarrassment, he'd come to realize how much he relied on Orlynne to keep the place presentable. Leaned on her like something that wouldn't ever give way.

He went to bed early but came awake with a sharp awareness of an otherwise still night. He lay there for some time, only vaguely registered the scratching at the back window because he was unsure if he was dreaming. He sat up and the world reeled. Everything seemed magnified yet vertiginously distant. Still, he knew those sounds were human, thought he heard a man's grunt as he tried to force his way inside the house. Kyle felt his way back down the darkened hallway toward the office, reached into the desk drawer where he kept the .380. It wasn't loaded and it took his clumsy hands a minute to turn over a box of shells and feed them into the pistol's magazine, rack a round into the chamber and go back out at the sound of busted glass.

He waited for a whisper of movement inside and when he heard it he stepped around the corner and saw the shape of a man. He raised the gun and fired twice. The intruder made an alarmed sound and staggered back and as he crashed into the sideboard.

"Oh my God, I'm shot! Oh Jesus!"

Kyle flipped the dining room switch and saw, sprawled and clutching his left thigh, Laura's husband, Peter Carson. Blood had begun to soak through his flannel trousers and his face had paled with terror. Kyle saw no weapon, only a cell phone that lay broken on the floor.

"You motherfucker," Carson whimpered. "You tried to kill me."

Kyle set the .380 on the dining table and snatched a hand towel from the basket on the sideboard, gave it to Carson and told him to press down hard. He tried but was useless with panic. Kyle knelt beside him and pressed the hasty bandage in place, told Carson to keep it there. The flow had already begun to subside.

"You're a goddamn fool, you know that?"

Carson made a sound that approximated assent as he tried to stand. Kyle helped him up and headed toward the door. Somehow, he managed the useless weight out to the truck.

They rode together without talking. At first, Kyle had thought the wound was serious and that he was hauling a dead man to the hospital, but in time he could tell that Carson's life wasn't threatened.

"You going to tell me what exactly you had in mind?"

Carson lifted his head in what must have been intended to be a defiant pose, though it only made him appear strained and theatrical, a man claiming his abject moment with a flourish.

"Was she there?"

"What?"

"My wife. Was she there?"

"I don't know what the hell you're talking about."

Carson weakly laughed.

"I wanted to get a picture of you both. Something to rub in your faces."

"I think you're confused."

"Don't patronize me. I've followed you, seen it. More than once. Your little getaway in Abingdon. That was me that followed you up here a while back. Should have known you were crazy then. Shooting at my car. Jesus. What kind of person does that?"

Kyle tightened his grip on the wheel as he turned for town. He set the hazard lights and stepped down on the accelerator. A few streetlights streaked the dash, their bulbs glancing down like canted eyes.

They turned in at the hospital by Sycamore Shoals. Kyle went inside and brought a man out with a wheelchair, walked in with Carson in and told the woman at the desk what had happened.

"A gunshot? You mean you're telling me you shot him?"

"Yes ma'am. It was an accident."

Carson laughed, shook his head. The duty nurse looked back and forth at them.

"Sir, is this man a threat to your safety?"

Carson said, "What does this look like to you, a paper cut? Can you get me a fucking doctor?"

"I'm going to have to call the sheriff's deputy that's on duty," she told Kyle. "We have to report all firearms injuries. You need to take a seat in the waiting area."

He sat next to the coffee machine, poured some out in one of the little paper cups but left it untouched. He wrung his hands a minute before he went ahead and called Laura.

"Hey, is everything okay?"

"Not really. Can you talk?"

"Yeah, wait a minute. Let me get up and turn the light on. It's been a hell of a night."

"What do you mean?" he asked.

She told him of a petty fight that erupted between her and her husband, how he'd called her a goddamn whore and told her to get out. She had, went and rented a room at the Holiday Inn by the interstate until she had a chance to get her feet under her. Kyle realized that it had likely only been part of the plan to provoke her to flee and then catch her in the consoling arms of her adulterous lover.

"Kyle, what is it? What's going on?"

"It's nothing," he said when he saw the deputy's cruiser pull up in the emergency lane. "I just wanted to check in, see how you were doing. I've got to run, okay? I've got to see to some things. I'll talk to you soon."

He ended the call without waiting for her answer and then went out to meet the law.

20

DELILAH RODE THE MAN UNDER HER, FELT NOTHING BUT THE DULL ache of her flexing muscles until he gave up what he'd been holding back. His eyes went blind and his mouth tightened into something that looked like it had been stabbed. She patted his chest and rose, went to the bathroom and washed out his leavings from between her legs. She tied her hair back and leaned over the sink, pulled some cold water up to her face.

"Come on back to bed," Jonathan said.

She could see his pale legs in the mirror. The rest of him was hidden behind the wall. Like he was nothing more than disembodied bones inviting her back for another joyless fuck. Loathing flooded her, something that seemed as though it was borne along her blood currents. Still, she knew to play her role, to make him believe she wanted to rub up against him like a scratch that had just found its favorite itch.

"I'm coming, baby."

He had propped himself on a small bank of pillows and watched her when she crawled into bed next to him, put her face against his damp chest so she wouldn't have to endure his face. She placed the tip of her finger over where his heart was supposed to lie, mapped a circle there, as if diagramming a scene of later excavation. At her touch he made a small sound of pleasure.

"Sweet boy, you haven't forgot what I asked you for, have you?"

"No, baby. I sure haven't."

"Well, you gonna let me have it?"

"I'm not sure you're going to like it very damn much. It's not pretty, you know."

Damn fool. As if she would be lowering herself to this if she was worried about things remaining pretty. She knew Harrison had something on the side, some slut he saw when he was out of town for days at a time. But knowing it wasn't the same as having the proof in front of her, seeing the face of what she'd been passed over for. She needed to have the picture in her head, the image that would bind her hate fast.

"You can show me whatever it is, sweet boy. You aren't jealous, are you?"

He laughed, pushed himself farther up on his pillow buttress.

"Hell, no. I got nothing to be jealous of. You're in my bed, ain't you?"

"That's right. I am."

He slid out from beneath her and fished the phone from the backpack he'd slung on the arm of the desk chair. He tapped the screen and started to scroll through. Its blue light limned his profile.

"Hand it here, baby," she urged, tried to keep the irritation out of her voice. "I'm a big girl. I can take whatever it is."

He glanced up at her, then back to the screen.

"I knew there was something wrong with that motherfucker. You sure you want to see this?"

She kept her hand extended until he finally gave it over. She placed her finger on the edge of the first picture. Harrison entering a brightly colored house. Then he was let in. Some black man. She kept going. The pictures hazy and blurred. The fool couldn't even figure how to get a goddamn picture taken properly.

"This ain't nothing, Jonathan."

"Keep looking through."

She passed through another few shots. Now she was looking through the window at Harrison and the man sitting next to one another on a piece of shit little green couch. Smoking something. Their legs were touching. Something big and dark and hollow swung out from underneath the base of her stomach. She scrolled once more and they were holding each other by the waist, their mouths on each other like they were trying to take air out. One picture more and she felt that sickness overtake her. She ran to the bathroom, slammed the door.

She had Jonathan take her back to the compound that night. Harrison was out. She went through his things in the closet, looked for signs of what she already knew. There was nothing more that incriminated him. Everything cleaned and organized. She had the address where Jonathan had followed him to Knoxville and knew how long it would take to drive there. She didn't yet know what to do with this information, though she could feel it taking shape in her like a sickness running through the many doors of her body.

Around midnight she'd heard Jonathan come scratching at the wall outside her room, speak her name in a hoarse whisper. She ignored him, pretended to sleep.

21

SHEPARD DIXON CAME UP WITH GERALD TO SEE KYLE AT THE HOUSE. They sat out on the porch and drank a beer before they got down to the business that each knew had to be settled. Dixon wore a tight polo shirt. Above it his patrician face looked as though it could have been lifted directly from a coin. Gerald was wearing overalls that appeared like they'd been pulled out of the bottom of a laundry hamper. A razor hadn't touched his face inside a week.

"There's no way around this, I'm afraid, Kyle," Dixon said, tugged at the peeling edge of the bottle label. "Not with what's already happened."

"It's a bunch of bullshit is what it is," Gerald angrily broke in. "That man breaking into your house, for godssake. You had every right to kill him on the spot as far as I'm concerned."

"It's more than simple legalities, Gerald . . ." Dixon began to explain before he was cut short by Kyle.

"We all know this extends beyond the law," he said. "It won't take long before it gets around why he was out here. There's no way I can't resign. It would put the board in a hell of a position if I refused to. I shot the husband of the woman I'm sleeping with. That's the fact and there's no way in hell that won't tear the town in half. We've got enough of a circus on our hands already with what Gavin Noon is trying to pull."

"Kyle's right," Dixon said. "We need to find a way to get ahead of this, and quick, too. There's going to be a special election announced as soon as we bring this to the public. We have to have someone to back."

They passed the old names back and forth for several minutes, but the familiar reasons for dismissing them seemed to rise up of their own accord. Too clannish. Too dull. Too old.

"What about Frank Farmer?" Kyle suggested.

Gerald passed his hand across the bridge of his nose, held it there as if given to sudden pain.

"Farmer, the black fellow that runs the arbor business?"

"Yeah, he's been here in the county for years now. Family man. Well-spoken and with business ties in the community. Hell, he can't be more than thirty-five years old."

Dixon leaned in, his jaw propped on his joined fists.

"It could work. It would sure piss off Noon and his people. You know he will make a run for your seat. Hell, he'd do it on principle alone at this point. What better than to have a solid black man as his opponent. It will get people out to vote, for sure. He played ball for Tennessee, didn't he?"

"Yeah, he was a hell of a cornerback for a couple of years," Kyle said. "If there's one thing that can get a man some traction it's that he spent some time as a Vol."

"But what people will it bring out?" Gerald asked. "It's just as likely to help Noon as it is to hurt him. You two are playing with fire. I'm not saying that Farmer can't pull it off, but we're not even sure he'd agree to run in the first place. You know, not every single man in the world thinks that sitting down with a bunch of boring old farts hashing out zoning laws is the second-best thing to getting an early ticket to Kingdom Come. Farmer might be a touch smarter than to suffer all of that."

"Well," Kyle said, "let's hope he isn't."

Dixon said, "Listen, this is all going to take some doing. We're going to have to run some kind of Republican. Officially speaking,

I can't be a part of this or we're walking into a minefield of collusion. That being said, a three-way race gives you all a much better chance of pulling this thing off. I'll get together with my people right away. You'll know soon enough who we will run. Getting Farmer is going to be up to you all. But I have to say, I really do wish you all the luck in the world."

FRANK FARMER was unloading a pair of chainsaws and a safety belt from the back of his pickup when Kyle and Gerald pulled into his driveway. He nodded hello, set everything down at his feet and stood wiping his oily hands while they got out and came to speak with him.

"Howdy, Frank," Kyle said, offered his hand.

"I don't want to dirty you up, Mister Pettus. I just got in from a job near the college. A big old elm that couldn't be saved."

"Why hell, Frank. I'm a politician. There's no way to keep my hands from getting dirty."

He smiled and they shook hands. Farmer was a thin but sinewy man, the muscles in his forearms defined from years of hard outdoor work. He wore a ball cap propped up on his balding skull. It read THE TREE DOCTOR.

"You mind if we step inside, Frank? There's something we'd like to talk to you about for a minute, if you can spare it."

He told them to come on, and they followed him through the open garage door and entered a tidy kitchen. He offered coffee, which they accepted. While Frank puttered around the kitchen for mugs and a filter, it gave Kyle a chance to take in the Farmer household. A framed portrait of his family in what looked like Easter clothes. A credenza with Frank's plaques and trophies from years of high school and college football. Above it a big action shot of Frank in Volunteer orange crashing into a Vanderbilt receiver, shoulder matched against shoulder. He remembered there had been talk of Frank having a shot at the NFL before he'd gone down with a knee injury in a bowl game his senior year. What had looked like nothing on television added three-tenths of a second to his forty-yard dash at that year's combine, which made all the difference in the world at a position that depended on speed. It must have been terrible to be that close to living a life among gods and then have such promise ripped unceremoniously away. But if Frank dwelled on the life he'd never had, Kyle could see no evidence of resentment.

Kyle asked after Farmer's wife, Gloria, and the kids, and he said they were doing well, and should be home from a visit to their grandmama's soon. Nice to have family close by that could relieve them of the kicking and screaming that twin girls brought into a house. They softly laughed and agreed.

"We do want to talk to you about something specific, Frank." Gerald finally brought the subject around.

"I imagined you did," Farmer said, his smile undimmed.

It was Kyle who continued.

"Frank, there's something that's about to come to light. Something that's going to force one of us to bow out of the commission. Normally, that wouldn't worry us all that much, but with this business with Gavin Noon and his group . . ."

"You mean the white supremacist? I thought you all had decided you weren't going to give them the time of day. Last I heard old Gerald here was going to hold out to the Second Coming before giving up his seat."

"It ain't me that's leaving," Gerald said. "Though if I had a plain lick of sense left it would be."

"It's me, Frank," Kyle said. "And we need to run somebody that we trust, somebody that will serve the community's interests."

"What kind of hornet's nest have you kicked over, Pettus?"

"That's not important right now, Frank. What's important is that regardless of which party you run for, the sitting members of the commission are willing to throw their weight behind you. Unofficially, at least. They'll field a Republican candidate, but it's all just following what's expected of them at this point. I don't think anyone doubts that as soon as Noon has a chance to disrupt the board he will seize the opportunity. We can't afford for a man like that to gain political power. So, after a little bit of talking, we've decided our best shot is a three-way race."

"And you figured a little local black boy would be just the ticket, didn't you?"

No one said anything for a while.

"Frank," Kyle broke the silence. "There's no way we can hope to run someone successfully unless they polarize the race. If we sit some faceless nobody that no one knows one way or the other then it gives Noon a chance to energize the people that support him, not just the ones that live out there praying to the ghost of Hitler, but to all the others in the county that are happy to go along with it. With you, we'd be making a stand. A real stand that shows everyone we won't allow men like this to take over our country. That damn thing in Charlottesville last summer, that was just the beginning. They marched and chanted and got everyone on Facebook stirred up, but look at what happened a few weeks later. It was on to the next outrage. Everyone had moved on to hating something else. But those bastards with their torches and their fascism don't forget."

Frank laughed, tugged at the brim of his ball cap.

"You think black folks don't know that, Pettus? My God, you all are in my house sitting here delivering a lecture to me about what it means when you let scared white men get a hold of something they don't understand. You think we ever stop thinking about it? Look, I don't doubt you're doing what you think is right, but you're asking me to get involved in something that would put me and my family at risk. Do you think there's a chance in hell that those men and those who support them are going to just stand off to the side while some nigger tree cutter stands between them and what they want? I know what year the calendar says, but I also know I live in Carter County, Tennessee. I know that means certain things. I've built my life around knowing that."

Before anything else could be said, they saw through the kitchen window Farmer's wife and girls pull into the garage, heard the car doors slam shut. His daughters burst through the door, exact duplicates of one another, charged forward to embrace their father.

"Well," Kyle said. "I guess we better be off."

"Yeah," Frank told him. "I guess you better be."

KYLE MET Laura at the Mexican restaurant on the main strip in town, sat in a booth near the back where they ordered the margaritas on special and shared an order of nachos though neither had much of an appetite. She had visited Peter in the hospital that afternoon. He had told her to do him a favor and put a bullet through her skull. She had remained in the room for a while after that, tidying flowers and just sitting there under his gaze, but nothing else had been said. Finally, she had told him she would check back in when she could and left.

"I can't believe I was such a fool," she said.

"We both made mistakes."

"I've told you it's not the same, Kyle. Look, I wasn't going to say anything, but I went to see Orlynne a couple of days after we went out to her place."

Kyle puts his hands flat on the table, leaned back. "I wish you wouldn't have done that," he told her.

"That's what you don't understand. I need to be a part of your life if you want this to work. And it doesn't matter if you and Orlynne are having a fight right now. She's as much a part of you as if she were your mama. It's not hard to see that. It's especially important for me to do what I can when it's the fact of us being together that's the problem you're having with her. I've got to make some kind of peace with her. A woman in a small town leaving her husband for another man can end up isolated in a hurry. I need all the friends I can find. Anyhow, I knew there was something upsetting her when we were there, even if she was trying to keep it to herself."

"What did she say?"

"She told me what she tried to warn you about and how you'd back-talked her."

"Back-talked? Jesus Christ. That's a hell of a way to put it."

"Well, she wasn't wrong, was she? Look where this has gotten us."

Kyle pressed his thumb and forefinger against his eyelids, leveled his breath.

"I'll smooth it out with her, okay? As soon as I can catch a minute."

Her hand encircled his, drew it back down to the table.

"What did the sheriff say about charges?" she asked.

"That Peter had broken and entered, so it doesn't look like the DA is interested in getting involved. He could bring a civil suit, though I'm not sure what good that would do him."

"He doesn't let things go. Obviously."

Kyle shrugged.

"He can have his day in court. It'll just end up costing us both money we can't spare, but maybe that's what it will take. It doesn't change the way I feel about things."

She smiled, reached across the table and squeezed his hand. He squeezed back.

"When are you going to announce your resignation from the commission?"

"We can't wait past tomorrow evening. We'd hoped to get someone committed to running for the seat, but everything's a mess. I don't know. We'll see."

He moved food around on his plate for a minute, not looking up.

"What's on your mind, Kyle?"

"I was thinking it's pointless for you to keep staying out at the hotel."

"You were thinking that, were you?"

"I was."

"You don't think we might be rushing things a little?"

"Not for me. I'm old enough to know what I want."

"That's good to hear. I think maybe I am too."

THEY DROVE over to the Holiday Inn to get the few things she had taken with her and then back to her car where they'd left it at the restaurant. It was just slipping over the warm edge of twilight by the time they got back to the house. He carried her bags back to the master bedroom. He had her brew a pot of tea for them while he went down to check on the greenhouse plants. She brought a pair of mugs down and they sat on the edge of one of the big watering tables and listened to the evening birds come in to roost while they sipped the tea.

"I think I can get used to this," she told him.

"I was hoping that might be the case."

The next few days offered a refuge. It was the weekend and Laura didn't have to drive to work, didn't have to leave the place she preferred. They lived and worked beside one another, often with few or no words exchanged. The days were long and hot but not unpleasant. They ate their meals in the shade of the porch and watched the mountains.

She didn't attend the night of the commissioners' meeting, waiting on him at the house with a bottle of wine instead. He counted on needing it. He got to the courthouse early to finish up some paperwork. From his office he could see a crowd had already gathered on the front lawn. As he'd expected, word had gotten out. The newspaper was there, as were some of Noon's gang. Shepard Dixon was out on the front steps wearing his thin sports jacket and unassailable smile. Old Gerald was there too, arms crossed and as stony faced as a carving affixed to a memorial.

The other commissioners nodded hello as Kyle entered the boardroom, though none offered more than the briefest greeting. He could feel their eyes shift as soon as he moved on and took his place at the table. Strange to be exposed there like a specimen. He cracked open his plastic bottle of spring water and sipped, waited for the public to settle in.

The chairman brought the session to order, processed through a few routine matters before he turned the floor over to Dixon.

"I want to open this session with the note that the following is a general address to the public for the sake of transparency, but that in no way is it an open format for debate. Therefore, please refrain from making comments or addressing the board with direction questions."

A few dissatisfied comments animated the crowd.

"If the meeting is disrupted, the board has the right to conclude the remainder of this evening's business in closed session."

The public fell silent.

"Very well. Commissioner Pettus, you have the floor."

Kyle nodded, unfolded his prepared statement. His voice was composed but foreign sounding in his own ears. He spoke of his years of service to the county, of his pride in what had been accomplished in the community. And then he came around to it. He was resigning his position on the board due to personal reasons that would become apparent in the coming days. He thanked those who worked alongside him regardless of party affiliation, thanked the law enforcement officials who were partners in ensuring the local government served its people, thanked the people themselves, regardless of their vote, for the trust they invested in the office. When he'd finished, he felt exhausted and got up and left the room before any of the shouting really got started.

22

THE PAPERWORK APPEARED TO BE ROUTINE. GAVIN SAT THERE IN THE courthouse lobby and filled out his vital information, then carried it all down to the Board of Elections office, handed it over to the woman who ran her eyes over each item to ensure it was properly noted. She smiled and told him everything looked fine, that he could now begin organizing any fundraising as well as commence production of campaign materials in pursuit of the special election. He decided to test his pose as a statesman, so he thanked her, pressing his hat over his heart as a sign of gratitude. She nervously giggled.

He stepped around the corner to the newspaper office to ask after the reporter, Mister Sealy. He found him in the back cubicle sorting through a short stack of press releases. When Sealy looked up, he popped to his feet and wrung his hand, asked him to have a seat and a cup of office coffee. Gavin accepted with pleasure. "Am I right to offer congratulations, Mister Noon?"

Gavin submitted a thin smile and shrug.

"I suppose that depends on things yet undecided, but if you're referring to my candidacy, then yes, I believe it's now official that I can say I will be putting my name forward for consideration in the special election."

Sealy smiled and wished him well even as he grabbed a notepad and pen from his cluttered desk. They moved naturally into interview, the questions something the young man had framed ahead of time. Gavin knew he needed to remain cautious here. Sealy may well have been sympathetic to the goals of Little Europe, though it was far more likely that he was simply looking after his own career. Still, if handled right, the press had its particular uses. With this in mind, Gavin discovered that he enjoyed the exchange immensely. The back and forth about giving his all for the county and how it reflected his deeper commitment to the country that had such potential but had fallen under many years of apologetic self-hobbling. There were rays of promise, of course. The rallying cry of working whites who had lifted the president into office after the socialist disgrace that had preceded him. But in many ways he felt the most exciting stage in politics was in the local arenas. That was where the DNA of a country was truly sorted out, where it could realize its perfection of form.

"You know," Gavin said, "there's an entirely different aspect of what's going on here that we've failed to touch on. It's something I've been thinking about since you brought the good lieutenant governor's support to my attention the other day."

"That was something else, wasn't it?"

"It was. It struck a chord, as they say. It really puts the contemporary problems we face across the country into sharp focus. We're told that our nation is about defending the rights of the individual, but that only depends on you being the right kind of individual. Can you remember what it was like to hold an unpopular viewpoint and not be whipped like a bad child for it?"

Sealy gently laughed.

Gavin continued, "But that's not the way it is now. You look wherever you want in the mainstream media. It's nothing short of puritanism. I think it's an American obligation to dissent. It think it's practically constitutional, in fact. If not for the courageous few who live as men thinking, we would live under the boot of whatever orthodoxy the empowered have decided to enforce. Men thinking, that's what we are. You know the reference?"

Sealy stammered, "It rings a bell, but . . ."

"Emerson. Ralph Waldo Emerson. There was a man who understood how a revolution could be packed inside a sentence."

Gavin cut himself short. No one wanted to be lectured.

"Well, I'm sure I've taken up enough of your time as it is, Mister Sealy. I'll leave you to your good work."

Sealy clumsily came to his feet, invited Gavin along for something to eat at the corner deli, but Gavin declined, said that he had campaign business that needed his attention. Sealy followed him to the front door, clapped him on the back. It was a bit familiar, but Gavin let it pass.

AFTER JONATHAN took him home, Gavin asked Harrison to come up and see him. They sat in Gavin's bedroom with the window thrown open. Harrison handed over the leather zip packet of money and the accounting sheet. Gavin gave it only a cursory glance, set it on his desk.

"I'd feel better if you'd count it," Harrison said.

"Really? Why's that?"

"Numbers aren't up for argument."

"Are you expecting us to have an argument?"

"No sir, but I know the weather has a way of changing when you least expect it."

"Fine, give me a moment."

He drew the bills out and laid them flat on the desk, methodically counted through and tallied the sum against the calculated columns.

"As I expected. Everything zeroes out perfectly. It must be difficult making sure that's the case."

"I don't follow."

"You carry something with you that looks like it might get expensive from time to time."

"You mean Delilah."

"I do."

"Yeah, well. I don't know what to say. I guess I kind of understand women."

"That's a precious talent."

Harrison had nothing to say.

"Well, that's immaterial," Gavin continued. "I do have something I'd like for you to take care of for me. A side task to our previous business arrangement. It shouldn't take too much of your time, but I need someone I can trust to do a comprehensive job, someone with a proven eye for detail."

"Shoot."

"I assume you've heard about my intention to run for local office."

"Yeah."

"I'm having some campaign signs printed. They should be ready for pickup tomorrow afternoon. I'd like you to place them strategically throughout the district. I've gone ahead and marked up a map," he said, handed a folded paper across. "I can have Jonathan drive you. I know he and you don't get on terribly well, but let's think of this as a team-building opportunity, all right?"

Harrison stood.

"You're the man signing the paycheck."

"Yes," Gavin concluded. "I am."

THAT NIGHT Gavin spent nearly an hour posting on several of the *Storm Front* threads. He listed his candidacy and his campaign philosophy. Almost immediately congratulatory feedback registered, different accounts chiming in with CONGRATS and WELL DONE and SIEG HEIL. He felt a pleasant buzz each time he refreshed the screen and saw the support tick up. He was beginning to grow tired, but before closing out he refreshed once more and saw a message of KEEP THE FAITH from the username of SirGallah00d. He clicked on the name. He was still online. He opened a dialog box for a direct message.

GNooner:	Thx for the comment.
SirGallah00d:	np
GNooner:	Btw I'm a fan of the Batman stories you've been posting. You should try to publish them somewhere.

Several minutes passed without a response. Gavin was again ready to log off when the speaker chimed.

SirGallah00d:	Sorry. Had to tuck the kids in. Glad you liked them. Didn't know if anybody even paid attention to them things.
GNooner:	Absolutely. They're better than anything I've read in a long time.

He hesitated before clicking send and then blustered through the next discharge of text.

GNooner:	I've been writing some too but haven't posted anything to the boards yet. Wondered if you might be interested in taking a look. Mabye some feedback :)

A long time passed without a response until Gavin became irritated.

GNooner:	U there? zzzzzzz
SirGallah00d:	Sorry man. Wife wanted me to do something. Sure send something along. I'm not a professional or nothing but I would like to see what you come up with. Gotta buzz off, bro. Sieg Heil.
GNooner:	Yeah, me2. SH

He logged off and shut the laptop down, sat there in the darkness with nervous excitement piling up in his chest. It was one thing to have these stories on his hard drive, recorded there as proof of what he conjured out of nothing, but the prospect of sending them out to a reader, a reader whom he admired and who would take these stories, these invisible things that he'd created, and make them part of his larger world, that was far more than he could have hoped for. He got up and stood at the window, watched the moon slide from its camouflage of tree branches, the light telling against the twisted irregularity of natural shapes. The tree limbs had grown and knotted toward daylight, disobeyed gravity, but only here in the night under the scrutiny of the moon was their hypnotic power evident, the way shade and angle transformed them into something terrible and profound. Beholding it like this, Gavin had never felt so strong and ready in his entire life.

23

HARRISON TOLD JONATHAN TO KEEP THE VAN RUNNING, THAT HE'D grab the signs on his own. His help would have been useful, no doubt, but the chance to be spared a few moments of his company was worth the tradeoff.

Inside, the print shop was loud and it appeared the air-conditioning was busted. All they had going was a rattling box fan set on the counter. The man behind the desk was boxing up reams of color flyers. Looked like advertisements for a local professional wrestler.

"You the boy for the Nazi signs?" the man asked, one hand hitching his waistband. "They're all pretty and lily white for you. Just like ordered."

Harrison nodded, slid the cash envelope across.

"You don't care much for my jokes, do you?" the man smiled as he gazed at the money.

"Is that what they are, jokes?"

The man shrugged, wet his finger, and began to count the bills.

"It don't mean a damn bit of difference to me. Just a bit of print on a surface, idn't it? This country is protected by freedom of speech, by God, or I'm not a Christian."

Harrison had no desire to debate the sign maker's ethics, asked him to show him the signs. The man laughed and told him to follow him around back.

Three trips to the car had everything stowed in the trunk. Harrison got in and directed Jonathan to the first installation, all the way down the highway to the border with Washington County. Midday traffic was mild, so they cruised through town, out past the high school and the Sycamore Shoals historical park where people still dressed up in colonial costumes and pretended to be mountain men who bred and broke treaties with the Cherokee. All in the name of preserving the past. From there they cleared the vestiges of town, left the history behind them until it was all straight velocity, thinned and tanned with endless drought.

"You think these signs are gonna make a damn bit of difference?" Jonathan asked.

Harrison glanced at him. Had no reason to trust him. Had no reason to share his mind.

"It's what the man wants done, so I'll do it. That's what we're here for, isn't it?"

"You tell me."

"I thought I just did."

Jonathan started to say something but stopped himself. Harrison was happy to let him privately foster whatever thoughts he had.

A few minutes later Harrison told him to pull over. They crossed over the rumble strips and parked. Jonathan made no effort to help when Harrison got out and opened the trunk. He held the sign. Red lettering on a field of white, the black German cross stamped at the top.

GAVIN NOON FOR COMMISSIONER
HERITAGE NOT HATE.

Incredible that he could be holding something like this. Equally incredible that his hand could be the one driving it into the ground.

The earth was baked into cracked clay. The iron prongs were sharp but as soon as they went, in the soil split and there was nothing to keep it standing in place. He tried another spot farther up the road, but it was no different.

"It kicking your ass?" Jonathan called. "Need Daddy to come up there and handle it for you?"

"Knock it out of the park, big man."

Jonathan peeled himself from the car, strutted down and snatched the sign from Harrison's hands.

"All it takes is a little bit of goddamn elbow grease."

He jabbed his boot down on the centerpiece until it seated.

"There. Look what I told you."

Jonathan's self-congratulations barely cleared his mouth before a shiver of breeze caught the vinyl edge and the sign flagged over in the dirt. He swore and kicked up dust.

"I think I see the problem," Harrison said. "You forgot to hit it with your purse."

Jonathan walked back to the car.

"That your solution?"

Jonathan gave him the finger.

Harrison picked up the sign, folded it under his arm and went up on the highest part of the highway shoulder where some grass was still able to grow. It wasn't ideal, but he had a decent vantage of the passing traffic and the earth still retained some of its moisture. He planted it there and tugged it to test how well it held. One soldier in a rank, he supposed. He walked back to the car.

"The hell kind of good is it going to do up there?" Jonathan smirked.

"Better than laying flat on the ground. Come on. Let's get to the next spot."

They spent until well past suppertime posting the campaign signs across the designated areas. The last one was next to the State Line Drive-In, just short of where the Warlick community began. So rare to see one of these old theaters still in operation. Big and bulky monuments to an outside world that held on to a kind of reverent strangeness. Harrison remembered one from when he was growing up east of Knoxville, set there on the banks of the Holston River. A summer eve with the car radio turned up and the enormous Hollywood faces framed and fixed against the night. The stories they showed didn't matter all that much. What mattered was the odd magic of seeing the remote and beautiful brought down to where you could drive right up to it, fill your eyes and your head with those impossible images. Made you believe you could one day find yourself in a place that seemed as important as that.

"Hey, daydreamer. You done or what?"

"Yeah," Harrison told him. "Let's head on."

When they got back to the compound Delilah was down in the kitchen helping put some dishes away. She didn't stop when he came up and placed his hands on her shoulders. For an instant it seemed as though she flinched.

"There ain't any leftovers," she said.

"That's okay. I can make a sandwich."

She toweled and racked the plates.

"Is something wrong?" he asked.

"Not that I'm aware of."

Despite this, the tightened muscles in her neck seemed on the verge of snapping.

"Well, I'm gonna grab a shower."

"You do what you need to."

WHEN HE lay down to sleep that night she was quiet beside him, though he could sense by her breathing that her mind was restless. After a while she said his name. When he didn't answer, she slipped from her side of the bed and dressed by the dim light of the closet. She left without making any noise. It was easier for him to lose himself in sleep once she was gone.

He woke to an empty bed when it was just shy of dawn. He sat there and smoked a couple of cigarettes waiting for her to turn up. When she didn't, he got dressed and left the compound without telling anyone.

It was still early by the time he turned off for Knoxville, so he stopped at the convenience store and bought a couple of coffees, loaded them up with the cream and sugar he knew Emmanuel liked. Harrison could drink coffee any way it was brought to him, but it pleased him to match Emmanuel, made it feel like a kind of rite to fold his life into another's.

It was just eight o'clock by the time he stood on the stoop waiting to be let inside. He knew Emmanuel would be up, so he didn't hesitate to knock. The early morning was when he always got started on his painting. Harrison had planned to come out here and watch him work for a while. Not talk, just sit there and absorb the atmosphere of Emmanuel and what he tried to illustrate with his pictures. Seeing him like that was its own kind of drug.

He tapped at the door again, surprised that the lights in the front room weren't on. He peered through the window and saw only lamplight in the back bedroom. Then slow movement.

When Emmanuel came to the door his eyes were red.

"Oh, honey," he said, brought him inside, and collapsed his body against Harrison.

Harrison simply held him and waited.

"It's my daddy," Emmanuel said after a while through tears. "The home called. He had a stroke last night. He was gone before the ambulance had time to get there."

"I'm sorry."

They sat together on the couch. Harrison pulled him to his chest and let him tell him what he could. He knew that Emmanuel and his father had been estranged for several years, but that seemed to fall away now and the loss was sharp. Emmanuel spoke of regrets and guilt and love and Harrison did his best to soothe him, though he could see that his words struggled to grab hold.

"I'm going to try and cook something."

"I'm not hungry," Emmanuel told him.

"That doesn't have anything to do with it."

He went in and turned the electric burner on under a skillet and set the oven to broil. The refrigerator was largely bare, but there were still a half dozen eggs and a block of cheddar cheese. A loaf of white bread on the counter. He pinched a couple of slices from the top and slid them into the oven. He got a bowl from the cupboard, cracked in four of the eggs and began to whisk them with a fork. Thin shavings of cheese after that. The slurry splashed into the skillet with a hiss. As it thickened he turned the setting folds and scooped them onto a plate. He placed the toast on the side and carried it all out.

Emmanuel took the plate and ate a few placating bites before setting it on the coffee table. Harrison did not try to urge him beyond that. They sat there and watched the morning light comb through the blinds. Harrison drank both coffees, not bothering to heat the second one when it had cooled.

"Would you let me take you somewhere?" Harrison asked.

Emmanuel smiled faintly. "Okay. Let me get dressed."

Harrison cleaned the kitchen while Emmanuel pulled himself together. There wasn't much to do. Emmanuel had always kept just what he needed. No surplus to confuse the method of matching one day to the next. As Harrison worked he thought about the few times he'd been around Emmanuel's father. He had been a quiet but burdened man, as if silence concentrated his distaste for the larger world. That sharp look he would turn on someone he saw as a threat. Eyes like gunsights. Harrison remembered coming to the house and how that man had known what he was, what his son was too, and how he'd never seen a clearer expression of hate.

"Is this supposed to be a secret, where you're taking me?"

Emmanuel was dressed. He had showered and looked better.

"It doesn't have to be."

"No, that's fine. I don't mind a surprise."

They stopped at the grocery store for a few things to take on a picnic. Hard cheese, a salami, a baguette and some wine and cigarettes. Harrison packed it all in a backpack and set it behind the driver's seat. Once back on the road they turned west on the interstate, cleared the in-town traffic and before long they were on the slow grade up to the Cumberland Plateau, Knoxville sinking behind them like a gravity they'd just escaped. The radio signal soon weakened and Harrison had to shut it off, but the silence was easy and clarifying, and neither of them wanted to intrude with talk.

He drove for an hour and exited near Crossville, took secondary roads according to directions he'd scratched on a scrap of ruled paper. Finally they came to a gravel road that terminated with a locked gate and a NO TRESPASSING sign.

"Jay, are you sure you're got this right? It doesn't appear terribly inviting."

"Yeah, it's okay. Come on."

He slung the backpack over one shoulder and bent through an opening in the gate. As he walked the contents of the bag softly clinked. The gravel eventually gave out into a rutted dirt track that curved through a frowsy meadow. The structure when it appeared seemed to grow organically out of the banks of trees, an unlikely bulk that spanned the enormous arms of branches, enclosing entire trunks. Story after story of the building wound upward, and at the top a cupola surmounted the uppermost tier of leaves. A sign hung above the entrance. THE MINISTER'S TREEHOUSE.

"What in the world?" Emmanuel exclaimed.

Harrison turned his head over his shoulder, smiled.

"I thought you'd like it."

"You're right, I do. If I knew what it was."

"Come on. I'll show you."

They stepped through a passageway of closely joined tongue-in-groove boards. As they went forward, occasional panes of stained-glass windows cast cool light across them like bursts of water. Further on a series of carvings, men and women with hands raised in supplication, their faces impassive and medieval. From there the interior opened into a vast and winding space. Spray-painted obscenities vied with Bible verses arranged along the walls like cardinal directions. They paused to read a few and then went on, climbed the staircase to the landing.

As they reached the next level Harrison told Emmanuel what this place was. A man's eccentric aim to build the world's largest treehouse because it had been something he'd dreamed, something he'd attributed to the voice of God Himself. So he had come out and done it with his own hands, devised the coursing woodwork and tooled the details as an attempt to achieve physical prayer. But the old man hadn't bothered with the proper permits for public tours of the place and it had to be shut off from the outside world. Still, no one bothered to enforce the prohibition. If you were willing to take the risk of entering a building without any official maintenance, the law wasn't going to stop you. It had gotten to be a bit of a myth when Harrison was in prison. A legend of this sacred place up in the trees that spread between the men regardless of their group allegiance or loyalty inside. He had promised himself that he would one day find it, see if it held the meaning he hoped it might.

"It's amazing," Emmanuel said, his hand drifting over the bend of an oak trunk. It twisted and wormed its way through the overhead ceiling.

They climbed to the next story and then one more until they could enter the cupola and see over the verdant tree line. The soft blue distance of the land without the problem of people inside it.

"Here, let's eat something," Harrison said, knelt on the floor and spread the things he'd brought along. He snapped open his pocket blade and passed it over the meat and cheese until he had several stacks. They ate and wiped their hands along the seams of their pants. They opened the wine and drank from the bottle, passed it between them.

"I'm not much for church. But I do have to admit this is pretty alright."

"Yeah, I kind of think so too. You want a cigarette?"

"No, you go ahead though."

Harrison lit a cigarette. The light breeze unspooled the smoke.

"I wanted to talk to you about something," he said.

"Talk then."

"I wanted to ask if you might be willing to pull up roots. Shuffle down the road a ways where we might could be something on our own."

Emmanuel turned the wine bottle in his hands.

"Plan like that takes money."

"Hell, I can get money."

"Is it that easy?"

"It can be."

"That's what I'm afraid of. You're determined to get yourself thrown back in jail, is that it?"

"The place I could get it from wouldn't bother with jail."

"Get yourself killed then? That's your plan?"

"No, not if I don't get caught."

"Harrison, I sometimes wonder."

"Wonder what?"

"If you're a born fool or if you've just spent a hell of a long time studying it."

Emmanuel turned up the wine and gulped it to the finish. He set the bottle down and took a few steps toward the overlook. He wobbled a little and had to steady himself against the railing. Harrison placed his hand on his back, which he didn't seem to mind.

"It's still just talk, you know?"

"No," Emmanuel said. "It's never just that."

24

THE HOUSE WAS DARK SAVE FOR THE BLUE GLOW OF A RUNNING television. Kyle struck the door panel three times hard with the flat of his hand, waited as he heard the curses and fumbling of the man within. The door yawned open on a bedraggled figure in sweatpants and T-shirt with a distended neck. It was Peter Carson.

"I ought to blow you to kingdom come where you stand," Carson said.

"We need to talk."

"I don't have a goddamn word to say to you."

"Well, you need to listen then. And it might take a minute, so we can either stand out here while it gets done with you looking like you're about to pass out or we can sit in there where you're closer to your pain pills."

"Goddamn you," Carson said, though he limped back to the couch, left the door cracked as he went.

Kyle followed, cast a quick glance through the house. The kitchen sink cluttered, the living room carpet littered. Laura's absence in the place was as clear as if it had been written on the walls. Carson lunged for the couch, stuck a longneck beer bottle to his mouth. Half a dozen other spent bottles lined the edge of the coffee table.

Carson smiled.

"I'd offer you one, but I don't want to."

Kyle cleared a place in a recliner and sat down.

"You mind putting that thing on mute so you can hear me?"

He pointed the remote and turned the volume down a few notches, the gibbering voices of *Naked and Afraid* still audible.

"You've got balls, I'll hand you that, Pettus. Run up on a man in his own house after you shot him in cold blood. Course, you don't have much problem taking what you want from my house, do you?"

"I'm not here to get a history lesson."

"Of course not. There'd be nothing you'd gain by that, would there?"

"Shut up so you can hear what I've come to tell you."

Carson fumed but kept his mouth closed.

"Now you can run whatever bullshit game you have in mind with this lawyer saying he's going to sue me all you want. What it comes down to is that you broke into my house in the middle of the night. There's not a jury in the state that's going to see shooting you as anything other than justifiable. But if you want to throw your money away, that's your own business. What I do want you to understand, though, is that this problem between us needs to be done. That includes leaving Laura alone."

"This sonofabitch means to tell me how I am with my own wife."

"You're goddamn right I do. You don't come near her. Not at my house and not at her work. You do that and it won't be the law that's your problem, you understand me?"

"Is that a threat?"

"Fucking A it is. I've already put one hole in you. It's not much to do it again."

"Get the hell out here."

"You bet. Enjoy your bare-assed reality show."

When Kyle got back out to the truck he sat there until his nerves calmed. After a while he pulled the pistol from under his shirttail and put it in the glove box before he cranked the truck and drove back home.

THE NEXT morning Laura asked if he thought things were settled.

"I imagine you know better than me, don't you?"

She turned the coffee cup with the tips of her fingers.

"I don't think he's dangerous, no."

"I can always ride by the library and check in if you need me to."

"No, it'll be okay. I've got a phone, you know."

He bent and kissed her, told her to make sure everything was locked up before she left, and went on to set up for the weekly farmers market.

By the time he had the tent up it was already hot. On the drive over he'd heard the local news talking about a wildfire in Watauga County, just over the North Carolina state line. The smoke had drifted down the valley and even here in the shadow of Roan Mountain he could smell it, see the faint shadow of smoke in the sky. The girls from the organic farm said it was bad the way they had come, a couple of roads shut down for lack of visibility.

Business sputtered throughout most of the morning. It was a pattern that seemed to happen toward the end of the summer before the last little flurry of tourist traffic in the week leading up to Labor Day. He had decided to pack up early and had just started taking up the guyline stakes when Frank Farmer pulled up in his work truck.

"I should look into running a nursery. You folks keep an awful short workday."

"Hey, Frank."

"Hey yourself."

He came forward, peered at the rosemary and lavender, a row of orchids.

"You looking for something in particular?"

"I could take some of those flowers there," he said, pointed. "Keep the wife happy."

"You do something that needs flowers to make it better?"

Frank smiled, passed a palm across his chin stubble.

"Not yet, I haven't. Though I'm likely to."

"Premeditated mischief, huh? Sounds like a sunflower problem to me."

Frank turned a few pots, looked the flowers over from several angles, as if checking them for flawed manufacture.

"You hear the radio this morning?" Frank asked. "The local station?"

"Afraid not. I prefer a little bluegrass in the morning to that bullshit."

"Bullshit is a pretty good word for it. They had that man, that Gavin Noon on there, talking about the special election. Taking calls from the public. Talked about his campaign and how it had nothing at all to do with being a white man. Said it was about standing for the principles that made this country what it was. You know, I sat there listening to him, and I thought to myself, this man actually believes the words that are coming out of his mouth. And that made me realize, he thinks he's doing right, he's out there believing this mess he spreads as sure as the sun comes up in the morning and sets at night."

Kyle said nothing, sensed that Farmer wanted him to merely listen.

"You need some help packing these things up?"

"I could use a hand if you don't mind."

They worked swiftly, struck everything down and loaded it into the back compartments of Kyle's truck. Seeing that business appeared done for the day, the girls from the organic farm decided to pack it in too. They shouted good-bye as they turned out of the lot and onto the highway just as Kyle and Farmer were finishing up.

"I see why you set up out here," Farmer said, smiled as he waved at the girls.

"Don't you start poaching on my territory. A man figures out the important things in life, and he's likely to get possessive."

They shared a laugh.

"I'll tell you something, Kyle. I'm about to say something and I think it might be the dumbest damn thing I can say, but I don't think there's any way around it."

"What is it they say in the church house? Speak your truth, brother."

Farmer shook his head, toed the ground like he was looking for a foothold.

"*If* I was to agree to what you and your commissioner buddies were wanting me to do. If I was fool enough to commit myself to something I have every reason to avoid. If that were to happen, I'd expect the men who asked me to do it to make damn sure they were there beside me trying to make it happen because I'm going to tell you right now, I'm not interested in being some kind of goddamn symbol that ends up at the end of the day without a pot to piss in. I'm not interested in being your token, you hearing me?"

"I am."

"You damn well better be. You've always seemed like a decent man. I don't know if it was the right thing for you to step down, but whether it was or it wasn't it's what we have to deal with now. I've lived here for the past few years, built a business that houses and feeds my family, and I'm not willing to turn loose of my home. Not for some damn Nazi pretending to be something else. And we all know that's exactly what he is. He can pretend he's part of this new America all he wants to, but he's determined to poison this place if he can. Maybe he will, but I'll be goddamned if he's going to do it without a fight. You tell who you need to that I'm willing, with one provision. You're my campaign manager."

Kyle laughed, swung the tailgate shut.

"I was afraid that was the provision," he said. "I really was."

25

GAVIN HEARD THEY WERE RUNNING THAT BLACK TREE CUTTER WHO lived in Elizabethton. He was unsure whether to be concerned or amused. What resulted was an uneasy combination of the two. Certainly it would get the attention of the media, which should drive people to the polls. The wheels of democracy on the move. He just had to make sure it was headed in the right direction.

He spent most of the morning going over some addresses he'd canvassed the week before. He still had another three weeks before the special election, which meant he should be able to get around to most everyone in the area he thought likely to turn up and vote. That meant Farmer was working at a pretty steep incline in terms of getting his name out there to the public. Sealy had called the night before to tell him what he already knew. That Pettus was working with him, running the whole monkey show, so to speak. Unable to let things rest and each man rise according to his own talents.

Gavin called Jonathan, told him to get the car ready. They were going to do a little personal campaigning. Reach out and touch someone.

Jonathan was leaning up against the hood of the car, smoking. Gavin handed him an address.

"Put that in your phone. It'll get us where we're going."

Jonathan ground the cigarette underfoot and slumped behind the wheel.

A quarter of an hour later they were sitting in front of Kyle Pettus's greenhouse. Pettus stood in the doorway of the upper enclosure, wiping his hands on a rag and likely speaking some unheard obscenity.

"You stay in the car, Jonathan," Gavin told him. "In case the pistol-packing ex-commissioner attempts a repeat performance."

Jonathan pulled out his phone and started to play with it.

Pettus stayed where he was, didn't say the first word when Gavin walked up.

"I've heard the news," Gavin began.

"I would have imagined you had, given your friendliness with that newspaper reporter."

"Well, Mister Sealy is merely excited to have a bit of real news to cover, I imagine. I don't think he intends anything particularly nefarious, from my point of view, at least."

"Yeah, you've got a hell of a point of view, don't you?"

"I do have principles, you know. The things I believe aren't merely a matter of trying to rhetorically convince someone. Don't you think that merits some degree of respect, even if you don't hold those same values yourself?"

"I think it merits treating you like something that's liable to bite."

"No way to talk to a man trying to unburden himself to you."

"Is that what this is?"

"I want to ask you something, with deepest sincerity."

Pettus said nothing, waited.

"I know you don't care for me or for the people I represent. We have fundamentally different worldviews, as they like to say in the press, but that doesn't cancel out the fact that we're both white men."

"That doesn't mean a goddamn thing to me."

Gavin's laughter came up like a strong cough.

"My Lord, Pettus. Of course it does, regardless of what lie you've told yourself. I realize that you think of who you are in a certain way. So many of you people who've gone off and spent a few semesters over at the state university like to believe they've cleansed themselves of their truer selves. That's fine. Every tribe needs its outliers. Makes things more interesting, don't you think?"

"I'm still waiting to hear why the hell you're on my property."

"Well, that's fine. A man with no patience for reason. I can see the virtue in that. Let's come to the point then. You might think this yard ape you're running in your stead is your little black savior, but I'm telling you right now that you're forgetting what this country really is at the end of the day. These people up here in these mountains don't need to be told by others how to think. They have the wisdom of the common man. They trust in their blood, their belonging to one another. You can pretend you're not a part of it all you want, but no one makes you live where you do among people like this. One thing I've learned in life is that you're not always born in the place you belong. This place, these mountains, they called to me, attracted me here like something pulling me from deep inside the ground. It would be profane for me to ignore that. If you don't feel at home here, Pettus, maybe that's because you're not. Just because you hold the property deed to this mountain, doesn't mean it belongs to you."

"I plan to walk back to my house right now. If you're still standing here by the time I come back out I'll be carrying a good deer rifle and I'm pretty dead on with it."

"I have no doubt. You've already proven your marksmanship, haven't you. Very good. I won't be in your way then."

Gavin did not rush back to the car. What was the word? Sauntered. Yes, he sauntered back and slipped into the passenger's seat, felt a warmth overtake him, a kind of fulfillment that seemed to brim and spill over.

THAT EVENING Gavin sat alone on the porch going over a notebook of talking points. It was a brief sketch he had begun to develop after supper when he received a call from the election commission, an invitation to a formal debate scheduled the week before the election. It would be held at the county courthouse. He had consented with pleasure. There was no doubt in his mind that the fact of his participation would force Farmer's hand. Couldn't afford to be seen as the coward, not if he was to be the symbol of all that he was purported to be.

It was pleasant to sit there and address himself to the task of delivering his position. The effort of concentration removed him from the immediacy of his physical environment, freed him in a way thoroughly meditative. Perhaps there was some danger in giving himself over to this, some faint amnesia, because he had become so absorbed by his own thoughts that he didn't immediately realize that a pair of voices were speaking hoarsely to one another in the deep shadows at the far end of the verandah. It was impossible to know how long they had been there. Only a few minutes, maybe, but enough time for him to tell that they were arguing but trying not to be overheard. His pencil scratched but he had no mind for what he wrote. Instead, he made out fragments of words, sounds reaching toward him but failing to take hold. Then silence fell, the unseen voices aware of their detection. Footsteps—quick, decisive. A few seconds later a form gradually resolved itself in the pitched light above the front door. It was Delilah, alone.

"Out here all by your lonesome, huh?" she asked huskily, trailed her hand along the railing at the edge of the concrete.

"Just thinking," he said, aware of how she tried to behave as though she wasn't taking pains to conceal something. So very odd. But so much about her was.

"I heard about you going out there to poke at that man that gave up his place on the commissioners' board. You sure that's the best way to go about things?" she asked with the faintest turn of a smile.

It was as though she couldn't help but insert flirtation into everything she did, even though she clearly loathed him. Gavin was struck by how successfully survivors could adapt themselves to any number of unpleasant circumstances. He wondered what things had happened to her, what had shaped her into the chameleon she had become.

"Well," he said, motioning for her to take the seat beside him, which she did. "Matters of strategy aren't typically straightforward, are they? There's some force that must be applied in order to understand what the rules of the game are supposed to be. It's a kind of physics, really. Perhaps a little less frequently observed but true nonetheless. I feel like you, of all people living here, would understand what I mean."

Though she wasn't looking at him, she smiled.

"Yeah, I have a pretty good idea."

She interested him. In his own way he felt a kind of paternal affection for the young woman. Anyone motivated by hate like hers was worth study and admiration.

"I have noticed something," he said.

"I bet you have," she answered, the words coming with such natural quickness that it seemed she couldn't have had time to mentally form them, the defensive tone as instinctual to her as an animal's use of its claws. He felt uncomfortably stimulated.

"You've noticed Harrison isn't the only object of my attention, haven't you? Wondered where it all stands, is that it?"

"Yes, that's right."

She laughed from a place inside her that shaped the sound into something desolate.

"Well, Gavin, I'll have to say, it is still possible to be surprised by people in this world."

"You misconstrue my interest. I wanted only . . ."

"Bullshit. You think through your dick, just like the rest of them. Hell, I don't fault you for that. Must be all this politics talk got your balls caught on fire. Found your little freak, huh? To each his own, I guess."

He didn't try to contradict what she said. Instead, he wanted to see what she might do when she had the power to act however it suited her. She moved closer, placed each of her hands on the arm of the chair as she stood over him. He could feel the heat of her body like something that might bring calm sleep. But she came no closer, stayed deliberately out of reach.

"Is this what you're after, Gavin? Is this what this Manson Family horseshit is supposed to get you? Pussy? A bunch of damn fools running around every time you give the word? Hell, you're smart, Gavin. That's easy enough to see. But you're not the only one who is. We're all just using each other out here, if you haven't figured that out yet. That's why this place has a chance to do something. Not because of your ideas. What makes this place something different is that it's full of people who are hungry, hungry in a way that people who've had plenty to eat all their lives can't ever understand. And it's them not understanding that makes them act in a way a hungry dog can smell. If you're really smart you'll leave all those speeches you've got planned in the trash. You'll smell things out like that hungry dog."

26

KYLE HAD COME TO SETTLE THINGS WITH ORLYNNE. SHE'D BEEN reluctant to let him past the threshold of the camper when he turned up in the evening asking if he could talk to her and Gerald for no more than a minute despite the fact that it was the dining hour. In truth, it was Gerald who'd got him past her and sitting down at the card table where the old man had already poured out a couple of goblets of homemade sangria. Taco night, he explained with a wink.

Orlynne sliced avocado, pretended Kyle took up no space there while she readied things. She talked through Gerald, asked him if they should invite Kyle to eat with them. Gerald grimaced over his wine.

"Lord God, Orlynne, let's bury the hatchet with this nonsense."

She made a sound that seemed significantly short of agreement. Still, she fixed Kyle a plate, slipped in beside Gerald and began to eat.

"You got a reason for coming out here?" she asked him.

Kyle had to finish chewing. Before he could answer, Gerald broke in.

"Honey, just listen to him, will you? I think you might want to hear what he has to say."

She laughed, bit down in her taco so that the shell popped and split in her mouth.

"So, a conspiracy between you two, huh? You better pour me one of them sangrias, Gerald, before you're looking for a new place to hang your hat tonight."

"I talked with Laura about what happened between you and me," Kyle said.

Orlynne relaxed her crimped mouth just a little.

"She tell you she and I had talked too?"

"She did. Told me a few things that made me understand her position a little bit better. Maybe made me understand your position a little bit better too."

Orlynne said, "Men do have a problem with what's right in front of their eyes sometimes. Lord knows a long life has taught me at least that much. So, that it?"

"It's the start of it, I hope. I came to tell you that I can see how I didn't realize the kinds of things I was asking people to do for me, what I was expecting them to do, and I'm sorry. I have never wanted to hurt those I love. Not Laura and not you."

She eyed him a moment, let him wiggle on the pointed tip of her stare.

"You know I don't hold anything against her personally, don't you? I even liked talking with her when it was just her and me. It's the only real way for women to get to know one another, Kyle. If you want it to mean something it has to come down to us apart from you. That's just how people are."

"I know."

"Good. Why is it then that the look on your face says there's something else that needs settling?"

"I'm not too excited about saying something that's going to undo the repair we just managed," he said, but as he did a smile worked its way behind the words.

"Oh Lord. I knew the peace couldn't last too long. Go ahead and tell it then," she said.

He explained his arrangement with Frank Farmer and of the strict time line they faced if they were to give his candidacy a chance of success. He needed her help. She knew the county as well as anyone and she would get people to the polls to vote. People who would understand that this was more than any other local election. That there was something real at stake.

"Gerald, honey. Will you clean the table?"

He did.

"You know, Kyle, this is one of the most foolish things I've ever heard of. Running the campaign of the man who's trying to replace you because you went and embarrassed yourself. I can't figure out which is worse, Farmer asking you to or you agreeing to it. The only grace you have is that this is the moral thing to do, even if it is a dozen kinds of stupid. So, taking all that into consideration, I guess I'll help you. Lord knows you'll need it."

He came around, hugged her. She patted his arm, told him to get off her, she had some phone lines to burn.

THEY HAD to organize as quickly as they could. Frank Farmer's place ended up becoming the campaign headquarters by default. His wife Gloria wasn't pleased at having her home upended nor with the prospect of her husband becoming the most controversial man in the county, but she suffered the trespass stoically, if not warmly. At first, his children seemed enthralled by the busyness of everyone's comings and goings, but they soon grew indifferent and preferred playing in the backyard in their plastic playhouse. Orlynne had a second short-term phone line installed so that she could canvass efficiently. Kyle and Frank went over current regulations and proposals due to be reviewed by the commissioners' board. Laura had come along to make herself available for running errands. Gerald, mouth at work over a pinch of Kodiak snuff, largely occupied the role of mascot.

They decided they needed a way to formally introduce Frank to the race before the actual debate with Gavin Noon and the Republican who was running. A way to show him as a member of the community who had come forward out of duty to the place where he belonged.

"How about an open meeting? Kind of like a town hall?" Frank said. "Something where I can shake some hands and kiss some babies."

Gloria peered over her glasses.

"Better than kissing hands and shaking babies, I guess."

Frank reached across the table, pulled her hand toward him and delivered a loud smack. Though she tried, even she couldn't resist his charm. Her laughter got everyone else going.

"I agree," Kyle put in. "This is the Frank Farmer the people need to see. Right here. We need a place where we can set something up on short notice."

"The library conference room hasn't been scheduled this week," Laura offered. "We could do it there. It's not huge, but it's something."

"What do you think, Frank?"

"By all means. If we're going to get this train going, we need to get out of the station."

Two nights later Kyle found a discreet place at the back of the meeting room while Frank took the podium at the front and answered questions from about two dozen townspeople who had come to hear him speak. After he'd talked for a while about living and working in Carter County, he opened the floor to questions. It was all pretty friendly. A couple of cracks about how poorly the Vols were doing these days with the pickings for All-American cornerbacks being so slim. Then some talk about zoning and local property and use taxes. He fielded it all with the good humor and approachability that had made him successful as an independent businessman. As Kyle watched, he realized Frank had something that he'd always struggled with himself as a commissioner. People simply liked Frank. He carried himself with an ease and lightness that had never felt true to Kyle. Perhaps it had something to do with Frank's natural athleticism, his intelligent response to continually changing circumstances. He moved in his mind like he had on the field, and his voice could fill a room.

At the end of the hour Frank thanked everyone for coming and shook the hands of those who wanted to have a final word with him. Kyle moved back toward the stacks to wait for him when he felt a hand on his shoulder. He glanced over to see Turner Whist at his side.

"Hey, bud."

"Hey," Turner said. He looked good. Combed hair. Even looked like he had a fresh shave. Hell of an improvement since the last time he'd visited him at the hospital. "You part of all this, Kyle?"

"Indirectly, I guess."

Turner laughed, a good sound. "I find it hard to believe you'd be indirectly involved in anything. I was sorry to hear you had to resign. A lot of folks think the world of you."

"Well, there's a time for everything. How are you doing now? I mean . . ."

"Yeah. It's one day at a time, brother. You know how it is. They got me on some new medicine. I've been staying with my cousin in Johnson City. Probably will for a little while. Melanie and the baby are up at her sister's place, which is probably best for the moment. I did want to ask you something, though."

"Ask away."

"I wanted to see if I could get back in the group. I'd like to work out there until we get the whole crop planted. I know Buckhorn's done, but I thought there might be some places we hadn't got to on Woman's Back. I'm a pair of hands if nothing else."

Kyle patted his shoulder. "I imagine we can find a spot. Here, step over this way with me. I want to introduce you to somebody."

Frank had just freed himself from one attendee who'd asked him to autograph a Vols Football calendar when Kyle got his attention.

"Frank, this is Turner Whist. He's one of the men who've been part of the reforestation group I've told you about. He's stuck a fair amount of greenery back on these ridges in the past few months."

Frank smiled, warmly shook Turner's hand.

"Glad to meet you, Turner. Good people like you keep a man like me in business. I need as many trees in this county as we can get."

"Frank owns an arbor business," Kyle explained.

"Sorry," Frank laughed. "My wife says I only tell the kind of jokes that are funny to myself. I'm glad you brought this up, though. I think it would be great to go up there with you guys sometime. Put my hands in the earth."

"I think that's a hell of an idea, Frank. I was just telling Turner we needed his strong back back on the job. And two is always better than one."

"It's hard to argue with that."

After telling Turner good-bye, Kyle and Frank went out to the truck. Kyle had driven to give Frank a last-minute chance to review his notes. Now, it seemed just as well because Frank's hands were shaking like a branch in a hard wind.

"Man, I'm glad that's over," Frank said.

"Nerves?"

"Feels like I just jammed my fingers in a socket."

"Doesn't show. Looked great up there. Made me a little jealous, in fact. Made me think if I was the one running against you, I'd have something to worry about."

Frank settled back, watched the town lights thin as they turned for the highway and headed toward the bulk of the mountains. "Well, that's good to hear," he said. "Maybe it means somebody else will have something to worry about too."

A FEW days short of the debate Orlynne began making a final push. She had a list of influential residents she believed could be swayed to Farmer if he went out and talked to them in person. Gerald remained unconvinced.

"We need to work the phones," Gerald said. "It's what's always made the difference when things have come down to the wire." He pointed at a list of names he'd pulled out.

"Oh come on, Gerald. You're telling me that Maynard Cobb will be brought around by a little sweet talk over a telephone?"

Gerald laughed, crossed out that name and three others.

"You'll play hell getting him to vote either way. He's been dead six months. Dropped a couple of hours after that meeting we had about a power line easement down around Hampton. He was furious that we voted it through. I felt kind of bad about it afterwards, but he was always riled up about something. Remember that, Pettus?"

Kyle glanced up from his work with Frank, nodded.

"Still, at least he died doing what he loved," Gerald continued.

"What's that?" Orlynne asked.

"Being miserable."

"You can be a hateful old thing, can't you?"

Gerald shrugged.

"I agree with you, Orlynne," Frank said. "I need to be out there. We'll go as soon as you get the names and places ready."

An hour later they were on the road, Frank driving his work truck. It was good for getting back in on some of the unpaved roads of the hollows as well as being a kind of unofficial advertisement as he rolled through. He had stayed in his work clothes too. No reason to hide the man in a suit and tie. He was simply one of them coming to talk about why he was the best person to protect the community from an old threat dressed up new.

By suppertime they had visited and talked with half a dozen business owners and otherwise civically minded people. They made no effort to distinguish between traditional Democrats or Republicans. This was more important than party lines, they said. This danger too severe. Overall, they were received with cool politeness when they knocked on doors. But once they sat down and took a cup of coffee or tea, the social ice began to melt and Frank would start talking, and when he talked it became obvious why he was the right man to run. He spoke with ease, avoided the kind of baggy rhetoric of someone who was conscious of being heard rather than understood. He spoke with directness and paused to listen to what others said in turn.

The last stop of the day was at the Reverend Joseph Winter's place. He was in the side yard watering several pots of begonias. Winter was a large hairless man with a head as round as a brass doorknob. He was flushed from the heat and he'd broken into a considerable sweat. He patted dry the back of his neck with an embroidered handkerchief. Along the stitching appeared a palisade of tiny blue crosses.

"It's the green thumb of Carter County," Winter said in his mellifluous voice. A voice long practiced to pitch itself to the back pews of the church house. He rested his watering can on the porch ledge and shook hands all around.

"We'd like a minute of your time, Reverend," Kyle said. "If you think your garden could stand a moment of neglect."

He smiled with an air of professional beneficence, welcomed them inside.

They sat in the cool of the living room, offered lemonade by Winter's wife, though they refused, citing full bladders from a full day of campaign visits throughout the area.

Winter politely laughed.

"I had heard you all were on the warpath today. I'm impressed you haven't dropped from the heat. I can't remember a summer like this, can you all? It's giving my growing season absolute fits. I can only imagine the professional problems it's giving you, Mister Pettus."

Kyle allowed that it had become more than a passing concern.

"So, Mister Farmer, I suppose you've come here to press me into the service of the good fight?"

Frank smiled, leaned forward in his chair.

"I think as that we're both Christian men, we might find that we have a great deal more in common than you would with Mister Noon."

Winter smiled slightly, lifted his open hands as if to beg for a moment of patience.

"I'm certainly not disputing the fact of your relationship with Jesus Christ as your personal Lord and savior, but a great many issues we hold in local elections have more to do with what's going on in our neighborhood than what's transpiring on the stage of national political theater. It would be naive to expect people to vote against their own interest. Surely, you understand there are limits to the kind of influence a man like me can wield from the pulpit."

Frank and Kyle exchanged a glance.

Frank said, "Reverend Winter, I'm not expecting you to turn your church into a platform for endorsement. However, don't you think the nature of this election, the fact that the man is an avowed white supremacist, doesn't that change things for you in the slightest?"

Winter retained his impassive smile.

"I really do applaud what you all are doing and I wish you the best of luck. But I'm afraid I'm not in the position to enter into the political fray. I'm sure you understand," he said, standing. It became clear that he had nothing more to say.

By the time they'd gone back out to the truck Kyle wanted to put his fist through the dash.

"Did that bastard just say he thought it wasn't his place to side against a racist? Did I imagine that?"

Frank turned the key, gassed the engine until it thrummed.

"Calm down, Kyle," he said. "You're getting a lesson, is all."

"A lesson in what?"

"In how easy it is to be a coward."

LAURA MET him at the house. She had stopped off in town and brought some chicken and vegetables home, kept the plates warm in the oven. They sat down to eat, split a bottle of Côte du Rhône poured into water tumblers. He was quieter than normal, though she didn't need to pick up on that to see that he was bothered.

"You want to talk about it?"

"Not sure I know how to. I thought things were one way. I've spent years working for what I thought was right, and now it seems like it was all a joke."

"I thought the campaign was going well."

He shrugged, drank.

"Maybe it is. It's just that there's a rot beneath the surface. Something that makes me feel ashamed, useless."

She reached across the table, took his hand.

"You're doing good work, Kyle. All of you. I'm proud of you. Others are too. You can't control everything. Be a little easy on yourself."

He said that he would. They talked pleasantly for a while, let the pattern of routine conversation cleanse what had stuck to them from their time apart over the course of the day. It was easy to lose themselves like that for a while, perhaps even necessary. Later, they moved out to the living room and listened to music, finished their wine. With her head on his shoulder it was possible to witness the gradual spread of evening through the front window and let that be enough.

27

THE NEXT DAY WAS SUNDAY AND FRANK WAS UP EARLY ENOUGH THAT IT was still dark outside. He stood in the kitchen and drank two cups of coffee before he went into the girls' room to make sure they were up and ready for church.

"But it's too early, Daddy."

"Too early for Jesus? I surely hope not. Shake a leg, you two. We're going somewhere new today, and I don't want to show up late."

They groaned about it, but wrestled themselves out of bed. Frank closed their door. Getting to be big girls, and he knew they needed their privacy, though privacy was about to be a rarity for any of them pretty soon.

"Don't take too long now, okay?" he said through the door before turning back down the hall to the master bedroom.

Gloria was still in bed. He slipped under the covers next to her and felt the good, warm pressure of her body against his. Fourteen years now they'd slept in the same bed. That was a long time to build yourself into another's unconscious physical habits. Impossible not to develop a kind of symbiotic regard for what the other person was feeling. The body expressed certain things that weren't said. Even as he held her, her limbs conveyed an unsettling he had felt in her since he'd decided to make a run for the commissioner's seat. Not surprising. It had to have been a kind of natural disaster in the middle of her life. She had grown up with alcoholic parents who'd only gotten dry once she left the house for college. Yelling and tears at all hours of the night. Petty theatrics, really. That was what her young life had been. So she'd built her adult world around what could be reliable. A hardworking husband. A counseling job at the university. There was a commitment to clarity in the way she lived. To wake up one day and find the careful hedge of protection she'd cultivated exposed on this scale, it must have terrified her, even if she revealed little on the surface.

Truthfully, even he could only partly understand why he was doing it. The reason he'd given Pettus, that it was a question of taking a moral stance, that wasn't untrue. But something more had chewed his skin. It had been a long time since he'd found himself in a serious struggle, and he missed it. The excitement of putting himself on the line was just as important to him as keeping a refuge was for Gloria.

He nudged her and she made a displeased sound.

"That's no way to start the morning," he told her.

"There better be a cup of coffee in your hand if you're talking to me right now."

He reached for the nightstand and held a mug above her nose. Her eyes opened with little friendliness. Still, she pushed herself up on her pillows and took the mug by the handle. He let her drink for a minute before broaching what he had decided in the middle of the night. That they would attend Reverend Winter's church, show the old hypocrite that he was willing to walk into the lion's den and sweet-talk those lions until they were curled up and purring.

"Sounds like a waste of time to me," she said. "Do more good to go to Mars."

"But Martians are outside the district. What good would that do?"

"Will you shut up and let me get dressed? Lord."

All the girls cleaned up good, he was pleased to see. Maybe not Easter good, but close enough. He liked going to church as a family. It felt like putting things in order. Everything was sorted and snapped into place. Sitting down and listening to scripture eased his nerves, and having the contentment of his family with him solidified whatever the preacher had to say that Sunday because he knew he was lucky enough to have the proof of blessings within his immediate grasp. It hadn't always been that way with him, and he knew it was dangerous to fail to appreciate such a fragile gift.

The church parking lot was already crowded by the time they arrived, but Frank found a place down near the back tree line where a small creek edged into the deeper woods. He went out to look at the water and watch some of the other recent arrivals while Gloria finished fussing with her makeup. By the time she got out he had counted a dozen families on their way toward the pews, and none of them a shade darker than cream of wheat.

"You sure this is a good idea?" Gloria asked, seeing the same thing he did.

"No, but we're beyond that now, I'm afraid. Come on, kids. Let's see what kind of Christians they grow out this way."

When they entered, several faces turned, some kindlier than others. He smiled at a couple sitting at the end of the pew and asked their pardon as they seated themselves halfway down the row. He scanned the program as he listened to the organ play "All Creatures of Our God." As it concluded, Reverend Winter took his place at the pulpit. He welcomed everyone and beamed a preacher's smile that looked like it had been practiced in front of a mirror since seminary. It was the kind of thing that was so obviously insincere that it amazed Frank anyone could see if for anything other than a hoax. Amazing what people could put up with if they thought that was what was expected of them.

He closed his eyes when Winter said it was time to pray, though his mind wasn't on prayer at that moment. Instead, he thought of what he would do if he should lose the election. It was one thing to rearrange his and his family's lives for the sake of civic service. But what would it mean if he risked an essential part of himself and then have it rejected, discounted? Surely that was a strong possibility. He knew it was naive, but he believed being a good man mattered, that it mattered to others as well, despite so much evidence to the contrary. But how would you feel if you staked yourself against someone like Gavin Noon and lost? The idea of it made him ill. As Reverend Winter said his amen, Frank swallowed back a taste of bile.

"Frank, you okay?" Gloria asked, squeezing his hand.

"Yeah, baby. I'm good."

Winter opened his heavy gilded Bible and began to preach. It was something about friendship and David and Jonathan, though Frank only periodically followed the line of reasoning. When Winter spoke, something else came out between the words. Something equal parts honey and horseshit. Like a poison flavored as a candy. He glanced around to see how his flock accepted his message. Their solemn and sleepy faces held little he could read.

Somehow the hour eventually spent itself and everyone stood to receive the benediction. But before Winter delivered his final words his eyes caught Frank's.

"I do hate that it's time to go," Winter said, "but I want to remind everyone that they are welcomed to attend the after-service coffee which is held, as always, in the basement fellowship room. We have such good talks down there. And you absolutely never can anticipate who might drop in for a visit."

Frank felt a nudge in his side.

"Why do I feel like that was for your benefit?" Gloria asked.

"Because you're a wise woman."

She made a sound of reluctant agreement.

The press of bodies slowed their way down the carpeted stairs, so that by the time they made it to the after-service gathering a line had already formed at the coffee urn. The girls had already had enough and were picking at the sleeves of their dresses, saying they were itching. Frank told them they could go on outside and play as long as they stayed out of the creek as well as the parking lot. They didn't give him a second to reconsider, vanishing in a ripple of bright taffeta.

"Mister Farmer, I thought that was you," Reverend Winter said, his smile theatrically bright. Neither offered to shake the other's hand.

"This is my wife, Gloria."

Gloria bent her head and pressed her lips for a civil greeting.

"Lovely, just lovely," Winter murmured. "I thought I saw your children as well?"

"They needed a little air," Gloria answered. "Too much adult conversation drove them to it."

Winter laughed, brought out his handkerchief to dab above his shirt collar.

"I can certainly sympathize with that, Mrs. Farmer. I'm sure Frank has already mentioned we had some of that kind of boring talk regarding his political ambitions here lately. I really do deplore that kind of thing. It's a terrible burden to put on a house of worship, this question of which ballot to stuff. I've never been a political man myself. I prefer to let the word of God speak for itself. Activist preachers are the pharisees of the world today, from what I can gather."

Frank filled two paper cups with coffee and handed one to Gloria.

"I'm not sure taking a moral stance is contrary to the gospel, Reverend," Frank said. "Fact is, many might see it as an obligation."

"You sound like you have very certain ideas about how biblical interpretation should be situated in public life. Such certainty can only be found in the minds of prideful men."

Frank didn't care to continue this line of talk. He hadn't come here to change Winter's position. Instead, there were people here who needed to see that he wasn't afraid to advance himself, that he could stand up to public scrutiny and not wither. And most importantly, he needed to do it with a smile.

"There's the man himself," a voice rang out.

Frank turned to see a broad-chested man with pale grey hair come toward him. At his side was an elegantly dressed woman with dark hair and a Mediterranean profile.

"Doctor Vasquez, good to see you," Frank said, took his hand warmly. The sight of a familiar face helped dispel the sense of contagion resulting from his recent interaction with the reverend. "Mrs. Vasquez, you look lovely as always."

"Hello, Frank," June Vasquez said. "We've been hearing a lot in the news about you lately. I asked Jamie if it was *that* Frank Farmer that the reporters were talking about, and he assured me that it was."

"Yes, we were thrilled to hear it," Jamie Vasquez excitedly continued. "I've told several people at the office that any man who is an absolute Michelangelo with a chainsaw would be uniquely qualified to set about pruning the thickets of political life."

Frank had maintained the Vasquez's three-acre lot with its many old hardwoods for the past several years. They had reason to keep him on regular notice. Their three-story Johnson City home was a cornerstone of the town's historic district and both lived in the fear that some windy evening one of the massive limbs would come crashing into one of their stylishly appointed rooms. The Vasquezes had no children, and perhaps as a consequence they set great store in their possessions.

Frank turned to see if the reverend wanted to speak a few words to the Vasquezes, but it seemed he had happily alit somewhere else.

"You know, Frank," Jamie Vasquez said. "I've got a patient who was in the office the other day. He works at the radio station here in town. He's a bit of a political aficionado. Anything from dog-catcher on up. Anyhow, I bet if I were to get in touch with him, he would be falling all over himself to get an interview with you before the election. Especially, given the controversy of your opponent."

"That would be wonderful, Doctor Vasquez."

"Jamie, please."

"Alright, Jamie."

Frank realized that the election was just like when he was back on the field. Some people might despise the fact of your notoriety. Others wanted to pretend you were as close as family. He smiled and listened to Jamie Vasquez talk, knew that there was already a line forming of others who wanted to do the same.

28

IT WAS SOON CLEAR THE DEBATE WOULD BE STANDING ROOM ONLY. News media from as far away as Nashville had turned up on the courthouse's front lawn. Several press vans were illegally parked along the adjacent streets. Sheriff Holston had ticketed them himself with no small degree of pleasure. The rumor of Gavin Noon's special guests had been leaked deliberately, and everyone was eager to frame a shot of the candidate standing next to uniformed members of the American Nazi Party.

They were not disappointed. Three men wearing black fatigues with red patches on the shoulders appeared half an hour before the event. Each of them stopped and spoke to the reporters with practiced elocution. They had come straight from the national headquarters in Arlington and were fully aware of the spotlight they occupied. When Kyle was asked for comment by one of the television reporters, he pretended that he hadn't heard and went in instead to find Frank.

He was already in the conference room seated on the first row, his wife and children beside him.

"You ready?"

"No," Frank said, smiled, though he appeared collected and focused. He turned his head to scan the crowd. "Looks like we're pretty popular. Guess we should thank our competitor for some of that."

Kyle turned to Frank's wife.

"How are you holding up?"

She said that they were fine, that everything was just fine, though Kyle could see the unease beneath her reserve. It was as though they all shared a single long nerve that was being stretched each minute. He had never really thought much about the strain an election put on a family. He had never had to.

Gerald and Orlynne filed into the row behind them, each patting Frank on the shoulder before they took their seats. The debate moderator, the morning news reporter for the local radio station, approached the microphone. Kyle quickly wished Frank his best and threaded back to where he could view everything from the rear of the room.

Gavin Noon entered with his bigots. They spaced themselves throughout the audience. Noon found his reserved place up front. Kyle could see that several of those in the vicinity were not uncomfortable to sit beside him.

Shortly, the Republican candidate Shepard Dixon had dug up came in. Wenton Keane was a potbellied man in a suit a size too large. He ran a heating and cooling repair shop just outside of Elizabethton. Kyle knew him only in passing, and what he knew didn't distinguish him much from a piece of human-shaped cardboard. He sat down on the front row and began rifling through some notes. Even from a distance his face appeared clammy.

The moderator asked for everyone's attention and the crowd's rowdy stirring eventually subsided. He then introduced himself and emphasized that no disruptive behavior would be tolerated.This debate was a means of hearing each of the candidates speak to the issues that concerned the community. A well-informed citizenry was the cornerstone of the structures that kept this country great, he claimed. Once he was satisfied that he'd chalked the necessary ethical lines, he turned and called each of the men to the lecterns. There was some cheering and booing before he could pose the first question. After the moderator shot a chilly glare at the general area, everybody quieted and he was able to begin.

They talked around the edges of things for quite some time. Opinions on zoning, county obligations on matters of infrastructure, the expansion of the volunteer fire department. The raw material of what the routine occupation of a county government official entailed. Kyle saw that a few of the attendees had begun to nod off, the heat and poor ventilation having its inevitable effect.

"With my next question, I'd like to turn to the issue that's been on the minds of many people," the moderator said. "That would be the fitness of character to hold public office."

Wakefulness jolted through the gallery.

He continued, "There has been discussion about who each candidate is and how they see themselves fitting into the community they intend to serve. Could each candidate please speak to their idea of how their belief systems and personal ethics qualify them to the best and most representative candidate for the voters of Carter County. Mister Noon, the question falls to you first."

Noon stood silently for a moment, head bowed and hands clasped to the wings of the lectern.

"Thank you for that question," he began. "It is agreeable when what's foremost on our minds is brought into the light. I will say that I am the superior representative of this community because it is a community I have chosen, a place I have sought out. This is a place that is often not understood by outsiders. These mountains are either a momentary stop for tourists looking at autumn leaves or some strange half-imagined place they call Appalachia, though they don't know what that means or how it has persisted through history. These kind of people think this place is backwards, an embarrassment. Then too, there are the well-intentioned liberals. Those who have descended on the hill country like a new breed of carpetbaggers, bringing their trust funds and patchouli. They would hold themselves up as saviors of this land. The absurdity of this is self-evident.

"But this is a proud country and it should not hide its face from the world. It needs men who know what they are and are willing to stand for principled beliefs. There is no greater strength of character than that. I have made no secret about the ethics I hold dear, and I have made my home here in Carter County because I believe it is one of the few places decent enough to acknowledge who they are and what their heritage is.

"These mountains harbored the pioneering spirit of European immigrants who sought a better life for their families. They didn't expect handouts. They didn't expect their lives to be without conflict. That's because they were made of better stuff. They drew strength from their heritage. I believe the descendants of those people are still here today. I think many of them are sitting in this very room tonight.

"I believe my character is true and respectful to the people of Carter County. I believe my honesty is necessary because others who have believed the same have felt belittled and hushed for far too long. But they aren't willing to be quiet any longer. And neither am I."

Voices in the crowd fluttered. The moderator told everybody to keep their opinions to themselves. After a time they did.

It was time for Wenton Keane to address the question. He did so in such a fumbling and shaky way that it was hard to say if he actually understood what was being asked of him. Still, when he concluded he smiled with what seemed to be great confidence. No one saw the point in challenging it.

"Mister Farmer," the moderator then said. "It is now your turn to address the question."

Frank nodded, glanced at his page of notes, then turned the sheet over and began to speak.

"I know there are a lot of you here tonight who don't know what to make of me, why I would want to get involved in something like this. I'll have to tell you the truth, none of you are asking anything I haven't heard from my wife."

Some laughter.

"But I will say that it's not something that I've agreed to lightly. I'm not a politician, have never had the desire to be one. My father once told me that more evil in this world was accomplished by men who wore suits than those who didn't. I imagine that his words had something to do with the vocation I chose. I've worked with my hands, gone out to see many of you sitting here, cut down limbs and tangle that threatened your property and homes. I like that kind of work. Being outside in the sun through summer and winter. It's not always comfortable, but it is something that feels real to me. And that matters. It matters too that I feel that work is for the good of the people who employ me, the people of the county.

"Now, you may have noticed I'm a black man."

Again, a ripple of laughter.

He smiled, said, "This has clearly become worth mentioning in this bid for county commissioner because of the man I'm running against. He has said this is a place that is defined by its past, by what it once was. He sees this as a strength. But I will tell you plainly. I think there are many things about the mountains that are not what I would have them. I've been called nigger by a white man to my face more times than I can count on one hand. I've had to hear that and hold myself to my own standards of behavior of not saying anything back in anger because I knew deep in my heart it made me a better man than him. And I can tell you now that that is the same reason I stand here as a candidate. Gavin Noon can claim this county belongs to the past and to all that means to him, but that's not the truth. Carter County belongs to the people who live and work here, who have been working here. At the end of the day, regardless of what the votes might say, I know I am a better man than Gavin Noon and it matters that I've taken a stand."

The debate turned next to the subject of what community initiatives each of the candidates would prioritize. Frank discussed the veterans group with its reforestation project while Noon pointed out his desire to have a formal program that policed pollution of the watershed. Wenton Keane stammered for a few minutes about the need for more game wardens checking for out-of-state fishing licenses on the Watauga. But Kyle realized that Frank had his feet under him now. He considered his responses, made the ideas stick together in a way that people could follow. He was on the right path. All Kyle needed to do was make sure he didn't get in Frank's way.

GAVIN HAD the men from Arlington drive out to Little Europe for a toast after the debate had concluded. He was euphoric, his chest light. He felt he had the world between his teeth.

Before leaving for the compound, they had explained that they regretted not being able to have more officers present to watch the debate in person, but the last thing they wanted was to disrupt the proceedings, make it all about the Nazi Party officers when Gavin was the one who deserved the crowd's focus. It was a chancy thing to insert themselves too egregiously. Gavin said that he completely understood.

The dining room had been cleared, a long table brought in. He had wanted candles to be set up but there hadn't been sufficient time. The dimmer switch wouldn't work either, which spoiled the effect he had wanted to create. But these were minor things. He wouldn't be upended by trivial disappointments. Too much had gone just as he had needed it to go.

The three officers entered—handsome and efficient in their pressed fatigues. Gavin welcomed them in, introduced them to those they hadn't yet had a chance to meet. They stood politely for a few minutes before taking their places at the table. Jonathan came around, inexpertly poured out a couple of bottles of champagne he'd been told to bring back from the Food City. It sizzled beneath their noses.

"I would like to toast our visitors," Gavin said, rose to his feet. "Commander Hopkins, and Captains Varner and Stone, it is a great honor that you have visited us here in Little Europe, and that you have shown the support of the American Nazi Party. We hope that the results of the upcoming election will justify the backing you have extended."

Hopkins bowed his head in acknowledgment, swallowed his champagne.

"Thank you, Mister Noon," he said, wincing briefly at the taste. "It has been our pleasure to assist in any way we can, even if it was just a short show of public support through the website and our press releases. It was the absolute least we could do for someone who is so driven. We were delighted when you reached out to us. Too many communities like those here at Little Europe prefer to conceal their identities from the general public. It is refreshing to see your own directness, particularly given your ambitions for political office."

His two captains nodded reflexively, as if trained to an established series of verbal cues.

"Yes, well, I do hope it is part of something larger," Gavin said.

"Something larger? I'm not sure I understand."

"The support. The support of the national office. What we're doing here, what's happening is part of a change throughout the country. Look at what happened in Charlottesville. This is a movement, a desire to claim a part of the country for ourselves. We have a real chance to seize political power in this country. The will is there. All we need is people with the ability to organize . . ."

Hopkins arrested Gavin's building speech with the slightest lift of his hand.

"I do appreciate your enthusiasm, Mister Noon. It has clearly served you well. But you must remember that what you're talking about is far more complicated than a few rallies and some properly placed television coverage.

"It's true that what happened in Charlottesville was important, but it was important because of the reaction it caused, not because it was a sustainable political overture."

"Now it may be me that doesn't understand."

Jonathan shook his head, drank off his tumbler of oversweet champagne.

"Hell, Gavin. He's saying he thinks we're all just little pissants down here in the cove, raising hell but not much else. Ain't that right?"

Hopkins pressed his mouth into an expression of tolerance but added nothing more.

"Jonathan," Gavin began, though his eyes did not leave his guests. "I believe there might be a few more bottles of something to drink in the trunk of the car. Something a little more spirited. Please bring some back for the officers."

If Jonathan had any sense of being dismissed, he did not show it.

As soon as his assistant had left, Gavin said, "Commander Hopkins, if you will elaborate. Now I am better able to hear what it is you are trying to tell me without distractions."

Hopkins shrugged.

"I don't want to dampen your enthusiasm, Mister Noon."

"Not possible. Please continue with what you were saying."

The Nazi administrator cleared his throat before reluctantly stating, "Our situation, despite certain admirable gains, is relatively unchanged on a national level. We are happy to show our faces here, happy that you want the association between your campaign and the party, because our greatest power on the national stage is in the imagination of those who detest us. We are the minority. That doesn't mean that we can't have an effect on the way the world is going. But we're in no position to make real strides. Charlottesville was a handful of young men with a coherent, unified ideology. But their involvement isn't sustainable. They still have to go to work on Monday morning. They are middle-class people. What they did was a kind of performance art."

"Performance art?"

"Maybe that's an unfortunate choice of words. Forgive me. As I said, I don't want to dampen your enthusiasm. Your commitment to the cause is commendable. We rely on exactly that sort of dedication to retain the focus of the national media."

Gavin's drink settled bitterly on his tongue.

He no longer tried to continue the conversation. He simply concentrated on behaving well, pretended that he was unmoved by what had been said. The liquor circled the room. Despite the steady seep of the alcohol, his nerves failed to unknot. He had to hold himself together for the next hour until Hopkins and his men were ready to leave. After they had been shown to the door and thanked one last time for their visit, he went up to his room, shut himself within. As his head sank against the pillow he was grateful that he no longer had to suffer their talk.

He had nearly gone over the edge of sleep when his phone buzzed on the nightstand. He swore quietly and swung his fleet onto the floor, saw one of the few names he could bear to look on just now.

"It's late, Mister Sealy."

"I apologize, Mister Noon. I wouldn't have bothered you this time of night unless it was something I'm sure you'd want to hear. Something that involves the history of your opponent, Frank Farmer."

"Go on."

Sealy began to talk and Gavin couldn't have imagined any words that might have sounded so dear.

29

FRANK HAPPILY ACCEPTED THE HELP OF THE VETERANS GROUP IN THE last few days leading up to the election. They stuffed mailboxes and knocked on doors from one side of the county to the other. He had felt a shift in the kinds of conversations he was having with people since the debate, and he knew he had to take advantage of his momentum while he could.

There was one stretch of the county he hadn't had a chance to show his face, up in the north end, just shy of the Carolina border. It was back in the deep end of some hollows with roads named after the families who had lived back there for a couple of centuries. Old-time mountaineers. Pettus suggested he take Turner Whist from the veterans group with him. Said he knew a lot of the folks out that way, could point him to the households willing to give Frank a fair shake.

As they turned back and followed the dirt road deeper in, the sunlight was soon cut off by the high ridgelines flanking them on either side. They passed a couple of trailers with satellite dishes stuck to the roofs. A big rottweiler barked from the front porch of one of them. Even with the windows rolled up, you could hear the rattle of its chain. A little further on they passed a brick building in a cleared lot next to a creek. Across the way was its barn with a brightly painted quilt square. A tin-covered lean-to abutted the barn; beneath it a full three cords of firewood were stacked as neat as needlework.

"I'm going to take you up here to my uncle Virgil's place," Turner told him. "He lives in a cabin that Daniel Boone was supposed to have stayed at back in the day."

"Daniel Boone, huh?"

"That's the story. It's pretty old anyhow. You'll see."

And he did. The cabin seemed as solid as an oceangoing ship, composed of planed timbers and hard chinking. It wasn't difficult to picture it having been here when the white frontiersmen pushed west with their whiskey and violent ambition. Living in a house like that had to have an effect on how you perceived the problems of the day-to-day. Time on a different scale. Walking the floorboards, it would be impossible not to listen for the ghosts of those who had come before.

Turned banged on the door. An old voiced roared within like a creature roused from hibernation.

"And this is one of the friendly ones?" Frank asked a moment before the door flung open. Out stepped a man a good six and a half feet tall with shoulders that nearly brushed the doorframe. He wore overalls only. Beneath it his massive naked chest labored with the effort of moving such bulk so quickly. His china blue eyes screwed up against the sudden flood of sunlight.

"Turner, by God, you're the only kin that could knock me out of a nap without taking a ballpeen hammer to the skull. How are you, son?"

The big man wrapped Turner in a smothering embrace, then stood him back up as tidily as he would a bowling pin.

As soon as Turner regained his breath, he said, "I'm good, Virgil. Didn't mean to disturb. Just was out this way with my friend Frank, and thought he's somebody you'd want to meet."

"That right? Well, good to meet you, Frank," Virgil said, extended his hand. "I've seen some of your signs up in town last time I was down there. Read your name in the paper too. Let me get a couple of chairs out here on the porch. Musty as hell inside."

He dragged out a couple of dining room chairs from the front of the cabin and set them next to his only rocker, which he took for himself and began to pack a pipe so that he could listen to them.

"You all smoke? I've got a couple of old corn cobs in there."

Frank said that he would take one if Virgil didn't mind. On the contrary, it appeared to please the bearish man immensely. Once they had settled into a congenial circle and the smoke was running, Virgil began to talk.

"I've followed your entry into the race with interest, Mister Farmer. You and that feller Noon have certainly put a spark into local politics that is a bit more exciting to what we're used to. As you might imagine, being this far into the back of beyond, we typically don't involve ourselves overmuch in what goes on down in Elizabethton. I've got a sister, she's over fifty years old, lives just over that ridge there. She hasn't been out of the county three times in her whole life. People like to think folks like us are a myth. But there's plenty of us that stick to our own. That doesn't mean we're bad or ignorant. It just means we value a different kind of life. I'm sure you can appreciate that."

Frank told him that he could indeed. There was a lot to be said for keeping to yourself when so much of the world seemed to be determined to prove it wasn't fit for any decent use. Virgil nodded, let the smoke spill from his mouth.

"But there's more to it than just that," Frank said. "I'm not sure it's something I realized until I agreed to get involved in this whole mess. The thing I worry about is what I would tell my children if I didn't stand up for what was right. That's about as personal as you can get. I've spent their whole lives telling them that they have a right to be who they are. It's no more complicated than that. They have the right to be who they are and to live how they decide is best for them. And if other people start to say that isn't the case, they have an obligation to fight for themselves. So, I guess you can say that doing this thing in public, in making myself a target for what men like Gavin Noon hate, I'm just trying to be consistent. I'm trying to be the example I want them to follow."

They talked for a good while longer, soon at ease with minor differences of opinion. But what surprised Frank most was how much agreement he could find with this man. He realized quickly that Virgil was an important man to convince. He listened well, but Frank had no doubt Virgil could speak in a way that could get the attention of people like him. He was a shrewd man, and no camouflage of attire or accent could conceal it.

After an hour of visiting, Turner noted that they needed to be pressing on. There wasn't much daylight left to burn, after all. Virgil walked them down to their truck.

"Mister Farmer, you seem like an honest man," Virgil told them. "I don't see a reason in the world that anybody with a reasonable head on his shoulders wouldn't be able to tell the same. I know that's what I'll be telling the folks that give me the time of day, at least. And I wish you the best of luck."

Frank said he was glad to have Virgil's good word and climbed up into the vehicle.

THEY STOPPED at a Dunkin' Donuts attached to a convenience store in Hampton to go over a list of the names they'd been able to contact. Nearly a dozen, with eight of those committing favorably to turning out for Frank on election day.

Turner went for a refill while Frank pulled the notepad around and checked the names once more. He had been pleased with the reception they received. Hospitable if taciturn at first. Though they were quick to share their mind once they had a chance to form an opinion of him.

"I'd call today a victory, wouldn't you?" Turner said.

"A step in the right direction anyhow. I'm grateful for you taking me back up there. I would never have been able to find some of those places if I wouldn't have had you as a guide. You think they'll actually turn out to vote?"

Turned tugged the brim of his ballcap, watched something out the window.

"Virgil will. He's a tough old bird, but if he likes you, he'll go to the ends of the earth for you. Some of the others will. Some won't. I'll tell you the truth. There's a damn good chance you were the first black man who ever stepped in any of those houses."

"I imagine you're right. What about you?"

"What about me?"

"You ever had a black man in your place?"

Turner shifted in his seat, wouldn't meet Frank's gaze.

"I don't know what to tell you," Turner finally said. "The world around here just isn't that way, is it? Maybe someday, but not now."

Frank agreed with him and said he thought it was time to go to his own home, get a night's rest before putting in another full day tomorrow. Turner said to go ahead and crank the truck while he went next door for a pack of cigarettes.

Half an hour later Frank stepped across the threshold to a quiet household. The kitchen light was the only one burning. The clock above the stove said that it was a quarter to midnight. On the counter was a note from Gloria saying that his supper was wrapped up in the fridge, but he wasn't hungry and didn't bother to check what it might be. Instead, he slipped his shoes off on the linoleum and stood them next to the back door, eased back down the hall with as little noise as he could.

She had fallen asleep reading with the lamp on. He carefully picked up her book and folded it with a grocery store receipt between the pages to keep her place then switched the light out. She startled at the sudden sound.

"Hey, it's okay. It's just me," he told her.

He put his hand over her bare shoulder. She lay there breathing for a while before saying anything.

"I was having bad dreams," she said. "I dreamed you were gone."

"I'm here, baby."

"Right now you are."

He kissed her and slipped beside her. When he put his arms around her he felt like he had hold of something bigger than he could ever manage to keep.

When he woke the next morning he found the bed empty. He turned his head and saw on the clock radio that it was nearly nine o'clock. Hadn't slept that late for as long as he could remember. Felt more exhausted for having slipped so far under. He sat there for a minute to get himself together. He glanced at his phone and saw he already had three missed calls from Pettus. He'd deal with that as soon as he had a cup of coffee in him.

Gloria was sitting at the counter with her tea, looking through the newspaper. She was already dressed for work. Of course she was. The world didn't stop turning just because he was laid up in the bed.

"I know I was supposed to take the girls to school," he said.

"You needed the sleep. Coffee's fresh in the pot. Pour yourself a cup, Frank. I need to talk to you about something."

He circled warily toward the carafe and poured out a cup.

"I am standing here thinking," he said.

"You are?"

"Yeah. I'm thinking the number of times you called me by my first name since we were married and it being for a good reason are enough to count on one hand."

She told him to sit down, that he wasn't wrong. But instead of talking, she pushed the paper across to him. It didn't take him long to see what she meant. It was all right there on the front page. He leaned back, studied the pattern of reflected overhead light in his coffee.

"Well, I should have expected it, I guess," he told her.

"What are you going to do, baby? This is the last thing in the world the kids need to see right now."

"I'll take care of it."

"There's no taking care of this, Frank."

He started back to the bedroom to get dressed.

"Of course there is, Gloria. I've got to call some people now. Don't worry about this. I know what to do."

She said nothing, though a moment later he could hear her leave by the front door.

An hour later he was seated in the broadcast radio office in Elizabethton. He had called in that favor Jamie Vasquez had offered. Kyle Pettus was there with them, though they hadn't said much to one another after they'd gone over the news and what it meant for the election. It was on Frank's shoulders now. He was the only one who could turn the narrative back to where it needed to go.

Ted Fallon, the morning show man, popped his head into the lobby and waved them back to the recording booth. A prerecorded segment on a charity softball event was running, which gave Fallon a chance to explain how the microphones picked up sound and how much time to take with each question.

"I appreciate you making time for us on short notice, Ted," Pettus said.

"Not at all. I'm proud to do it. I imagine we'll get about twice as many people listening as normal. You ready, Mister Farmer?"

"Let's go ahead and run it," Frank told him.

Fallon counted him in and introduced the segment. Frank said he was pleased to be invited and was eager to talk directly to the people of Carter County, that he believed it was important that they hear the actual voices of the people who meant to represent them.

"Mister Farmer, I want to make the best use of our time this morning," Fallon said, "and that's going to mean delving into something uncomfortable right here at the outset. I'd like for you to give our listeners a response to the newspaper story that ran this morning. According to the *Carter Citizen* it says your father, Demetrius Farmer of Dekalb, Georgia, was convicted in 1994 of a double homicide in a drug-related exchange in Atlanta, and that he has been serving consecutive life sentences at a state penitentiary since that time. Firstly, is this report true, and secondly, how would you like to respond to this piece of news and how it affects your run for office?"

Frank leaned toward the microphone, kept his voice even.

"These general facts are accurate. My father was involved in a very dangerous and destructive life. Even as a boy, I could see what kinds of things he was caught up in. So did my mother. It was why she and I left when I was eight years old and she and her sister raised me in Murfreesboro, Tennessee, which is where I began playing football once I started middle school. I have visited him across the years and seen what a life in prison does to a man. It's not pretty.

"I want everyone who's listening to understand something. I love my father. The last thing in the world I would ever do is pretend that he isn't part of me. That's exactly what the people who leaked this information want me to do. They want me to try to shrug this off so that it looks like I would do anything to protect myself. Well, that's impossible. This isn't the kind of thing you can set aside. It's forever part of who you are. It's made me be the kind of husband and father I am. It's made me the kind of man who won't back down when a political opponent tries to smear me.

"But here's why it's important to those of you who are hearing my voice. This was reported because my opponent wants you to fear me. He doesn't want you to see me as a man willing to serve this county. He wants you to see a criminal, a threat. He wants you to define yourself by fear and suspicion. I want you to vote for me because we have a chance to say that Carter County is better than its worst parts. We have a chance to deliver a new future. But I need your help to do it."

After the interview, Fallon walked them back out front, shook Frank's hand and wished him the best. They said the same in return and went back out to Frank's truck and sat there a minute.

"You think it'll make a difference?" Frank asked.

"Hell, Frank. Just you saying something makes all the difference. I believe you're a smart enough man to see that."

They then drove out to beat on doors to see if he was right.

30

HARRISON LEFT TOWN THE MORNING BEFORE THE ELECTION. HE HAD to take the opportunity while he had it. Once the votes started coming in he knew that Noon would expect everyone to be gathered around him and there would be no chance to slip away.

He had packaged some of his money and put it in with a gym bag he would later fill with weed. There had been the temptation to move ahead with everything now, to go ahead and steal the rest of what he needed from Gavin's stash, but it would be foolish to move forward before everything had been set to rights.

Delilah didn't ask why he was going. She had stopped asking him a lot of things in the past week. A part of him wanted to take her aside and talk to her, to make her see what he was doing had to be done, but there was something in her that had begun to trouble him, something that seemed to back her up and leave her cornered. He could no longer trust her to side with him. Delilah would always make sure to look after herself, and if that meant shifting her allegiance he had no doubt she would. So he had not lingered when he told her he would be back the next morning in time to help with whatever errands Gavin might require on election day. And she had made no claim on his attention. As he left she'd said she liked having the bed to herself anyhow.

When he got into Knoxville Emmanuel's car was gone, so he sat out on the front porch until he got back. Already, it was hot and even in the mid-morning shade he was beginning to sweat. He pulled out his phone and checked the forecast. A line of strong thunderstorms were supposed to roll in from the west over the next couple of days, bring some of the first rain they'd seen in nearly five weeks. That would probably concern Gavin. He would need strong turnout, which probably meant he'd had them all getting out and driving as many people to the polls as they could. Still, Harrison would believe it when the weather actually materialized. Hard to believe there was anything still green in the ground. Weather like this was enough to make a man doubt the wisdom of living where he did. Take away everything, and so much of a life was still subject to the sun and how it beat down on your body.

Emmanuel was pleased to see him. He had counted on that. They had talked about him coming up for another supply of weed, but that wasn't supposed to be until the weekend.

"I do always appreciate your surprises, Jay. You're quite accomplished at them. Come inside so I can appreciate it more thoroughly."

Harrison helped him with his bags. He had just come from the art supply store and was carrying some canvases and some new paint. They placed them on the counter of the breakfast bar before Emmanuel went into the kitchen and poured them each a glass of freshly squeezed lemonade. It was good to be there like this with him in the cool of the shaded house with something cold to drink in his hand.

He lifted his glass toward the bags of art supplies.

"You about to commence a new masterpiece?"

Emmanuel smiled, tipped his head forward.

"Well, I did have a project in mind. A bit of a departure for me, though. I was considering a self-portrait."

"Really?"

"Yes, really. I wanted to get an early start on it."

"Don't let me get in the way. As long as you don't mind me visiting."

"You know I don't mind that. Sit over there, though. You're blocking my light," he said, smiling as he motioned toward the open curtain.

Harrison moved along as directed, watched as Emmanuel prepared his impromptu studio. The light was coming in from the front window and it warmed everything in its subtle blush. Emmanuel stretched the canvas then placed it on the easel, readied his paints. The problem was the mirror. It was sturdy on its stand but the surface area was small and he had to be exact in its angle of adjustment to make sure he would see enough of himself to begin.

From where he sat, Harrison had only an oblique glance at the canvas, but even so he was surprised at how quickly Emmanuel worked. The color came from his brush as though it took its source from some hidden reserve. All poise, loop, and tempered fire. There seemed to be no connection at all between what was being accomplished on the canvas and with the face of the artist. How strange that was. But perhaps it wasn't. He didn't know what it was to want to create something like that, though he admired Emmanuel for wanting to do so. It seemed important and ambitious in a way that felt beyond him. He respected this difference, suspected it might have been what kept him interested in Emmanuel across all these years. It had been so hard to admit these things to themselves when they were friends in high school. So much had been held back, but seeing him now as he worked, Harrison knew that he needed to know as much about him as he could. He was starving for these details that belonged to the man he loved.

Emmanuel made a face, painted a large black X across the surface of the mirror. Harrison couldn't check his laughter.

"What, that bad?"

"It's not working," Emmanuel said, cleaned his brush. "It's not the same when you're sitting there."

"You've been able to paint while I've watched before."

"That's because I was painting something else. Here I am trying to paint myself and it doesn't work. I'm different when you're here."

"Is that a bad thing?"

"No, it's not bad. It makes things more complicated, though. More difficult to grasp. That's okay. It's a start. That's all that's important right now."

Emmanuel put everything away and sat next to him. They remained like that for a while, merely impressed against one another until the awareness grew into something more impulsive. Harrison leaned in to kiss him. Emmanuel's skin tasted clean and dry and warm. When Harrison was kissed in turn his insides hollowed until it felt like he could gather all of their lives together inside the frail and abandoned house of his body.

They found their way to the bed in a delirium. It was a slow and pleasant diffusion, each touch somehow discovering what was familiar but new. Harrison gripped Emmanuel by the bicep and pressed him to the mattress. They were both already hard. Harrison smelled everything he could as he flattened his hands along Emmanuel's side to keep him pinned in place as he slid down lower and put Emmanuel's cock in his mouth. As he moved his head over him he could feel Emmanuel's fingers rub his scalp. The pressure and warmth against his head was its own kind of benediction.

THEY SLEPT and fucked and talked about how they could make a life together through the course of the day. They didn't leave the bed. Neither bothered with their phones to see what time it was. They had the shifting angles of sunlight for that. Eventually, though, they became hungry and decided on the spur of nostalgia to order from the Chinese dive they had frequented at teenagers.

"You know, I just realized something," Harrison said as he finished punching their order on the website.

"And what's that?"

"I guess I've never thought of it this way, but we were kind of high school sweethearts, weren't we?"

Emmanuel laughed a full-throated laugh. He slipped from the bed and dressed in his kimono.

"Are you just now coming around to this piece of wisdom, dear one?"

"You're making fun of me."

"Only a little. Do me a favor, will you? While we've got a little bit of time to wait for the food I'm going to try to get some painting done. Stay in here though so you don't ruin my concentration."

"You want me to stare at the walls?"

"Anything but staring at me. Take a nap. You've been putting in a full day's work after all."

"We've been sleeping all day," Harrison said and winced as Emmanuel went out to the living room, but even as he spoke he could feel the pleasant burden of a nap closing down on the top of his head.

When he woke he was aware that more time had passed than he intended. The light had softened to the late afternoon. He sat up to rid himself of the grogginess, remained sitting there stupidly for a minute listening to Emmanuel work in the next room. Once his head cleared he dressed and went out to chide Emmanuel for letting him oversleep.

"Oh, it hasn't been that long. I'm working well anyhow. Why don't you run up there and bring the food back. I'd like to squeeze out another few good minutes if I could."

"All right. I just hope it isn't cold."

"We've got an oven in there, don't we? Now go on, shuffle."

Harrison went out and climbed into the Taurus. He'd forgotten to let down the working window and the car had sat closed up in the sun throughout the day. The seat was hot enough to sting his ass through his jeans. As soon as they got clear of town they would unload the damn thing. They could use Emmanuel's vehicle for a while but they'd need to discard that relatively soon as well. There could be nothing left that tied them back to their old lives. There was too much to risk. Gavin might not be terribly intimidating to look at, but Harrison had no doubt he would have a long memory for those who stole from him. The best way to catch a bullet in the brain was by underestimating the commitment of those you'd crossed. Even when they were gone he'd keep a close eye on what might be coming after them. He owed that to Emmanuel. Maybe he owed that to himself too.

The Wok'N'Roll was empty save for the preteen girl behind the counter. She glanced up from her phone and asked for the name of the order and went back to the kitchen to grab it. Harrison heard her speaking to a man in some language he didn't recognize, relatively certain it wasn't Chinese. Their voices were quick and, it seemed, contradictory, as if words were things capable of immediate physical violence. When she came back her hands were empty.

"He said he forgot to put the order in even though I put it in the computer. If you can wait a few minutes he'll have it ready for you."

"Yeah, okay."

She turned and fired a salvo of clipped syllables at the kitchen. A muttering in return. Then in a few moments the pan began to sputter as contents were tossed in. The girl went back to her phone.

Harrison pulled a chair from one of the front tables and watched Magnolia Avenue through the glass front. It weighed on him if he sat here and thought about what this place meant. It was maybe a little better now than it had once been when he was a teenager and he and Emmanuel would walk here just to have a reason to escape the scrutiny of their separate home lives. A little better but not much. All day they would sit in school, both of them bussed all the way out to Carter High School a good fifteen minutes from where they lived in the east edge of the city. All hicks and hayrakes out that way, Emmanuel used to joke, but there was much truth to it. There were only a few black kids that got districted out that way, which would have made it hard enough for Emmanuel to get along, but once he opened his mouth everyone knew that was only the beginning of what made him different. Harrison had befriended him quickly, tried to protect him from the worst of what the other kids were capable of. He had the advantage of his complexion, at least.

Magnolia, though, that was where they really went to school, where they really began to learn about what life meant to do to you if you weren't careful. They saw the whores, the drugs. The way poverty could get down inside someone like an infection. The way it never let loose.

"Hey, your order is ready."

He passed cash across the counter, took the receipt. The warm bag in his hands felt good. He concentrated on that as he stepped back out into the world.

When he pulled back up to the house he sensed something was wrong. Enough time had passed that the sun had set and everything was slowed by that mood of early evening half-light. At first he wasn't sure what it was—a pressure change in the air, maybe, or some other slight maladjustment. Then he saw that the door had been left ajar, and despite the incoming darkness, none of the interior house lights burned.

He took his handgun from the glove box and carried it loose along his leg until he cleared the threshold. The living room was silent, the only shapes the slumped lines of old and empty furniture. He called Emmanuel's name but there was no answer. With the pistol raised, he moved down the hall to the kitchen, scanned the area and called back to the bedroom. There was a soft and strained moan. Harrison went toward the sound, his hands beginning to shake. The bedroom door had been left open and he saw Emmanuel splayed out on the floor, his head twisted toward him with eyes that rolled with pain. His mouth had shaped to say something but when he tried to speak there were no words, only a spillway of dark blood. Harrison reached for him, but in that moment his eyes were shuttered from behind by a bag snatched over his head and drawn tight. A moment later something smashed into the back of his skull, freeing him of every possible concern.

31

KYLE TOOK LAURA, GERALD, AND ORLYNNE TO BREAKFAST IN TOWN before they were to go on and cast their votes at the elementary school. They chatted while Gerald looked over the map Kyle had drawn up the night before that showed the pickup points for those who might need a ride to get into town and vote. He penciled in a few additions himself, relying on his memory of those old-timers who had been reliable Democrats going back for decades.

"Are you even sure these people are still above ground?" Kyle asked.

"Of course I'm not sure. But God knows they'll check the right box if they are."

Kyle lifted the paper, eyed it skeptically before he set it aside when his sausage and eggs came.

"Have you talked to Frank this morning?" Orylnne asked Kyle. "I was worried he might have a case of the nerves."

"Yeah, I gave him a buzz and asked him if he needed anything. He said he was going with his wife to vote and then head back to the house. I told them we'd stop over there a little before supper and wait things out with them."

She nodded, lifted her hand to get the waitress to bring another round of coffee.

"Hey, I've been thinking something," Gerald said.

"I thought I saw the lights dim," Orlynne put in and slyly winked.

Gerald's lips rounded into an amazed O.

"You all see the way this woman talks to me?"

"Aww, hush. It's good for you. Go ahead, Old Man."

"Old Man? Lord, the insults never cease. Anyhow, before I was unwittingly attacked I was about to propose something, though now I'm beginning to have my doubts . . ."

Orlynne petted his hand like something tied up that needed to be soothed into compliance. "No, go on ahead. You know it's just my way of fussing after you."

He eyed her for a theatrical few seconds before pressing on.

"Well, I was thinking we ought to split our attention. Kyle, you and Laura can stick to the north end of the county while Orlynne and me tackle everything south of town. That's mainly your old district out that way anyhow. I know we said that we'd have better luck if we turned up on the doorsteps all together, but I just don't know. That storm that's supposed to come in might make more folks hesitant to drive out than we first thought. It's a lot of damn ground to cover."

Kyle turned his head, looped an arm around Laura.

"What do you think, girl? You think you're safe with me all by yourself?"

"I imagine I can handle it. Let's get on and finish eating though so we can get our votes cast and on to work."

"There's a woman with common sense," Orlynne said, scooped her eggs. "Maybe you all might think of running her next."

KYLE AND Laura drove back along Gabriel's Cove to where several modular homes had been put up in the last decade. They ignored the houses decorated with swing sets, or those that had bicycles leaned up against the newly built decks. Young families would have been able to get to their voting stations without assistance. On further back, though, the gravel road thinned out until it was only sunbaked earth, and as they rode a cloud of dust rolled out behind them. Each few hundred yards was a step further back in time. From prefab to brick ranches to bungalows to cabins. As if the closer to the head of the cove you got, the closer you came to some ancestral habitation that had more in common with legend than fact.

Their first stop where someone was home was at a clapboard house painted yellow but going to a soft green hue of grime beneath the shade of a black walnut. There was an old Cutlass parked out front but one tire was flat and it appeared not to have moved for the better part of several weeks. Kyle had almost passed the place by, given it up as deserted, but Laura had urged him to knock on the door. When he heard the sounds of someone moving inside he mimed an expression of shock before they got there and started turning a series of deadbolts.

The door came open and softly rebounded against the stop. An old woman in a pale purple sweat suit stood watching him.

"What you selling?"

Kyle said, "Not a thing in the world, ma'am."

"Bullshit. Last week a man came out here asking if he could clean my carpet. I said, hell, why not? Then when he was finished he pulled out a clipboard and started writing me a bill. I said, what the hell are you doing and he says to me, I'm making out a receipt. And I says a receipt for you being a good Christian, and he didn't know what to make of that at all."

Kyle waited, expected her to continue, though she seemed to have lost her interest or concern with the subject.

"Well, ma'am, we're not selling anything. We were just driving through here looking for people who might need a ride so that they can vote in today's special election."

"The special election, you say?"

"Yes, ma'am."

"What's so special about the special election?"

"Well, ma'am. I used to serve on the county commission, but I had to give the post up, so they're looking to elect someone who can take over and do what's best for the county."

"Oh, I heard about that! You're that one that's diddling the married librarian."

She cracked a mischievous grin, leaned in closer.

"Is that her out there?"

"Yes, ma'am. That's my sweetheart, Laura."

Her laughter was nothing short of a cackle.

"Let me get my tennis shoes on. I can't pass up the chance to ride into town with such as you two horny toads."

In half an hour they'd collected another two residents willing to accept a ride to vote. An elderly widower named Castleberry and his middle-aged son. As soon as they were in the back of the truck cab, the sweat suit lady let them know the infamous company they were keeping.

"This is as good as my soaps," she said between titters. "I swear it is."

Neither of the Castleberrys had anything to contribute along those lines.

There were a few of Gavin Noon's men standing just outside the polls wearing HERITAGE NOT HATE T-shirts. They were handing out printed brochures but they didn't approach when they saw Kyle walking the taxied voters in. Once all three of the cove people had been escorted in, he went back to the truck to wait for them with Laura.

"Any trouble?" she asked.

He shook his head, rolled his window all the way down to catch as much of a breeze as they could.

"Just some Nazi goons standing out there pretending to be concerned citizens."

"I've been wanting to tell you something for a little while."

"Tell it then."

"I just want you to know how I much I admire you for doing this, for sticking to what's right when it would have been easy to let Frank and Gerald do everything."

He took her hand, held it for a long time without feeling the need to say anything.

She smiled, lifted his hand to her mouth and held it there for a while.

"You know," she said after a while. "I think sometimes I love you more than you do me."

He tried to tell her that she had no right to say something like that but she told him to be quiet, to hear her out.

"You don't understand," she said. "It's okay. I like that I love you more. It gives me something that I've never had before. I've lived my whole life in a small town, married to the man I was supposed to marry. I never stepped out of line, never strayed from what was supposed to be the path to a good American life. But I spent years hating myself because I never felt that it amounted to anything. I felt suffocated by it. Each day I'd work and then drive home and fix supper and it was all like I was looking down at this living woman doll carrying out a set of instructions without any idea of what it was supposed to mean. There were times I felt there was some invisible part of me that was attached to a rail and it carried me back and forth every day and there was never any way I could swerve."

He brought her next to him and they sat there until the others came back from the polls.

"Well, look at the lovebirds," the old woman cracked. She had a sticker that said I VOTED, HAVE YOU stuck to her chest. "Absolutely shameless! Come on and get us back to the house. Some of us have more to do than sit around in the shade making eyes at each other all day."

Kyle and Laura made several subsequent runs with a dozen more voters through the course of the day. By four o'clock they finished their last run and drove out to meet Gerald and Orlynne at Frank Farmer's place. Gloria and the kids were out front tying red, white, and blue balloons to the mailbox and the front gate. The children waved as they pulled in. Both of them were dressed in peony pink dresses with blooming sleeves.

"Frank's out back," Gloria told them. "He's getting the grill going."

They pulled all the way into the carport to leave room for the later arrivals and went around the side of the house.

Frank had just laid the charcoal and squirted enough lighter fluid onto it that Kyle was about offer a word of warning when Frank struck a match, lit the entire book aflame and pitched it in. The grill moaned, spat, and thumped with a momentary gust of yellow flame. He grinned above it all.

"Just in time! You all want a beer?"

He didn't wait to hear their answers, tugging a couple of Dos Equis longnecks from the pail of ice at his feet. He snapped the caps with an opener he had dangling from his key chain. Kyle took his beer and studied the sky.

"You not worried about the forecast?"

"Naw, that storm's not supposed to get in until midnight. We'll have plenty of time to enjoy the evening before then. How did you all make out today?"

"Good, good. We got a decent number of folks in. Have you heard from Gerald and Orlynne?"

"They called about five minutes ago. I asked them to pick up some bottles of sodas and paper cups in case we get more folks turning up than we're expecting."

Kyle was pleased to see that Frank was in a good mood. He knew first-hand how hard it was to preserve that appearance with your stomach turning somersaults while you waited for the call from the election board. Or maybe Frank was just better suited to it. Kyle had come to believe that it was important to understand when stepping aside was the better action, especially when a man who had the will to do the right thing was ready to assume leadership.

Several of Frank's supporters began to show up in the next half hour. Many of them from Frank and Gloria's church, though despite that affiliation they seemed to have little problem in accepting the campaign-funded beer. By the time Orlynne and Gerald arrived it was a generally mixed gathering of old and young, black and white. Frank had brought a sound system out and set it up on a picnic table underneath a dogwood tree. It was playing Stevie Wonder's "Superstition," which Kyle hoped wasn't a reflection of any kind.

"I didn't know this many black folks lived in the county," Gerald declared in a voice that drew a sock in the arm from Orlynne. "What? I didn't. It's great, though. Maybe this isn't the fool's errand I thought it was."

Before Kyle could offer comment, Frank came up and shook both Gerald's and Orlynne's hands, thanked them for the work they'd done.

"We were glad to do it, Frank," Orlynne said. "Did the election board tell you when to expect the call?"

"Sometime between eight and eight-thirty, they said. Plenty of time for everybody to fill their bellies. We've got hamburgers and hot dogs. We've even got a rack of ribs going."

"Ribs, you say?" Gerald asked, his interest piqued as he drifted away from the conversation and toward the billowing meat smoke. Frank went along, guided the old man by the shoulder.

"He has terrible manners," Orlynne observed. "I wonder why it is I find it so damn charming. If you two will excuse me, I'll make sure he doesn't go do some public damage with all that particular charm of his."

Kyle told her to go on.

"It seems like they're really well matched, doesn't it?" Laura said.

"Yeah, it does. I'm glad to see it."

"You know, I've got an idea."

"I like to hear your ideas."

"Well, I couldn't help but noticing that beer pail is running a touch low. And given this is an evening destined for victory, it might be a good idea if we made a run so that the stock wasn't exhausted when we'd find ourselves most in need."

"See, that's one reason I love you. You're a provident woman."

"You love me, huh?"

"Yeah, I do. Why don't we ride out there and get those beers. Maybe get a few minutes to do a little something else too."

She smiled, took his hand.

"Hand me the goddamn keys, then," she said.

32

GAVIN HAD ENTERTAINED A FEW VISITORS IN THE FRONT SITTING ROOM, had glasses of champagne brought on a tray Conner Polk carried, though it seemed the reserves were depleted more quickly than possible. He would have preferred having Jonathan there, but he needed him out in the community, getting out as many people as he could. Polk was already drunk, nearly spilled the bottle each time he poured. No doubt, the fool was drinking it off each time he disappeared into the kitchen. The newspaper reporter Sealy was his only reliable and consistently stimulating company for the evening. The day had started well. Victory felt like something that lived there in the house, but as the hours had slipped by he had noticed how deserted his surroundings had become. There was such busyness with the details of the election that, at first, he didn't notice it, but after he had cast his vote and he had returned to the compound he had become aware that those he had come to rely on weren't there to support him. Most upsetting of all was Harrison. When he had first joined him at Little Europe he didn't have a high opinion of the man. But over time, Harrison had become essential. Much more than a bodyguard or a drug dealer. He was intelligent in an uncommon way.

He drew himself away from his distraction, suggested Sealy go for a walk with him now that the sun was going down and the weather had cooled. The young man was willing, began to gather his notebook and recorder.

"No, leave that," Gavin said. "This is a walk, not an interview. I'll give you the interview after we know the results."

Sealy nodded, placed his things back on the sideboard.

The sky was odd and it breathed a tremor over the treetops. Gavin had never understood the source of omens in the weather. He remembered his father reciting the old mariners' dictum that a red sky at morning guaranteed a violent storm, but even as a boy he had questioned this. He had once had to shelter in a bathtub during a tornado when he was a small child and they lived in a trailer park not far from the Ohio River. His father was on the road driving his semi when it happened and it was only Gavin and his mother at home when the warning buzzed across the Emergency Broadcast System. What had happened then terrified him in a way that even now he couldn't fully explain. It was as though the entire surface of the earth revealed itself as an illusion and the terrible roaring thing that was beneath loosed itself with all of its indifference to those who lived. He wept hysterically. His mother had thanked God that they had been spared, but he knew in his heart that there was nothing left of Him to thank. What he did remember, though, was how clear the sky had been that morning, how it held nothing but a promise of calm weather.

"It looks like you've cleared a lot more land since the last time I was out here," Sealy observed, indicating the swath of hacked and burnt thorn bordering the river.

"Yes, everyone has been very industrious. They want to get it ready for winter greens. I hope we might begin turning a steady rate of business at the farmers market this time next year."

"I didn't know that's what you had in mind."

"Of course," Gavin said, pointed toward a path that would lead them closer to the river bank. "It's only ethical to be a farmer, if you intend to participate in a country as an upright citizen. Are you familiar with *The Georgics?*"

"Not since college. I remember old Virgil going on about how to read natural signs."

"Yes, he does. I have to confess I was never much interested in that. It always seemed to me that forecasts are so often better understood as postscripts. The context applied to the content as a matter of afterthought. However, I was always moved by how he understood the inherent hostility between nature and man and how in coming to terms with that hostility, by actually learning to seize it, we discovered a truer sense of ourselves."

"You would consider yourself an idealist then, or a realist?"

"I would consider myself a man who operates within a certain set of limits. Sometimes I've found that I'm the beekeeper, but sometimes I've found it more instructive to become the bee, even if for only a finite period of time."

Sealy walked along beside him until they could see the faint rush of rapids through a break in the trees. The humid air rose to meet them. Gavin could feel it move over him like a new skin.

"What do you think you've learned from that? From those times you were the bee?"

Gavin placed his hand on the reporter's shoulder.

"I've learned that the beekeeper is kept as much as the bee."

POLK WAS stumbling drunk by the time Gavin went up to his room for the night, but still he continued to drink. He poured the last of the champagne into a plastic Coca-Cola cup and emptied half a pint of Old Crow whiskey in, sipped it as he went out to the porch. After the board of elections had called there had been little left to say to anyone. He could have told Gavin how it would have turned out, but he knew the bastard was too proud to see it. He considered how satisfying it would be to stand there at his door and tell him that all the big words and ideas he'd held onto with the faith of a backwoods preacher were as worthless as anyone else's dreams were, but even drunk he was unable to do so. Polk hated himself for his weakness, but weakness had kept him alive this long. Cowards had their own kind of wisdom too.

He wondered how long the others would stick around before they scented blood. They'd already begun to drift away, as if they prematurely sensed the long slide into nowhere. The trick was to time your escape perfectly, not get pulled along with the collapsing gravity of it all. He would need money. He knew Gavin kept some in his room locked away, though he had no idea how much. It had to be significant, though. Harrison wasn't worth much, as far as he could see, but he didn't lack the ability to keep his clients happy. There was almost something to admire about that. Plus, there was Delilah. If he was about to split, there was that to take into consideration. He'd seen her running around with that silly ass Jonathan, but it didn't take much to see that that was all a game, her having fun at that fool's expense. She needed a real man, someone who measured his angles and understood how to be smart about not getting caught by circumstances, not some drug dealer with muscles and a buzzed haircut. There was no doubt that she flirted with him a time or two. Maybe that was just her way, but dammit it got to him, not knowing what she meant to do and leaving him here out in the middle of the damn woods trying to sort it all out. He emptied the cup in a long swallow and filled it again with the remaining half pint of Old Crow.

The night was making him anxious and his body needed to move; he needed to make himself kinetic in order to avoid going out of his head. He got the machete from the outbuilding and went out to where he'd been clearing thorn. He took a few swipes, heard the brush softly rattle by his hand. Even though it was much cooler at this hour and the work wasn't enough to draw sweat, the alcohol in his bloodstream made it hard to manage. He stabbed the point in the ground and stood there looking at a sky that held no stars nor moon. There was a pulse of lightning high above but no thunder.

He pulled out the machete and began to beat his way through the thorn. It quivered and split and snapped back against him until the barbs razored his skin. His blood ran. For a while that relief was enough to sustain him, but in the field of night he soon became aware of the enormity of his task and he slung the blade deep into the thicket. There was only one way to make headway against it all.

He found the can of gas in the back of the shed. It was already mixed so that it could be used for the chainsaw, but that didn't matter. It would still burn. He carried it out and dumped the contents among the thorn. The reek of the fumes was nearly enough to make him vomit, but he covered his mouth with his free hand as he struck the lighter. He edged closer, extended his hand to the end of the fuel trail. It took, ran, and writhed like a serpent composed of light. Then the flame found its voice and made a soft boom amid the undergrowth. The branches snapped and cracked. He watched it and felt like a god standing there.

Above him, though, the sky began to move.

33

HARRISON WOKE TO A DARKNESS SO COMPLETE HE BELIEVED HE must still be masked. But as he breathed, he realized that there was nothing over his face. The recognition gave little comfort. His back was against an iron stanchion and his hands were bound behind it. When he tried to move them he could hear the soft rattle of chains.

"Jay?" a voice called from a few feet away. It was Emmanuel's, though it was strained and weak.

"Yeah, it's me."

"How bad you hurt?"

"Just my head. You?"

"I think my arm's broke. I think they did it after they knocked me out."

"Have you seen them?"

"No."

"I wish I could touch you."

"Yeah. I wish I could touch you too."

They sat listening for a while.

"Is this a warehouse?"

"I don't know. I don't think so. It's dirt underneath us and the ground isn't level."

Harrison thought he heard some underlying sound in the near distance. A heavy door opened at the end of the room and a momentary intrusion of streetlight revealed the cinder-block walls against banked earth, a low ceiling. There was a confusion of silhouettes as someone entered and shut the door behind them. A flashlight switched on, the beam in his eyes so that he could see nothing more, only hear their scuffing steps as they advanced.

"This doesn't have to take long," a man's voice said.

"Where are we?" Harrison asked.

"It speaks," said the man

"It does. It's curious about its current set of circumstances," answered a woman.

Harrison realized it was Jonathan and Delilah.

"I want to do this on my own," she said.

"Are you sure?" Jonathan asked.

"He might be a badass, but he ain't nothing up against a bullet."

Jonathan lit a propane lantern so that they could see. Delilah drew a small automatic from the waistband of her shorts and held it at her side.

"You get on. This is between us now."

Jonathan said, "I'll wait at the car."

"Whatever," she said. "Just let me have the goddamn room a minute, huh?"

He filed out and closed the door with a weighted thump. Delilah set the handgun flat on the floor and bent over to turn the hissing lantern as high as it would go. The magnified light sharpened her shadow against the wall as if it were an imprint from a more vivid form. She raised the lantern and carried it until she was just beyond Emmanuel's reach.

"He's pretty," she said. "I guess I should have expected that."

"You don't have to do this, Delilah," Harrison told her.

She laughed, held the lantern up so that she could scrutinize every detail of Emmanuel's battered face.

"Of course I don't have to. I want to. That makes all the difference, doesn't it?"

"I get loose of this and I'll make a difference for you, bitch," Emmanuel said between clenched teeth.

"Yeah, I bet you would. There's no danger of getting loose though. We made sure of that."

She strutted back to Harrison, picked up the handgun. She looked more herself holding it.

"Let him go, Delilah. Let him go and do whatever you want with me."

"Fuck no, I'm not letting him go. I didn't do this so you'd have a chance to be a hero for your tarbaby piece of ass. I did this so I could make you hurt as much as possible, and I know the best way to do that is by making him hurt as much as possible. So don't fucking beg me. We're past begging now."

"Where are we?" he asked softly. He needed her to come closer.

"We're at the river. This is the utility storage for the old railway bridge. And once we're done with you two you will be rolled down the bank into the black waters of the Tennessee. Forever and ever, amen. And you can stop whispering so that I'll come over there and you can try to grab me. Those chains you are hooked up to are run through an eyebolt and looped back on themselves. You can't move your arms much more than about a foot."

He tested the truth of what she said and found that she was right.

"I've thought quite a bit about how to do this. Make sure it does everything I want it to. It would have been easy to just shoot you both in the back of the head. Roll you for whatever money you had on you and make tracks. But that wouldn't be enough."

"I'm sorry I hurt you."

"Hurt me? You didn't fucking hurt me. You still don't get it? This is about who gets to walk away at the end. It's about who's strongest, who's ready and willing to kill. That's something you and Gavin have both never understood. There's no reason to this. This is just impulse. That's what makes a difference between having and being had."

She produced a short clip knife from a case on her hip, flipped it to him.

"What the hell am I supposed to do with this?"

She cocked her head, mockingly coy.

"Just give me a minute to show you, baby."

She went over to where Emmanuel was chained, bent down and turned a key in the padlock. The clasp clacked open and she swiftly tugged the chain through the bolt. With the chain knotted around one hand and the handgun pointed at the back of Emmanuel's head, she forced him to his feet. As they moved, she torqued down on his broken arm so that he had to obey the pain. Once she had him faced to Harrison with their chests nearly touching, she stopped.

"You decide how this is going to happen," she said. "You can make him go out real easy. I know you know how. You can see that pulse in his throat right now, can't you? I swear it's bouncing just like a trampoline."

"Fuck you."

"This isn't a choice I'm offering you. Hell, this is mercy. If you don't put him down right now by your own hand I will have that other mean motherfucker beat him to death while you watch and know there's not a goddamn thing you can do about it."

He couldn't look Emmanuel in the eye. The blade had taken on a different weight. All the doors of his mind were flung open.

"Cut him!"

Instead, Harrison pushed hard against his own wrist and brought the edge across. His pale flesh opened with such ease that he felt no pain, marveled instead at the abrupt flow of red that in a delirious moment he believed might be a hue of paint.

"What the fuck did you do!" she screamed.

His head was coming undone and he couldn't be sure what he was doing with his hands. There was a further darkness crowding in around the near darkness, but it caused no fear. It crowned everything he could see. The knife dropped from his hand. There was more screaming.

She opened the lock and unwrapped the chain. She tried to close the wound with her hands but it continued to run. He saw her screaming in his face, though he couldn't make out any words. Then, in moment when everything collapsed on itself, her eyes widened with surprise when Emmanuel stabbed the knife into the base of her throat and a second later ripped it across. She came to her feet as if she had been electrically shocked, her hands a useless dam against the life overspilling. She took only a few steps before she fell face down into the immediate nowhere. Emmanuel tore his shirt over his head, crying in pain as he brought his hurt arm free and pressed the balled material against Harrison's wrist.

"Hold this here, okay?"

Harrison nodded, clutched the shirt in place. Emmanuel found the gun a few feet from Delilah's body. He picked it up and moved toward the door with the lantern. Before he opened it he killed the light.

His footsteps padded back a minute later.

"Hey, you still with me?"

"Barely."

"The other one's down by the car. It's maybe a hundred feet up the way, but I think there's a trail the other way that gets us back up to the paved road. Can you move?"

"Yeah, help me up?"

Though Emmanuel bore the brunt of him, every step was exhaustion. But as soon as he was outside and could see Jonathan at the car smoking a cigarette, his physical weakness fled. Fear quickened him and he was able to mount the trail without Emmanuel's help.

They got to the side of the road and crossed over, careful to stay beyond the cast of streetlights. It was late and there were few cars out on this side of the river. Still, it was much too far to walk. Finally, they decided to cross at the bridge and make their way to the transit terminal. Just as they arrived, the night bus headed for Magnolia stopped and hissed. When the doors rolled open the woman behind the wheel took them both in, shook her head.

"There's rules about who I can take on the bus," she told them.

"Yes ma'am, we don't need to go far."

"Honey, it looks like far is exactly where you two need to get."

She shook her head but waved them aboard, told them to sit far enough back so that she didn't have to put up with their smell.

As they rode through the next two stops they didn't say anything to each other, their eyes on the night flowing around them like a shared nightmare. When they came to their stop, Harrison stood at the rear door but Emmanuel had remained seated. When

Harrison touched him on the shoulder he began to weep. The bus driver glared at them in the mirror.

"I don't know what's wrong with you, but you need to get him off my bus right now, you understand?"

He got Emmanuel up and down the exit steps. The doors rolled shut and the bus lumbered on. Harrison asked him to be quiet as he guided him through the narrow streets and back to the house. Once there he told him to pack everything he needed as fast as he could. In a couple of minutes he had put some clothes and a sheaf of papers in a small leather suitcase. Under his good arm he had the unfinished self-portrait. There was nothing else he needed, he said. Nothing else that he would give a damn if it burned to the ground.

"Where's somewhere we can go, somewhere safe until tomorrow?" Harrison asked.

"I don't know. Nowhere."

"There's got to be somewhere, Emmanuel. Someone you can trust."

He paused for a moment.

"My cousin Felicia. She's up on the other end of Skyline Road."

Emmanuel unlocked the doors of his Cavalier and slipped behind the steering wheel. "Might need a team effort here," he said, glancing at his busted arm hanging on the ignition side of the steering column. Harrison reached over and twisted the key until the engine caught, then eased the shift in reverse so Emmanuel could turn around and put them on the path toward any future better than the one that would find them here.

34

JONATHAN KNEW IT WAS TAKING TOO LONG. HE FELT SOMETHING sick settle into his stomach when the stopwatch on his phone clicked up to a quarter of an hour. He took the pistol out and circled around to enter from above so that he would have a clear sight of the situation. Even from there he could see that the lantern remained burning inside.

He dropped down and kicked the door aside and saw her. He did not need to go any closer to know that she was dead, though there was nothing just then that could keep him from doing so. Once he cleared the rest of the room he holstered the handgun and then went forward.

There was so much blood that it repulsed him. He had not expected that. He had not expected to be afraid of it as well as ashamed. Perhaps that was why he didn't take her in his arms and instead simply registered the basic fact of her subtracted life. He wasn't sad. Not exactly. He simply felt cheated, tricked.

He sat on the concrete floor, drew his legs against his chest. Wondered at the immediate fact of her body being there but everything else not. He supposed that was where people got their religion, in this space that was a tease. Something should have been over there in that pile of bones, just as there should have been something filling his chest right now, though each was as empty as punch holes.

He didn't have any more time to bother with her, so he closed the door and padlocked a chain in place as guard over her tomb, went down to the car and drove out of the place and through the darkened city.

The car was gone when he got to the house. He knew that it would be. Still, he went inside, checked each of the rooms to make sure there wasn't something worth seeing left behind.

He went back to the bedroom, opened all the closets. Stacks of paintings fitted against one another with thin diaphanous padding placed in between. He carried them to the bed and looked at them. Pictures of people and places, but they didn't look real. Instead, there were bright swatches of color that seemed like they came from out of the eye rather than the thing between the frame. Was enough to make you dizzy if you looked at it too long. He didn't have much of an idea what he was supposed to think of that. As a kid he remembered watching TV shows with people talking about what made something into art. Seemed to him they were always talking in a way that sounded as though they knew some trick you never could. There was even one time a urinal was hung up in a museum and idiots came there and looked at it like it meant something.

He got up on the bed and unzipped, pissed on the canvas then stamped his foot through until each painting had his own special signature on it. He hopped down and went back out to the living room.

He sat on the couch and tried to think. He thought he should call Gavin, but he didn't know how he might explain things. He thought too maybe he should run.

No, he wouldn't do that. Enough of his life had been finding the quickest exit. That kind of thinking wore on you after a while. He was tired of being worn down.

He went back to the van and drove out of the neighborhood and headed back toward Little Europe.

35

FRANK'S VICTORY WAS ANNOUNCED JUST AS THE STORM HIT THE western edge of the county. There were jokes about omens and auspices, but the jokes soon died on the tongue when the emergency broadcast came over the radio, telling everyone to get inside and away from windows. Farewells were shouted as everyone took off for the prospect of better shelter. Kyle clapped Frank on the shoulder as he left, said to take care of his family while he and Laura headed back to his place on the mountain.

Over the next half hour the wind tore across ridgelines and howled down the length of the valley. Trees bent and sheared. What had been forecast as essentially a string of thunderstorms had converged that afternoon as the front raced through the central part of the state. In that time they had become a solid squall line bearing down on the mountains.

When the storm reached Carter County the sustained winds were above seventy miles per hour. The wind simply picked up the brush fire set by Polk at the edge of Little Europe and flung it across the river and up the shoulders and sides of the mountains in a matter of minutes. It was a rhapsody of flame. The firestorm detonated as abruptly as a bomb and the earth ruptured. Anyone could see that there could be no rescue, only escape.

Kyle saw the fires as they came. After he and Laura had got back to the house they had sat up late, too excited by the election results to sleep. They were on the porch because they knew the winds were coming and they were ready to be thrilled by the spectacle, wanted to welcome it as something that matched their optimism about the future of the county. They had won the vote. The calamity that followed made no sense.

"We need to call somebody," Laura said, rushed into the house to find her phone.

The smoke flung across the burn line. Kyle could hear the distant sound of trees cracking. The smell of it all was sharp and acrid. As the wind gusted again the inferno bounded closer.

"There's no signal," she said, back now and staring at the oncoming firestorm.

"Is there anything in there you can't do without?"

She shook her head.

"Come on, then. We need to get out of here before we get caught in the cove."

She didn't need to be told to hurry.

Once they reached the bottom of the drive and turned onto the dirt road there was a ridge between them and the advancing flames. But even though they lost direct sight of the fire, they could see the stuttering pulse glowing there above the mountain. They passed the fork in the road that would take them into town.

Laura pointed at the missed turn.

"Where are you going, Kyle?"

"We've got to get up there to Orlynne's. If they don't get out this way they'll be shut up in there."

He tore along the road faster than he ever had, felt his stomach flip each time the tires barked and skidded through a curve. His hands gripped the steering wheel like it was trying to throw him. The road became as much his enemy as anything or anyone ever had. It slipped through the night and it slipped through him, a destiny made up of dirt, rock, and calculated angles. All he wanted was to stay on it just a little longer.

"Kyle, look!"

He should have seen it earlier; he had been too tightly focused. The fire had gotten in through a saddle between the mountains and jumped the river. Both sides of the road in front were ablaze. He didn't slow.

"We can still get through. It's not that much further."

They felt the heat before they even go to the fire. Laura closed all the vents but the smoke was still able to thread its way in. At the next turn everything got impossibly worse. Despite the unstrung chaos of all that burned around the truck, he could see the poplar begin to tilt in time to brake. A second later it crashed and blocked the road. The tree was too big to move, too big to cut even if he had the chainsaw. There was no room the turn around and the fire had encircled them.

He threw the shift in reverse and plunged his foot on the accelerator. The heat and smoke and wilderness of light slipped away like beads along a string. It became only the rush of darkness once they were clear, and each of them had to consciously decide before they could breathe again.

"Are you okay?"

Laura nodded but couldn't find her voice.

"There's still a way to get to them," he said as they pulled up to the road fork. "I'll just need you to run me back up to the house and then you can ride out this way."

She shook her head, told him she wouldn't be separated from him. He had little appetite or time for argument, so he drove on.

When they pulled up to the house they could see the fire had crawled and surmounted the big ridge. Ash blew across in gusts of warm snow. In half an hour everything under their feet would be burning.

He dragged the canoe and its gear out into the open before Laura could get around and heft the back end.

"I don't think we're going to be able to get to the put-in. There's a spot just up the road, though. It's steep, but we should be able to manage."

"Should?"

They carried the boat out to the truck.

A few minutes later they were overlooking a granite sheer. In daylight it couldn't have been more than a dozen feet to the water, but in the weird gloaming of firelight the distance magnified. They fastened their life vests and started down, tried to find footholds but it was all smooth and slick.

"Go ahead and jump in. Be ready to stop it if I can't hold on."

Laura turned and leapt into the pool.

"Throw the paddles down," she called up.

He pitched them down a few feet from her. Though the light wasn't good he could still see where they splashed and spun. She swam over and gathered them in her arms. He squared up and clambered toward the rocky edge, tried to keep his center of gravity as low as possible while he shoved the boat down in front of him, moved crabwise. He had extended the bow until it nearly touched the water when his feet lost purchase and he was over without a way to control his fall.

When he came up in the river he stung all over, but it seemed to be mostly scratches and light cuts. Where they were, the water came to his chest, so they had to float the canoe down to the next set of shoals before they could climb in and get a better look.

"Let me see," Laura said once they were aboard, held his leg to view the wound, see if anything was embedded. The cut was clean, not significantly threatening.

Laura moved forward and together they paddled for the main current. It pulled them in, still strong this far back despite the months of drought. The regular rhythm of work was good. It kept his mind off the pain in his leg. He tried not to think about Orlynne, about what they would find there at her trailer by the time it would take to cover this much distance, at least three miles, along the river. It was tempting to lay in with all he had but he knew that tiring out prematurely was a risk. There was also the river itself to keep in mind. Though he knew this run well, the fire would change things. As soon as they were past the fireline there would be the likelihood of falling and fallen limbs. Trying to paddle on too quickly could get them into problems because the rapids were still big enough in places to be a danger. Especially in the dark. No, he had to remain patient, keep a steady stroke and pilot them through. He settled in and gave himself over to the river.

36

FELICIA HAD NO INTENTION OF LETTING THEM THROUGH THE FRONT DOOR.

"Come on. I wouldn't be here if it wasn't an emergency," Emmanuel said through the chain-locked door. Harrison could see no more of her than a single glaring eye.

"Emmanuel, you have got to be crazy turning up on my doorstep in the middle of the damn night with a crazy-looking cut-up white boy with you!"

"Look, honey, look. There is too much for me to explain this to you, standing out here. Just let me in and I can set it all out for you."

"Don't you honey me."

Despite her refusal, she paused, took a breath.

"If I let you two motherfuckers in this house you better not wake up my kids. I swear to God I'll cut you both down to the spine if you do. And you, white boy, don't bleed on anything."

"Yes ma'am."

The door swung shut as she shot the chain free to let them in.

There were admitted to a small front room with a closed-off fireplace and a big gilded mirror hanging above a yellow couch. Seeing himself reflected there, Harrison could understand her hesitancy to welcome him.

"I know there's got to be a reason you're not wearing a shirt, Emmanuel, but I'm not even about to get into all that. And White Boy here looks like he should be in a hospital."

"His name is Jay."

"I don't give a goddamn what his name is."

She shook her head, closed her eyes and asked her god for long-suffering patience.

"We need to clean up."

She waved her hand in the air.

"You know where the bathroom is. I'm going to need some damn wine."

She left them for the kitchen. Emmanuel told Harrison to follow and showed him back through the short hall, switched on the bathroom light and closed the door behind them.

Harrison held his arm over the sink so that he could carefully remove the bloody shirt from his wrist.

"She's right, you know," Emmanuel said. "We do need to take you to a hospital."

"Which is the first place he'd check."

When the cloth separated from the injury, the smell of dry blood was so sharp it made him gag. Emmanuel ran a trickle of warm water from the tap and helped him clean and dry the cut. He opened three large padded bandages and overlaid them. Harrison circled adhesive tape around the wrist until the material was secure.

"You need the doctor as bad as anyone," Harrison said, softly grazing the bicep of Emmanuel's hurt arm and kissing his shoulder. "But not tonight. I need you to stay here tonight."

"You need me to stay here? You told me we both were staying. What the hell are you up to now, Jay?"

"I've got to get back there to where Gavin's got that money. We're going to need it if we have a chance of getting clear of everything. We already agreed I was going to do it."

"My God, that was before everything that's happened tonight. Stealing from that man was always going to be dangerous, but now you're going to try and do it while you're walking around three pints light of blood? That's crazy, even for you."

"I don't have time for this argument right now."

He went back out to the front room where Felicia was sitting with her coffee cup of merlot.

"Do you have duct tape?"

"Duct tape? You want to start up home repairs to pay me for my kindness?"

He held up his bandaged arm.

"I might need something sturdier than this."

She pinched her eyes closed with her fingertips.

"First drawer to the left of the dishwasher."

He went in and wrapped the tape several times around until his wrist was stiffly encased. He tore the tape with his teeth and smoothed over the end. Emmanuel had come out from the bathroom and was wearing a large yellow towel around his shoulders.

"Don't leave the house until I get back," Harrison told him as he swiped the keys from where Emmanuel had dropped them on the coffee table.

"If you get back, you mean." Emmanuel said.

Harrison hugged him, said, "No, that's not what I mean at all."

HE DROVE the interstate with the speedometer notched on eighty. Any faster and he would have drawn the attention of state troopers, but this time of night they would let just about anything fly through east Tennessee. The mountains were dark for a while but there was some kind of strange light just beyond them. Harrison had no idea of what to make of it until he smelled the smoke. He angled his foot down and the road fled behind him.

He first caught direct sight of the fires as soon as he exited for Elizabethton. The roads were a confusion of people driving away from town and several volunteer firefighters hurrying toward the blaze. There seemed to be no official coordination, only this general apocalypse.

Once he was through town the highway out to Warlick had been blocked by deputies. He was stopped by one of them.

"It's all shut down through this way. It's burnt clear up to Roan Mountain."

"I've got to get through. I've got to get to some people."

"I'm sorry, sir. All the people that are still up there are coming out on their own. Letting you through would just give us somebody else to worry about. I'm going to need you to turn around, please."

He rolled the window up, sat there a minute before he jerked the wheel hard and stomped the gas, bounded across the grass median until he was running up the incoming lanes that had been left open for evacuees. He heard shouts but no gunshots, so he drove on, moved to the emergency lane when he saw vehicles coming toward him. In this way, he slalomed back toward the cove and turned into the heart of the fire.

The road was surrounded by the cracked red embers of what had already burned, everything blackened and baked by the violence that had run its course. He could feel the heat inside the car, heard something pop a second before the headlights flickered and died. He banged the dash to get them going, but it did nothing. He had to slow to little more than a walking pace, guided by the strangely mystic confusion of the firelight.

When he finally reached Little Europe, he was amazed to see that it still stood. Everything around it was burned, devastated. But the old asylum remained there on the brow of the hill as if it were constructed and affirmed by the same force as the fire itself. It glowed with an odd but presiding beauty. He parked and went in to see who was still there.

He moved through the foyer and noiselessly up the stairs. Along the hall on the second floor, several of the rooms had been left open and there was no one inside. They must have had ample time to get clear. They must have known. He paused at the room he had shared with Delilah, pressed the door open on a hinge that moaned. There were some things of hers there. A blouse and a box of pictures of her with her brother. It was almost like there had been a soul in her body. He got the rest of the cash and his extra revolver from the closet. He stuck it in the back of his waistline next to the other one, the one Delilah had meant to kill him with, then he went on toward Gavin's room.

He opened the door and saw Gavin sitting at the window looking out at the fires. He was in his office chair, one leg cocked casually across the other, as if he were viewing a scene of outdoor theater instead the loss of everything he'd tried to build. A few feet across from him sat the idiot boy Connor Polk slumped in an oak stiff-backed chair, his forehead punched with a bullet hole. The ostensible source, a Smith and Wesson automatic, lay just within Gavin's reach on the windowsill.

"I wondered if you would come back," Gavin said. "I hoped you would."

Harrison circled around and rested his weight against the edge of the heavy desk.

"What happened?" Harrison asked.

"I lost my temper, I'm afraid. He was the one responsible for the fire. At first he wouldn't admit it, but I could tell he wanted to lay claim to something of import. It wasn't just that, though. He threatened me. Told me he was going to take the money he knew I had hidden here, and that if I didn't give it to me he would throw me out into the wildfire. I believed him. It looked as though the house was going to burn. So, I told him I would give him what he wanted. I opened the safe and he wasn't worried about what I might do. He thought I was weak. In his mind there was no reason for concern. I simply pulled the gun out and pulled the trigger. I was going to do the same to myself. I have no desire to burn alive, but as I sat here, trying to come to terms with things, the wind changed. It carried the fire away from here. There was no reason for it, only chance. So I've been sitting here thinking about that and then you walked in the door and I wonder if that's maybe the reason all of this has happened. Just so we can have a conversation."

Harrison could see the safe remained open and that the stacks of cash were still there.

"What kind of conversation would that be?"

"One where we tell the truth. I think that's something we owe one another at this point."

"From where I stand, it seems like each man has his own idea about what that means."

"Doubtless that's the case. But there are certain shared entanglements that can't be ignored. We were part of something here. You and I, even this poor dead fool. We ventured something."

"I was just trying to find a way to make a little money, get back on my feet."

Gavin shook his head, smiled.

"No, that's too easy. It's understandable to hear you say that, though. I think it's common for us to deny what we did and why we did it, especially here among the ruins. I will tell you what I think. I think you liked discovering your strength. You liked that you could build a reputation for yourself. You were valuable in a way that even I couldn't see at first. But you held the secret of your own value and that made you see that we were able to give something back to you that held meaning. It must have confused your cynicism. You understand violence in this way," he said, motioned toward Polk's body, "but I understand it too, though in a different key. I understand what it accomplishes in the mind, when it degrades and renders men worthless. Because I have fought against that kind of violence my entire life."

Harrison watched the fire heave in the distance.

"You think you've made a difference," Harrison said. "But I don't see that anything has changed. People die, but there's nothing new in that. There's nothing that won't keep them from doing the same tomorrow and the day after that. They die because that's what happens when there's no way around the suffering. Everyone knows that, whether they're willing to admit it or not. You can say it's because of the Blacks and Jews and Mexicans, but you might as well blame it on the weather. We all just want to find a way to ease the everyday hurt. So, yeah, maybe there's a part of what you said that's true about me. It helped to have a place here, but this isn't where I want to be anymore, and it sure as hell isn't who I want to be anymore."

Gavin reached for the handgun, though he did so without intent. He merely held it between flattened palms, as though it obstructed a properly composed prayer.

"I know you came for the money. You should take it. We couldn't have gotten it without you. The idiot here had no right to it. None of the others did."

Harrison eased from the desk, advanced without reaching for a weapon. He shifted the cash into the gym bag he'd brought from his room. When the bag was full he had to pinch the top together so that he could zip it shut. He walked toward the door without a glance in Gavin's direction.

"Harrison?"

"What, Gavin?"

"I hope you know I only wanted to make our world better."

Harrison shut the door and walked down the hall. A second later the handgun fired. Harrison heard Gavin's body strike the floor.

He grabbed a backpack from his room and filled a bottle with water from a bathroom tap, drank it to the bottom then filled it again and put it with the rest of his things. He hurried out to the car and tossed the money and other effects in the passenger's seat, cranked the engine and swung back for the dirt road that led out of the cove.

He turned to take one last look at Little Europe, impress it on his memory so that he could recall with clarity what he had escaped. Perhaps on any other night he could have seen what approached. But amid the flame he had missed the disturbance, the oncoming rush, as the white van slammed broadside into the car and smashed him into a wall of scorched earth.

37

HOLSTON HAD NEVER SEEN ANYTHING LIKE IT. THE ABSOLUTE magnitude of everything. Ash sifted down from what burned on the ridgelines and settled on the streets like an awful dry snow. He struggled getting all of his off-duty deputies to report in. They were scattered over the county and trying to beat back toward town so that he could put some kind of evacuation plan in place. The worst was the sheer chaotic noise of conflicting information. He would hear that one cove was completely destroyed or closed off only to learn fifteen minutes later that traffic was still flowing through there and that it was the next cove over that had been burnt. It got to be so bad that he didn't trust any single report unless he could confirm it with his own eyes. He headed out to discern the truth from rumor.

The highway checkpoints were manned, at least. He stopped by and told them to turn around any traffic trying to go past Hampton. He went through himself and turned toward Warlick, where the fire gouged the top third of the mountains. He rolled down his windows and could hear it talking even above the howl of his engine.

The wind had temporarily quieted. Little chance that would hold, but maybe the reprieve would allow people the few critical minutes they needed to get to a paved surface. The worst of it would be for those who lived down the back dirt and gravel roads, hemmed in with no way out. Since that was where the worst trouble was bound to be, he turned into the first hollow he came across.

The smoke made him slow. It camouflaged the advance of the flames, though, and he couldn't be sure how close to danger he might be getting. He was cussing the lack of visibility when a shape appeared abruptly a few yards ahead and he had to mash the brakes to keep from rear ending the tail of a pickup parked in the middle of the road. A tree had come down and landed across the hood. He recognized it immediately as belonging to Frank Farmer. Sickness welled within him.

He got out and cried Frank's name, though he doubted his voice carried far. He saw that the cab was empty. He couldn't call the sight of that relief, but it was better than the dread it replaced.

"That you, Holston?"

It was Frank coming from up the road. He had his chainsaw under his arm and he sweat like a man who had been spat from the belly of damnation. Next to him was one of those boys Pettus had in the veterans group.

"I'm afraid your truck is stuck, Frank."

"I'm afraid you're right."

Frank told him he had gone up the road to clear the way with the chainsaw and heard the tree come down less than ten seconds from when he'd stepped from the cab. He could get the tree off, he said. But the engine was smashed beyond repair.

"We need to get back through here, Holston. There's got to be a dozen homes back here. Most of them won't have any other way out."

"Hell, I know it. Hop in my truck. Let me run you up and you can work your way through a little quicker, at least."

Frank nodded and hurried back to the sheriff's vehicle.

They came to another downed tree a couple of hundred feet up the road. It was pine, at least. Should cut fast. Frank worked as close to the burning end as he could stand, let the heavy saw urge its way through. The trunk snapped and before he could set chainsaw aside Holston and the veteran boy were there, swinging it to the side like a gate. Without a word, they got back in and went on, moved like that through three more blockades before they got to the first house.

"This is going to take all night, Frank."

"Good thing I don't mind your company, Holston."

Despite everything, the sheriff couldn't stifle a laugh.

"Good damn thing."

FRANK WORRIED the heat was getting to Sheriff Holston, so he told him to stay in the cruiser while he and Turner worked up to the next line of burning trees. They still had at least half a mile more to cover, and he knew they were running out of time. He didn't need the look on Turner's face to tell him that. This was the cove he and the boy had worked just a few days before, talking to Turner's uncle Virgil and so many of those others that he claimed as kin. The boy's family was penned up there behind this wall of fire.

Frank knew they had to pace themselves if they had any chance of making it all the way back. He set the saw aside and tried to survey how many more road obstructions they would face before the next road bend. Before he could tell Turner to wait, the boy had set the saw and started in on a canted oak, but the angle was bad and the blade got pinched. They worked at it for a couple of minutes, but neither of them could get it to budge.

"Leave it," Frank told him. "We ain't going to get it out now. We're going to have to go on foot from here."

He went back to the police cruiser to tell Holston what they needed to do.

"No way, Frank," Holston said. "You've got a wife and two little girls back in town. You don't have any business going any further than you already have. Get in the car."

Frank smiled, placed his hand on the top of the cruiser.

"Are you detaining me, Sheriff?"

"I damn well should. Come on now, and get that crazy kid to come with you."

But Frank turned and he and Turner went up toward the gathering smoke.

38

THE SCENE SURROUNDING ORLYNNE'S TRAILER WAS BATTLE STREWN. Exploded and flame-guttered trees and still-burning second growth. Smoke that rolled and obscured any clear view of what may have survived. Kyle steered the canoe into a shallow notch in the bank until the bottom ground to a stop in the mud, told Laura to stay with the boat until he could see what had become of Orlynne and Gerald.

Once up the bank he could see the trailer had been partially burned but remained intact. The fireline nearest to it shot flat yellow flames more than a dozen feet from the ground, and even as far as the river the heat on his face was enough to draw sweat. He saw each of Gerald's goats dead at their stakes. It looked as though they had been put down with gunshots. He called Orlynne's name, but he heard nothing in response. Bracing himself, he sprinted the gauntlet of smoke and fire until he got to the trailer door and swung it open. Inside, he found them lying in bed clutching each other. In one of Gerald's hands a small pistol was held. For a moment, Kyle thought that he had been too late, but Orlynne opened her eyes and lifted her head.

"Kyle?"

He told them he was there to get them, that he had his canoe at the river's edge. He told them to hurry. They got to their feet and staggered toward him. They moved with awkward, hectic newborn jerks, their bodies having to freshly remember life when only moments before they had been prepared to resign themselves to its end. Kyle steadied them at the threshold of the door.

"I'll take Orlynne first, Gerald. Then I'll come back for you."

Gerald nodded, told them to hurry up for god's sake and not spend so much time with wasted words.

Kyle drew Orlynne tight against his side and encircled his arm around her mouth and eyes to try to keep the smoke out as they limped to the canoe. She kept his pace and they pressed through. Laura was out of the boat, reaching her hand up for Orlynne to take. Once he was sure she was down the embankment and aboard, Kyle rushed back for Gerald. When he got back to the trailer he found the old man doubled over, coughing with such violence that it seemed to be ripping through his chest. Kyle grabbed him by the bicep and dragged him forward. They had only managed a few steps when Gerald's entire body seized as if touched against a massive electrical charge. A moment later his legs went from under him. His eyes were rolled. Kyle hunkered down until he could gather Gerald across his shoulders and carry him out.

"What happened?" Orlynne cried.

"He collapsed. It was sudden. Like he'd been hit with something. I think maybe it was a stroke."

Kyle lowered Gerald to the embankment edge, got in the water himself before pulling Gerald along after. It was a messy business to get Gerald in the canoe and hard to get afloat with the extra weight, but eventually Kyle shoved the boat out to the channel and they caught the current. He climbed up into the stern and steered them through the next deep bend. The river would be getting big soon and with the added weight there was little freeboard, only a couple of inches between the boat's gunwales and the waterline. He glanced from reading the river to where Orlynne cradled Gerald against her. The old man's only movement was in the slight rise and fall of his unsteady breaths. Kyle knew he needed to handle the canoe without fault as they entered the rapids. If they took on much water at all the boat would slow and swamp, and if they couldn't stay afloat, there was little chance for Orlynne and none for Gerald.

They struck a big rock on the left bow. The blow thumped down the entire length of the canoe. Laura showed her pale face briefly over her shoulder, called back, "Sorry."

They had entered a stretch of dark water and their eyes were slow to adjust. Kyle had little more than memory of previous runs to aid him now. Even if Laura saw a hazard ahead it would be too late for Kyle to correct.

"Dig in!" he shouted.

The water had begun to feather and surge. Ahead, a smooth rush of river sculpted against a jagged log inches beneath the surface. Kyle swung his paddle hard against the current to back water, and the bow clocked abruptly to the left. They glided past, the bottom juddering.

They were in a steady run now, and Kyle patterned himself against the water, sensing rapids entries as much as actually perceiving them. The river turned again, took them toward the fires for a while so that the light improved as they shot a medium-size rapid. But soon the water shallowed and he and Laura had to stop several times to shove and drag the boat across a maze of slick ledges and footcatches. Gerald remained terribly still.

Once past the portage the water quickened so that Laura had her feet knocked out from under her before she could climb back into the boat. When she fell her paddle came free and floated out of sight. Kyle helped her back in and pushed off, pulling deep strokes to try and catch the paddle.

"I can't see anything!" she cried.

"There, look there. It's hung on that rock."

He leaned hard on the paddle and brought the canoe up beside where Laura's paddle had floated and been carried up by an eddy. They bumped and ground against the edge of the stone. Laura timed her grab and plucked the paddle up by its end, then turned it around and pushed off. The boat reluctantly slew over and they caught the main current, drifted forward once more.

"Hold on steady, now," Kyle told her.

Smoke flooded his view and he heard the new train of rapids well before he could see them. As they entered he could immediately tell the flow was running much stronger than normal. Before he could correct to the right side he struck a protruding rock so hard that he was amazed it didn't split them right there. He backed water but doing so took him toward the bank. A branch as big as his wrist slapped him across the shoulder. Nausea coursed through.

"Kyle, are you okay?"

He nodded, dug his paddle in, and guided them back to where the river howled.

39

THE COLLISION HAD THROWN HARRISON AGAINST THE DRIVER'S window, but he remained conscious. His immediate surroundings were all ring and hum. He shook his head clear and tried the door; it was wedged tight against the road bank and left no room to exit. On the opposite side, the door had been crushed and the nose of the van remained buried there. He heard a door creak open, saw Jonathan lurch free of the van. Harrison quickly lowered the driver's window, grabbed the bag of money, and slithered atop the bank still hot with embers. He pulled one of his pistols and fired off six blind shots before turning to run.

Behind there were shots. He both heard and felt them in the air around him. He ducked behind an outcropping, heard a pair of rounds dig and split the stone into a confetti of hard splinters. He snatched the second pistol from his waistband and took aim at the form coming up the road. Two quick shots and he saw him waver and disappear behind a rolling bank of smoke. He waited, focused his attention on the obscured area. A long time seemed to pass, but he didn't move, until finally he did.

A bullet struck and buried in his hand. By the pain, he knew immediately that the round had found bone. He ran, knew the shot had come from his flank. He had dropped his handgun and he felt that what strength he had was fleeing. The wound slickened with blood. Each few feet he staggered and caught himself against a burnt tree, tried to master his breathing. Another shot punched the bark an inch from his skull. A bank of smoke surrounded him.

Depth seemed to collapse and an odd calm overtook him. He heard the singing of flames. He had no other choice. He plunged into the source of the smoke, staying low to breathe. More shots screamed, but the weird dimensions of firelight cast against the smoke made them seem unreal. The only real thing just then was the pain in his hand. He wrestled his shirt over his head and tore a long strip of cloth with his teeth. The binding of the wound did little to staunch the flow of blood, but at least hid the injury from sight. He crouched behind a wall of half-buried rock, felt something hard beneath him. He shifted to see what it was when he saw the faint etching of a name. A few feet further he saw a small obelisk and beyond that a symbolic bell and a pair of marble hands. Refuge here in an old cemetery, forgotten for some indefinite period of time beneath the crawling vine and second growth but made new in the hungry fire.

Thirst came on him with impossible urgency. He knew dying men cried out for two things—their mothers and water. If he was going to die, he would want it to be in a place that mattered. A place where he could come and have all his bodily desire fulfilled. In that moment it seemed that he was at the center of a thriving garden of fire.

Like a wraith, Jonathan appeared in profile. Smoke parted and invoked him here amid the tombstones. The pistol hung at his side as he was blinded by the smoke. Harrison threw his full weight against him. Then it was all surge and reflex. Two animals kicked, strangled, and gouged at one another in the stinging heat until they came apart, the distance between a buffer against mutual murder.

Harrison's sense of direction deserted him. Everything was pain and radiance. He had staggered farther into the fire's belly. His skin blackened as he hurried through the flames and falling debris. He felt his throat closing down. He did not look back to see if Jonathan had followed him in, but if he had he would have beheld a figure at peace with the casual violence and how it dismembered him when the great burning limb crashed down. It came almost as a relief. Almost as an answer to something long sought and only here, in the end, discovered.

Harrison, though, fought through the heat toward some clearing beyond, took a step into the edge of a different borderland only to find the ground dissipate, and for several seconds he was suspended in the cool and dark air.

Then the river grabbed him.

40

FRANK AND TURNER GOT TO UNCLE VIRGIL'S HOUSE FIRST, BUT COULD find no evidence of him.

"Do you think he got out?" Frank shouted above the clamor. The fire had run to within a dozen yards of the house. It would leap to the roof within minutes.

"No, his truck's still here. He must have headed up to my aunt's place."

Frank remembered the woman named Meredith Sue. She had come to the door with a walker. A small lady with pale, distracted eyes. A woman who'd lived much of her life as a shut-in. Still, she had welcomed them, promised she'd be proud to vote if her brother Virgil would give her a ride into town. In the end, she seemed just to be happy to have someone to talk with her.

They got back out to the road. It got narrow this far into the cove and the heat from both sides was hard to take. There was no way around it. It would be easy to get cut off back here. That would be the end of things. Already, direction was hard to determine. If any more trees came down across the road they would lose a clear path.

When they topped the road crest they could see the house had already been engulfed in flames. Even from several hundred yards

Frank could hear the different pitch of burning as the weather-treated timbers roared with chemical accelerant. Turner charged up the rest of the way. Frank was about to call out to him when he saw a flicker of movement to the left down a shallow draw. A great paw waved.

"They're down at the creek!" Frank shouted, though his words were torn away by the inferno. Turner, not hearing, went on toward the house.

Frank got down to Virgil and Meredith Sue. They had found a good spot in the knee-deep water protected on each side by a tumbling of big granite. Remarkably, the air was cool.

"You better grab him," Virgil shouted at Frank. "There ain't a better place to hold up back here than where we're at. There's about two dozen burning trees up there. Any one of them is big enough to flatten a truck!"

As soon as Frank topped the run of rocks, the heat plashed down on him. Though his voice was swallowed by the din, he called Turner's name until he went hoarse. The house was now entangled in such a welter of flames that its hard geometric lines had gone liquid. He was about to turn back for the creek bed when he saw Turner. He had collapsed just feet from the blazing house. In moments, the whole structure would founder like a struck beast and Turner would be gone. Frank went to him.

Frank hooked Turner's motionless shoulder to drag him free from the immediate blast of heat and then worked him across his back. Crablike, he got to the edge of the draw and shuffled toward the creek. Virgil reached up a powerful hand and helped them both down to the safety of the waterline.

"We best stay put until this thing wears itself out!" Virgil yelled.

Frank nodded, the power of speech drawn out of him by the firestorm.

41

THROUGH MUCH OF THE NEXT HOUR KYLE STEERED THE RIVER BY memory. However, that memory was made imperfect by the changes worked by the storm. Rocks that should have been visible were lost by the smooth carving of strong current. Without warning, the canoe would transition from a sleepy drift into a tight, urgent run that had to be navigated expertly. It was hard to stay alert and ready for what the water would demand. The firescape had made the land into something broken and blighted, something conjured. If he looked into it too long, he felt as though he was losing part of himself.

Laura saw an odd shape pitched up on the rocks. At first it looked as if it were some broken remnants of a beaver dam that had washed up in the lee of the massive stone upthrust, but it was moving, and as they neared, Kyle could see that a man's face looked back at him.

He backstroked and brought them in line with a bordering shoal where the water calmed and they could hold in place.

"See that just below him. He lets go and he goes into that hydraulic. That's all undercut ledge there too. He gets into that and you'd be lucky to get him out with a winch. I don't have a rope to throw him either. The only way is to steer in there close and grab him as we go past."

"We've got to try," Laura said.

"We don't have enough room for him. He gets in and the whole boat will swamp at the next rapid."

"We have room," Orlynne said. Her voice seemed to come from an untested place in her throat. As soon as she said it Kyle realized that Gerald was dead.

"We have room," Orlynne repeated, with conviction. "I need your help lifting Gerald over the side."

"We can leave him on the shoreline. We can come back."

"No, I don't want him out there where he'll have to lie out in the sun. I want him buried. Here. He loved this river. He would have chosen this. Help me."

Kyle gathered Gerald beneath the arms and tumbled him into the water. The splash was gentle. He pushed him firmly into the current. The body flowed into the rush of movement. A second later the underpull seized him and he was lost beneath the stone and held there by the force of surging water. Orlynne wiped her eyes once, cried no more.

"We need to go on," she said.

Kyle agreed. He shoved off with the paddle blade and set them on as close a line as he could and still be sure to stay out of the upcoming hydraulic themselves. It was all planning and delay and then they were committed and everything accelerated. The water bounced them forward before it flung them into an enormous dip. Kyle jammed the paddle deep into a current. It fought him with the strength of an animal contesting death. When he could delay no longer, he swung back hard and the bow bucked up and away. He could see the man's eyes roll in recognition as they approached.

Laura and Orlynne grabbed hold of him and he was dragged along the side until they were beyond the crash of whitewater. He tried to lift himself but he had nothing left. Kyle took his hand and together they pulled him in. Almost as soon as he was aboard he passed out. For a moment Kyle thought they had exchanged one dead man for another, but from his chest came a troubled cough.

"Is there anything more to do for him?" Laura asked.

No one said anything, though Orlynne placed her hand across the man's closed eyes, sheltered him in her small way.

42

SEVERAL TIMES THROUGH THE NIGHT KYLE HELD THE CANOE BACK IN deeper water until the fire had fully burned the banks and spent itself in the ranging hills. They had come too far to lose themselves to haste. A cell of lingering fire could still trap them. For several hours they simply watched the country burn, commenting on its terrible beauty and how no one would ever see something like it again in their lifetimes. Eventually, it diminished in the gradual appearance of daylight.

They came off the river early the next morning after they crossed over into green country. The newly quiet surroundings astonished them. The man they had drawn from the river had lost a worrisome amount of blood, but late in the night they had been able to stop the bleeding. Kyle saw the hand, knew it likely to be the result of a bullet rather than a burn. He had also noted the bag strapped snugly across his chest and kept as securely in place as if it had been stitched. The man had regained consciousness while Orlynne watched over him but he had not spoken other than to thank them for the help. When Kyle paddled up to a place where they could take out, they dragged the boat up on the grass. While Orlynne stayed behind, Kyle and Laura went up to the road to flag down a passing vehicle.

"I wonder what he's carrying in that bag," Laura said once they were out of earshot.

"I imagine I have a pretty good idea. A man doesn't hold on to something at the risk of his own life unless it means the whole world to him."

"Aren't you curious to see, though?"

A pickup rounded the corner and its headlights came on through the dissipating smoke. Kyle lifted his hand to draw the driver's attention.

"Whatever it is, he's earned it. Maybe he'll even prove to be worth whatever it is he thinks it can do for him."

After the driver got out and helped them bring the boat and the rest of their party back up, they headed for the hospital. Kyle tried to get Orlynne to sit in the cab, but she insisted in riding in the bed beside the injured man. It was a warm morning, she said. Warm as a bath.

As they rode, the driver told them what he'd heard, though much was still caught up in the wild growth of rumor. Several thousand acres burned. Upwards of five hundred homes lost. The fires were still burning in the east, but they had diminished through the course of the night. They were expected to be contained within the next twenty-four hours. There was loss of life, yes, though the numbers conflicted. No one yet could say what had been the cause, only that it wrecked the county, made people understand what ruin and disaster truly was.

Once they got to the hospital, the injured man thanked him, told him his name was Jay. He said he wanted him to know that. Kyle couldn't say why this was important to the man, though it did seem to have been stated with gratitude. Kyle asked if there was anything he'd like him to ask the nurses for.

"I'd like a telephone. I need to make a call to Knoxville," he said.

Kyle told him that he would make sure they brought him one as soon as they could.

After he talked to the nurses, Kyle went out to the soda machine room and made some calls. Booked a room for Orlynne and one for Laura and him at a place in Johnson City. He tried to get in touch with Frank Farmer, but the line was busy, so he called for a cab to take them to the hotel.

After they checked in and saw Orlynne taken care of, he and Laura went down and shut themselves in their room, shucked their shoes and filthy clothes and showered together as long as the hot water lasted. They climbed naked into the bed and slept until late that afternoon when the phone woke them.

"Yeah?"

"You're alive."

"I am. Hey, Frank."

"I've been calling all around to run down as many people as I can."

"Yeah. Yeah, that's a real good idea."

"Can you get into town?"

"I can get a cab."

"No, don't do that. I'll come out and get you."

"Okay. Half an hour?"

"I'll be there."

"Hey?"

"Yeah?"

"You got any spare clothes I can borrow off you?"

"Yeah, I'll swing by the house."

When Frank got there, Laura met him at the door wrapped in a blanket, made a joke about a casual dress code. Frank apologized, said he should have thought to bring something for her as well. She said she'd take a gift card to Marshall's on the county and he told her he'd see what he could do, smiling.

Kyle dressed in the bathroom and went out with Frank, told Laura he'd bring back something to eat.

"Maybe a little something to drink too?"

"Maybe," he said, kissed her.

Frank went downstairs with him and they got a coffee and sat watching through the glass front where a news van from Knoxville was setting up for a live broadcast. The reporter had a big backdrop of burnt mountains behind him.

Kyle told him about Gerald. Told him the whole story of how they'd gotten out and what it had cost.

"I liked him," Frank said. He sipped his coffee. "He was about as good a man as he could be."

"Yeah, I guess so. How's Turner?" Kyle asked, felt something uneasy settle between them. Couldn't exactly say why. Some kind of change in the emotional air.

"Doctor said he should be able to check out tomorrow. Said there's a lot of folks that need his attention more than Turner does. He did a lot out there. We got to some people before that mess up there with his aunt and uncle. I think we helped."

"You think? Hell, Frank, from what I've heard people are calling you a hero."

Frank watched the television reporter run through his sound checks. He had his cell phone out and was checking how his hair looked. The cameraman began to count him in.

"Yeah, I've been thinking about that. I think heroes are supposed to be loved, don't you, Pettus? This place doesn't love me. Doesn't love me or my wife and girls. There might be a few individuals who care, but the world is a whole lot bigger than individuals. Bigger than people who like you because they recognize your name in the newspaper or hear your voice on the radio. I'm convenient for this place, but being convenient means you're just a thing."

Kyle stirred his coffee for a moment to let off some of the heat.

"I'd like to think that's only part of the truth, Frank. I'd like to think we did something to save a little bit of goodness."

"I know you think that," Frank said, and when he smiled, this time it was different. "We have to live with belief in something, don't we?"

Frank stood, said he had to see to some concerns down at the courthouse. He told Kyle to finish his coffee. There was nothing that needed to be done that wouldn't wait until tomorrow.

"Unless you're a representative of the people?" Kyle asked.

"Something like that. Tell your woman in there that gift card for clothes will be in the mail. Take care of the both of you. People like you two make me think better of the world."

After Frank left someone switched on the television to the news and Kyle watched as the man standing outside appeared on the screen. There was a strangeness to it that he couldn't quite explain. He talked about the fire and what it had done, what had been left, and yet it was as though it happened on an alien planet, though everything was there just the other side of the window.

He walked down the road to a wine store and picked out a couple of bottles to take back to the room. By the time he got back he found Laura asleep. He sat on the edge of the bed and placed his hand against the curve of her neck. She didn't shift. He wanted to go on sitting there with her like that until they were old and addled. Surely, that meant something good. He stepped softly to the kitchen and uncorked a bottle, stood by the window and its pale light and drank with what he hoped was contentment. If nothing else, it was thirst.

The next day, Kyle was able to rent a car. Went to Johnson City for clothes and some tools they might need, then drove out to his house to check the damage. Laura rode with him. They had to stop twice on the way up the drive to chainsaw fallen trees that blocked the path, but the damage to Kyle's property was less than he had expected. So many others had lost their homes, but only one side of his house had caught fire. Part of the roof would need to be repaired, but it was nothing he couldn't remedy himself. Might even provide a chance to build an addition, give Laura a project she could develop alongside him.

One loss was the bottom greenhouse. Most of the plants inside were dead, though some of the seedlings survived. He could raise those up, and in time they could reforest some of what had been lost. He knew the boys from the veterans group would be willing to get out and get their hands dirty, help bring back the trees. They, more than most, understood what it meant to cultivate a garden from what had been fire. He had never been happy with the location of the greenhouse anyhow. In the late summer it didn't get enough sun. There was a flat patch of ground above the house that would suit growing things better. That would be the best place to rebuild.

"Do you feel that?" she asked him. "The ground?"

He knelt. It rose to his skin and went through his body.

"It's still warm," he said. He swiped his finger through the ash, and it felt as though he touched something that would be hard to explain, the way that religion can be. Even in front of her, he felt embarrassed. Still, he didn't try to wipe away the warm ash.

They decided to stay on at the hotel through the end of the week while people came out to the house to assess the damage. They ate dinner in town, not bothering with who might see them together or what people might say. But most of the time they remained in the room to content themselves with the comfort of one another, a peaceable and sincere country fit for only two.

Acknowledgments

I want to express my gratitude to Rick Huard for seeing this book through its birth pangs, Nancy Basmajian for holding its feet to the fire, and Stephanie Williams for permitting it to keep such excellent company with the Swallow Press list. To Beth Pratt, Sally Welch, Jeff Kallet, and Laura Andre my esteem and thanks.

I refer readers to Chistopher K. Walker and Michael Beach Nichols' harrowing documentary *Welcome to Leith* for insight into how real and threatening the blight of White Supremacy is in today's rural America.

This book is because of A., E., and I.